His
Dark Bond

His Dark Bond

ANNE MARSH

BRAVA

KENSINGTON PUBLISHING CORP.

www.kensingtonbooks.com

BRAVA BOOKS are published by

Kensington Publishing Corp.
119 West 40th Street
New York, NY 10018

All Kensington titles, imprints and distributed lines are available at special quantity discounts for bulk purchases for sales promotion, premiums, fund-raising, educational or institutional use.

Special book excerpts or customized printings can also be created to fit specific needs. For details, write or phone the office of the Kensington Special Sales Manager: Kensington Publishing Corp., 119 West 40th Street, New York, NY 10018. Attn. Special Sales Department. Phone: 1-800-221-2647.

Brava and the B logo are Reg. U.S. Pat. & TM Off.

ISBN-13: 978-0-7582-6679-8
ISBN-10: 0-7582-6679-0

First Kensington Trade Paperback Printing: February 2012

10 9 8 7 6 5 4 3 2 1

Printed in the United States of America

For Zoe, Ethan and Lucy. Zoe and Ethan—no book gets written without your help. I appreciate everything you do. Bonus points for not pointing out that microwavable chicken nuggets are not the dietary staple in most families.

For Lucy—welcome to the world! Since the brainstorming for this book began when you were sound asleep on my lap and I couldn't go anywhere (because a wise auntie never, ever wakes the sleeping baby), I owe you one. Plus, you do a mean bear impression. Someday, you and I are teaming up on a bear shifter book.

And, of course, for Louis. As always.

THE FALLEN

Three thousand years ago, rebellion ripped apart the Heavens. Moving swiftly, Michael took action against the rebellious Dominions. For millennia, these angels had served the Heavens. The Dominions were bred to be Heavens' staunchest warriors and had never wavered in their duty. They fought. They defended. They killed, on Michael's command. In the war between good and evil, they were the first—the critical—line of defense. But murderous atrocities had come, and the Dominions had accused Michael. The Heavens' warriors had taken up arms against him—and lost.

When the Dominions fell, Michael condemned them to a near-eternity of punishment. On his command, the rebel angels were stripped of their wings and exiled from the Heavens. These Fallen ones were sent to Earth and condemned to live as Goblins, thirsting for light and goodness not to be found in their own corrupted souls. No Fallen could regain his lost wings and return to the Heavens—unless that male first found and loved his soul mate, the one female capable of redeeming his dark soul and teaching him love and light and peace. In 2090, the first soul mate was found.

CHAPTER ONE

Zer made the run to G2's, coming into the club from the roof because he had energy to burn and he got off on the sheer physical pleasure of pounding across the rooftops, leaping the empty spaces between the buildings. Beautiful thing about all that space was that you just never knew when your foot might slip. If only it was that easy to finally bite it. Put an end to millennia of emptiness. To the suspicion that maybe, just maybe, you'd been exiled from the Heavens because you *weren't* good enough and not because of a well-engineered setup.

Security met him as soon as his boot hit the rooftop, of course—because Zer's lieutenant, Brends, wasn't an idiot, and the male looked after his own with the tenacity of a starving hound—but the patrol recognized his face even before he snarled the password. Everyone knew who Zer was. The sire. The one who was supposed to lead the Fallen out of this shit storm and back to glory. Never mind that he was at least a thousand years overdue.

Two males, one on his left and the other flanking his right. If they'd wanted to take him out, they'd missed their chance. He'd been vulnerable when his boot hit the edge, but now he was on solid ground.

Leather duster flying around him, he took the stairs down

to the club floor, taking out his frustration and his restless energy on the anonymous stairwell with the stark linoleum and aseptic guardrails. Moving silently downward, his shadow gliding over the steps before him, he considered what he'd learned in the last week.

The nightly fights against the rogues preying on the human population of M City were only the tip of the iceberg. The desire to drink human emotions was worse than any drug. The rogues were Fallen who either no longer could or would control their urge to drink human emotions. Lost to that dark hunger, they rampaged out of control, insane and indulging in sprees of violence as they drank their human victims to death.

Worse, Cuthah, the corrupt Dominion who'd engineered the Fallen's exile from the Heavens, was clearly massing the army he'd threatened to raise. Sure, the motherfucker had flat out said as much during his last heart-to-heart with the Fallen, but Zer had hoped—for longer than he should have—that Cuthah had merely been grandstanding, doing a little posturing because the male had been on the losing end of the fight and was looking to save face.

No such luck.

Maybe Zer should have just let the rogues do their thing. The Heavens might have evicted the Dominions' asses, but they hadn't put out a kill order. Not yet. Some of the Fallen still fought for redemption. The others gave in to the soul thirst and became rogues. Fuck if he knew why he fought, though, other than that he was, like it or not, still the leader of the Fallen three thousand years after their disastrous Fall from grace, and he'd never walked away from a fight.

Plus, Zer and his brothers might be debauched sensualists who enjoyed more than their fair share of earthy pleasures, but they did not kill innocents. Seduce, yes, murder, no.

The humans grinding on the crowded dance floor gave him a wide berth when he strode into the club.

He planted himself in the club's private banquette and then propped his feet on the table. His seat in *his* world. He was king here and everyone—human and Fallen—knew it.

The gaping avenue in the dancing crowd closed up once he was safely stowed in the banquette, the music kicking up in volume to match the drug-induced euphoria of the crowd. Sin and sex. His humans stank of both vices. Like the addict he was, he opened his senses, drinking down the delicious cocktail. Unable to experience emotion themselves, the Fallen depended on the humans around them to provide it. There were a few ways to tap into that emotion, but the best was sex. And Zer was hungry for it.

Wanting more.

Always more.

"You find the females on the list?" Nael, one of Zer's lieutenants, didn't waste time with meet-and-greet. The leather-clad Fallen dropped into the seat across from Zer.

A female deposited a tray of bottles and glasses at the table, running her eyes down the hard muscles of Zer's forearms. The interest was automatic, as was the revulsion when her gaze hit the black ink on his wrists and she realized what he was. Not a Goblin-lover, that human, although clearly she was willing to take her paycheck and work the club floor. Her loss. She'd have made more from Zer in one night than she had at her job in a week.

He spared her departing ass a quick glance. The female moved quickly but sleekly, the muscles in her thighs tightening with each stride. She'd have been a hot ride, he thought regretfully. Able to keep up. Ride him half the night and then some.

He'd have liked to taste her.

Unfortunately, with the thirst riding him hard, one taste wouldn't have been enough. He'd have taken another. And another. Until he killed her, and he wasn't going rogue. Not tonight.

"I haven't looked." He'd been too busy killing rogues and hanging on to the shreds of his sanity. Without removing his feet from the table, Zer reached out a long arm and snagged a bottle. Popping the top, he poured himself a shot of well-iced Armadale.

"Soon," Nael suggested. "We get to them first, before Cuthah does, and we're one up on him if they're really soul mates and not just bond mates."

G2's was full of would-be bond mates—humans who were more than willing to temporarily trade their souls to the Fallen in exchange for a favor. One favor for one soul. Catch was, the larger favor, the longer the bond lasted. That wasn't Zer's problem.

No, his problem was that, when the Archangel Michael had exiled the Dominions, stripping them of their wings and their emotions and condemning them to a near-eternity on Earth as Goblins, he'd also dangled the promise of redemption. *If* a Goblin found his soul mate. One soul mate for each Fallen angel, or so Michael had sworn—one human woman who could redeem her predestined mate and restore his wings. It had taken three thousand years to find the first soul mate and Zer wasn't happy with the odds of finding more.

Michael's henchman Cuthah had already killed off every potential soul mate he could lay hands on to prevent the Fallen from regaining access to the Heavens; these four had to be next on his list. "We've got names, so they shouldn't be that hard to find." Truth. The only real question was to whom these females would belong. Wrapping his fingers around the slowly warming sides of his glass, Zer sprawled back in his chair, his eyes moving with deadly interest over the writhing crowd below them.

Most of the club's dancers were human. The hired ones paid with a weekly check were sliding sweat-slicked bodies along the steel-and-glass poles, flashing wicked, almost-there leather thongs and bracelets of diamonds on their wrists and ankles as they moved. The music was a primal beat that penetrated the dancing crowd like a lover, and, wherever Zer looked, he saw the telltale possessive flare in the guests' eyes as they eyed the wicked choices on offer.

G2's only rule was pleasure. But the currency of the realm was spiritual. You wanted the Fallen's favor, you paid for it. With part of your soul. At G2's a night of unforgettable pleasure could be the ritual sealing a dangerous bargain: the granting of a Goblin favor, anything a human might wish for, in exchange for a piece of that human's soul.

Surprisingly, all too many of the dancers there were ready to make that bargain. For the Fallen, it was the best way to slake the inevitable soul thirst.

Spreading out the crumpled page, Zer didn't need to read the words to know what they said. This hit list he knew by heart. Four names. Four potential soul mates. Recon the females, do a little search-and-forcible-retrieval. Once he had these females secured in G2's, he'd let his brothers do the picking and choosing. Match themselves up to their soul mates.

It would have been simpler if they could just choose a couple of tonight's dancers from the club floor. Those females wanted to be here, wanted what the Fallen had to offer. Maybe, these four would, too. Maybe, they'd be just as easy to seduce and wouldn't have any issue with offering themselves up, body and soul, for a little one-on-one with the Fallen if the price was right. No way to know unless he went after them.

"Find an address for me."

With a curt nod, Nael took a handheld from the pocket of his duster. The military-grade casing was an invitation to drive a Humvee over the ruggedized hardware. Like the brother, nothing short of nuclear holocaust would crack that case. Pretty as hell but Teflon strong. Nael had no issues with who or what he was now, and that made him Zer's right hand.

There was the click of ice cubes and computer keys as Nael did his thing. After a few long minutes, he looked up.

"Got one."

"Just one?"

"You need more than that for a start? Besides, she's close at hand. She must not be the clubbing type, or we'd have seen her in here."

Did you just look at your soul mate and *know*? Long experience told Zer that nothing ever was that easy. The out clause on Michael's sentence came with a lengthy list of caveats and restrictions. No way Michael had made it as easy as accidentally bumping into a female on the sidewalk. Or a dance floor.

They'd learned that when Brends found the first of them.

And, truth be told, he didn't envy Brends his soul mate; that was an emotional ball-and-chain, and Zer didn't do bondage. Not unless—a hard smile creased his face—he got to be on top. Domination was bred deep into his genes, and, whether Brends admitted it or not, he'd put his heart and soul into the hands of a human female.

Zer turned his glass in his hand, the damp-beaded glass reflecting the unholy glow of his eyes back to him. Damned beast.

Nael eyed him. "You want me to find another female?"

Nael would, too. God, the brother loved the Internet, databases, and a clever hack job. In this case, breaking code and violating at least a dozen human privacy laws to get the information Zer needed.

"No." It really didn't matter where he started. "Which one you got?"

"One Dr. Nessa St. James. Assistant professor at M City's finest university. Up for tenure this year and—get this—specializes in genetics and biblical studies. The human who developed the pee-on-a-stick DNA testing kit." Nael waggled his eyebrows.

Nessa St. James's life was about to do a 180. Zer hadn't expected to find the next soul mate gyrating on his club floor, but a teacher? Hell, his boys would chew her up and spit her out before breakfast. She'd require hand-holding, and he did *not* do hand-holding. Ever.

"She's one of the top geneticists in the world, Zer." Nael flipped the handheld around so Zer could squint at the small screen.

Ignoring the screen, he stared at Nael, and Nael stared back. The good doctor was on Cuthah's list—which marked her as a potential soul mate—and she had the skills to unravel Cuthah's little biological bomb. Cuthah had claimed the soul mates bore the equivalent of a biological bar code—a little hey-look-at-me in their DNA. While Zer wasn't sure he believed Cuthah's claim, he still needed to check it out. Yeah, opportunity was knocking here.

"We should get her," Nael pointed out, as if waltzing into a university and plucking out the particular human they required was just a walk in the proverbial park.

"She'll have a price." All he had to do, Zer decided, was find out what she wanted. What she *coveted*. Money could fix anything. He'd buy up her lab, cut off her grant funding. Then, because he was feeling *mean*, mean and thirstier than hell, he'd cut off her library card. She wouldn't get whatever it was she wanted from her life until she gave him what he wanted.

Her soul.

"You want me to juice you up?" Nael looked like he knew precisely how thirsty Zer was. Brother wouldn't have made an offer he didn't mean, though, and that was just one of the reasons Zer valued the male. Nael had his back. No matter what. If Zer went rogue and needed a helping hand with a blade to end it all, Nael would do it and wouldn't ask questions, either.

So Nael would seduce a human female and let Zer sip the woman's soul if that's what it took to make sure his sire left G2's at full strength. Christ. It wasn't as if the dancers minded. Hell, that was why they were *there*, doing the bump-and-grind on this particular dance floor. They wanted to be chosen, wanted to win that lottery ticket. Zer resented the desperate need coiling through him, but there was no avoiding it. He had to drink, soon, and he didn't trust himself to do the seducing.

Not anymore.

"Yeah." He jerked his head in a too-quick nod. He wanted to say something else, acknowledge what the brother was doing for him, but what was the point? They both knew Zer hung on by his fingertips and that the whole fucking mess would come crashing down when he let go.

"I love takeout." A slow, heated smile curled the edges of Nael's mouth, but Zer couldn't help noticing that it didn't reach his eyes. Brother knew he was pimping, and even for his sire, it had to sting. He'd find a way to repay his brother.

Beside him, Nael was running a discriminating eye over the dancers, like a housewife at a farmer's market. Too old, too stale, not right. He finally settled on a kitten-eyed blonde who looked like she hadn't done innocent since grade school. When Nael shot her that long, slow smile of his, she came gliding across the dance floor as if there was some sort of chain connecting her to Nael. Her hips writhed sensuously, never losing the throbbing beat of the music, and Zer would have staked his immortal soul that she felt that pulse straight down to her pussy.

She'd do.

Nael didn't bother with chatting the female up about the weather, just gave her the once-over and reached for her, wrapping his large hands around her corseted waist. When he kissed her, a deep, openmouthed, wet kiss, Zer felt the shock of her pleasure straight down to his own toes. She hadn't believed it could be like this.

She broke off the kiss long enough to ask, "He watching?" She gestured toward Zer, and he stared back at her.

"Yeah." Nael nipped at her mouth with his, his fingers pressing through her hair to find a sensitive spot on her scalp that made her purr. "You don't mind that. You just come on over here and tell me what you want."

When he pulled the female down onto his lap, her pale legs straddled him as if he was her favorite ride.

"Kiss me," she answered. The dark flush of arousal colored her skin. She smelled of expensive perfume and even more expensive beauty lotions. A consumer. Those shoes she was wrapping around his brother's back were five-inch heels, reducing her walk to a careful, sensual shimmy. The straps crisscrossed her ankles, snaking up to her bare knees like a lover's tongue. They sure as hell didn't reach anywhere near the microscopic leather skirt that stopped just south of her ass. Nael's hands smoothed the fabric away. He whispered a throaty question. Asking permission to go further.

The female meant nothing to either of them but a temporary way to stave off the hunger riding them. Nael touched her, because Zer didn't trust himself anymore. He couldn't give her the care, the pleasure that she wanted. That she deserved for giving herself to satisfy their carnal hungers. He was so damn thirsty for the taste of her soul, he'd have drained her dry.

He wasn't that kind of killer. Not yet.

Had Michael known what he'd condemned the Fallen to? That question tormented him, but it didn't stop him from drinking, sucking down the taste of the female's soul like she was water and he was dying in the desert. Stale water, yeah, but water nonetheless. He could feel the power flowing through him, the sick ecstasy of feeling, even if they were secondhand emotions. The female coming apart in Nael's arms thought she'd died and gone to heaven, but she had no clue.

Zer had been to the Heavens. He knew what she was really missing out on and what a faint substitute the bliss Nael could shower on her was. The Heavens were worth fighting for, worth protecting even if they didn't want the protection of the likes of him. He'd stop Cuthah no matter what he had to do, because for once in his too-long life he was going to make the right call. Was going to win the battle that mattered.

This was a race to get to the next soul mate first, winner take all.

If Nessa St. James was fortunate, the Fallen would get there first.

CHAPTER TWO

Nessa St. James stared across the fake teak desk at the bastard who'd just declared he was shutting down her lab. Putting her out of business. Tears burned the edges of her eyes but, God, she wouldn't cry. Maybe, if she didn't blink, the tears would stay put and she could play this out. On the other hand, if she gave in to the urge to sob, she could probably justify punching the bastard in the nose, because, if she were going to be unprofessional, she'd go the whole nine yards. Do something she'd really regret. The dean smiled right back at her, patting his tie into place as she breathed her way through the beginning of a panic attack. The cheerful pink and blue stripes marched straight down the line of buttons on his white oxford without missing a step.

"Clearly," she said, "I didn't hear what I thought I just heard."

"We're closing your lab," the dean repeated. His gaze dipped south of her jaw and then slid smoothly back up. She fought the urge to check the neckline of her own white blouse.

"Why?" *Don't panic.* She'd worked too long and was too close to the answers she needed to quit now.

"How long have you been working for us?"

"Three years." She was up for tenure next year. He'd promised in her interview that she'd be a candidate for early tenure, wouldn't have to wait the full six years for her review. His promise had been just one of the many reasons she'd elected to live in M City, to take a position here when she could have worked anywhere in the damned world. They both knew this. So, why was he threatening her?

"You're an impressive researcher." The dean settled back in his chair, increasing the distance between them. His wife had either bought the oxford at the start of their marriage or had idealized her husband's weight. The cheap cotton stretched over the well-defined start of a paunch. Too much fast food and too much stress; his genetics weren't coded to handle that double-barreled onslaught. His body's response to the overload had been to build him a spare tire.

"Thank you," she said cautiously. They both knew it was true.

"And that's why there may be a junior position we can offer you in Professor Markoff's new lab. That would be a good move for you," he continued smoothly, and this time his eyes definitely strayed from her face to the narrow vee of skin exposed by the collar of her blouse. "Given your unfortunate background." He leaned forward as he delivered his bombshell, folding his hands on the teak desktop. Either he didn't know her history with Markoff—or he didn't care. "Your research credentials are impressive, of course, as I've said, but most of our business partners prefer dealing with humans." He licked his lips.

"You don't believe I'm human." She loved her lab, her research. She'd never missed a day of work, and undergraduates actually bothered showing up for her lecture. Plus, she knew just how much money the university had made from her patent on an over-the-counter DNA testing kit. Pee on a stick; find out what you were. Apparently, none of those accomplishments mattered because of one extra chromosome.

A chromosome that marked her, clear as day, as belonging to the paranormal camp.

The problem was, she felt human.

"There is nothing in the university rules that prevents a paranormal from taking a teaching position." She felt compelled to point this fact out to the dean. "You hired paranormals prior to my arrival at this university. Nothing in the university's human-resources manual prevents it." She'd double-checked, twice, after her unfortunate discovery.

He looked smug. "You didn't disclose this information when we hired you."

"I didn't know it," she snapped. "Believe me, this is as much of a shock to me as it is to you. I didn't know until I took a DNA test that there *was* anything unusual about my ancestry. None of this affects my work here, what I've accomplished."

"Maybe we could work something out," he offered, and a new smile, one she'd never seen before, creased the corners of his mouth. "If you could bring in some more funding. And if you were interested."

God, she needed a shower. Surely, he wasn't suggesting what she thought he was. While she was no beast, she wasn't a beauty, either.

"Like I said, Professor Markoff is eager to work with you."

Over her dead body. Markoff had been a mistake, but she'd been lonely. He was interested and was no slouch in the looks department, so she'd accepted his dinner invitation. Unfortunately, Professor Markoff had been under the mistaken impression she would accept a lot more than that. He'd been livid when she'd refused his invite to spend the night. No way she was joining his lab now. He'd have her playing junior assistant forever while he took all the credit for whatever research came out of their happy little merger.

"I'm not interested in working with Professor Markoff." She blinked slowly, cautiously, but the tears still stayed put.

"That's too bad." The dean shrugged. "Maybe you should go home, think it over. Consider what your options are."

"Have you read my latest paper? I'm the principal investigator, and that's a peer-reviewed journal our entire field reads." Most junior faculty would have sold their souls to the damn Fallen for that sort of exposure. She'd worked nonstop for six months putting together that paper. Getting it reviewed and published had been a major coup. She had precisely the chops she needed to make it in this field.

"The twelve tribes of Israel." He nodded, but his face didn't change. His fingers stroked the smooth edge of his desk, tidied an already perfectly aligned pile of papers. "Professor Markoff briefed me."

Professor Markoff couldn't tell his ass from a hole in the ground unless someone else had already written about it, but now wasn't the time to bring that up.

"Thirteen," she said, and she savored the dean's wary blink. "There are thirteen tribes. One is missing from biblical records, and I've found it."

"Twelve." The dean levered himself out of his chair. "Everyone knows that there are twelve. Your hypothesis is an interesting piece of fantasy, but I'd question your research methodology. No one is going to fund that kind of fantasy."

"It's not a fantasy," she countered. "I can trace the DNA ancestry of that population. The region's right. There's a genetic affinity—and there's the paranormal gene. This tribe carries that gene. This is incontrovertible fact."

He blinked slowly. "You can prove this? And you have the funding to do so?"

"Yes." Damn it, she could. Prove it. Funding, however, was a little less certain. "I can. I'll be able to." If her hypothesis was correct. She squelched the uninvited niggle of doubt. She needed time to finish her experiment. Then, she'd have all the proof her dean required. And the answers she needed about her own unexpected bloodlines.

What had started out as academic curiosity, the thrill of discovery and of breaking new ground, had turned into a too-personal quest. No one in the academic community had done work on paranormal DNA. Hell, no one had realized the paranormals *had* DNA. DNA was, after all, a human trait, a recipe for building humans. Paranormals were, by very definition, inhuman. Except for the crossbreeds like her. And that had been her first clue.

The dean sighed. "Go home, Nessa. Think over my offer; let me know what you decide. I'd like to hear from you in three days. Give me funding and facts, and we'll talk. Otherwise—" He shrugged.

Otherwise, don't let the door hit you on your way out. He hadn't fired her, but he'd made it crystal clear that she either had to find funding, take a demotion, or get squeezed out of the department. That gave her precisely three days to rescue her career or watch everything she'd spent a lifetime working for head straight down the crapper. She was going to have to put her backup plan into play.

She cleared the door and made it past the department secretary before the tears finally spilled over. She should have made a beeline for the restroom, but she refused to cry in a stall because her reptilian dean had decided to destroy her career on what appeared to be a whim.

Besides, campus lately had a decidedly less than friendly feel. Maybe it was her paranoia kicking in, or maybe, it was the half dozen times this week that she'd caught *something* out of the corner of her eye. It felt like someone was following her.

Ducking into the bathroom still seemed like a bad idea, however, despite the cheerful flood of students streaming past her. Most of them were paired off in couples, arms wrapped about each other. She didn't know what they saw when they gazed into each other's eyes, but she knew lust when it strolled by her. Spring always hit campus hard, and her students were busy doing what came naturally. Maybe, there was something wrong with her, but she'd clearly gotten hit with the short end of the mating stick. Maybe, she should make more of an effort. Going home lonely night after night wasn't anything to be proud of. She needed a cat. Maybe, two cats.

If, of course, she still had a paycheck to buy the Friskies with.

With a timeline of three days, she wasn't going to have a choice. It was going to have to be the backup plan. Genecore Foundation had sent her a frozen DNA sample, requesting a workup. The anomalies she'd found had piqued her curiosity. Genecore had extended the possibility of a collaboration—a well-funded collaboration—but she'd only just begun checking out the group. She wasn't going to leap from frying pan to fire. But the foundation's president was very, very interested in her work. She'd make that call before her lecture, she decided. Let the guy know that she was seriously interested in signing on to the DNA project he'd proposed.

Elbowing open the door to the building where she had her lecture, she slipped inside, heels clicking on the black-and-white flooring that was older than she was. Heels were a vanity, but, damn it, she was short. She'd take all the extra inches she could get. Plus, the thin heels changed her walk, made her aware of the movement of her hips, the slide of the skirt's fabric over her skin. Made her feel different. More confident. Sexier.

She might not be married, engaged, or even dating, but nothing had ever topped the thrill of setting foot on this campus, of knowing that she *belonged* here. She wasn't leaving, and she wasn't working for Professor Markoff. There was a way to sort out this situation and she'd take it.

With a sigh, she flipped open her cell and dialed.

This was home, and she was damned good at what she did. Never mind that she was as meat-and-potatoes as they came and that the Stalinist architect who'd designed the campus had had a penchant for Gothic curlicues and stonework. On gray days like today, she half expected the gargoyles to come down and strike up a conversation, which meant she was even more tired than usual.

The call went through and a cool voice invited her to wait while she was connected to her party at Genecore.

Time to rescue her own ass.

Zer blew through the door of the building because the rogues riding his ass weren't going to knock first, and his was only a party of three. Get in. Secure the female. Get out. Quick action would minimize human casualties, as well, and that couldn't hurt his chances with Nessa St. James.

She was probably just as tenderhearted as most of *them* were.

He motioned for Nael and Vkhin to peel off. "Secure the lobby." Nael looked like he was jonesing for a good fight, but Vkhin would guard his back. That left Zer free and clear to fetch the good professor.

His booted foot hit the inner door, then paused, because his hands were busy palming weapons. Conveniently, one rogue stopped to mow down the campus security guard. The guard had been a squat, out-of-shape human male, his nose buried in a day-old paper. Most likely a rent-a-cop and from a piss-poor outfit, because the male hadn't even gone for his weapons. No, he had ducked and covered like a good boy, so Zer hadn't bothered with him. The rogue nearest Zer, however, had apparently disliked leaving loose ends behind to call for backup and had vaulted over the desk, blades flashing. Nael and Vkhin were moving in, but Zer's blades cut deep, and, sure enough, there was a high-pitched scream from the murderous rogue, a little quick splatter, and the hallway got a whole lot quieter.

Shit. He needed to pick up the pace.

He took stock. A voice was speaking inside the room. Smooth. Cool. Modulated. *Bingo.*

He burst through the shattered door and ignored the scream-and-run of the panicked students inside. None of them was dumb enough to run in his direction. A quick eyeball told him where the other exits were. Two more sets of doors. Good. He was going to need all the outs he could find.

His first sight of the professor stopped him in his tracks.

She was . . .

She was two kinds of sexy, and no way in hell was she a biblical scholar and world-renowned geneticist. The clothes were right: a buttoned-up, no-nonsense white blouse in some sort of synthetic fabric that wouldn't wrinkle if he drove his SUV over it. God, he was a dirty bastard, though, because he couldn't stop staring at her breasts. She turned away from the whiteboard, and the smooth movement pulled the supple material of her blouse against those breasts. Full, generous handfuls that made him want to suck each of those candy nipples into his mouth and tongue her until she came undone.

Hell, yeah.

She stopped speaking when he exploded into the room, her hands moving, gripping the edge of the lectern hard as they slid beneath its lip. *Panic switch.* He'd have bet his last breath that she'd have a panic switch installed under there. Good. A strong instinct for self-preservation would make his job easier.

She stared at him, so he glared right back and wondered if she had any idea just what a turn-on that damp, nervous little stroke of her tongue over her lower lip was.

Christ, she was sexy. And he'd bet that she had no idea.

She'd twisted her chocolate-brown hair into a neat chignon and skewered the heavy mass with a well-aimed pencil. Just as sweet as sugar. Her skin was pale from too much indoor time, and he could just make out her dark eyes as he took inventory. Two arms. Two legs. Two breasts. All the standard accoutrements for her kind and nothing special, so he shouldn't be so turned on. Then she opened her mouth. She didn't seem to raise her voice, but he heard her clear in the back of the lecture hall.

"Security has been alerted. I advise you to get the fuck out of my lecture hall. Now." That liquid voice ran straight down his spine and took up residence in his balls. That voice didn't match her prim, buttoned-up exterior at all.

Christ, she had no idea who she was baiting. What. That, or she just didn't give a flying fuck.

Her delicious, icy glare had him hardening, and he so needed to get a grip on his cock. "Down, boy," he muttered, as he headed down the main aisle. The slower students or the ones unfortunate enough to be trapped behind their companions scrambled out of his way.

He knew what they saw. Coldhearted killer with ice in his veins. They weren't wrong, and, from the look in his professor's eyes, she saw it, too. She abandoned her death grip on the lectern, grabbed her laptop, and made a beeline for the nearest exit.

If she'd been dealing with another human, she might have made it.

He didn't bother with explanations—because there just wasn't enough fucking time. He could hear the next rogue thundering down the hallway, mowing through the crowd of panicked students despite whatever Nael and Vkhin were throwing at him, and she wouldn't have listened to him, anyway. Shoving one blade between his teeth, he vaulted over the rows of seats one-handed. He kept the other hand weapons-ready. Three rows. Two. And bingo.

He cut her off, wrapping one leather-clad arm around her chest—yeah, he was a bastard, all right, because he noticed *precisely* how those buttoned-up breasts felt cushioned against his arm—and yanked her off her feet, releasing the blade in his teeth. She let loose with a multilingual barrage of curses that the entire useless U.N. couldn't have outdone as the laptop slid away from her.

"Shut. The. Fuck. Up." He hauled her up against him just to prove he could. "I'm on your side."

She stopped her cursing long enough to bring her fingers up to do her level best to claw his eyes out, while her feet did a number on his shins with her damn pointy heels. Again, too bad for her that he wasn't human. She had no chance at all.

He took her down to the ground because that was simplest and lowered his full weight onto her. No way that petite frame of hers was bucking off his weight, although she gave it her best shot. Three enjoyable seconds of that—after he shifted his weight just enough to pinion her legs as far apart as the fabric of that pencil skirt would let her move—and she stopped. Fighting for breath, he figured, because most humans prioritized living, and living included breathing.

Her brown eyes glared up at him. "If you're the good guy," she said, "who's playing the villain in this scenario?"

Genetics was predictable. The male pinning her to the none-too-clean tiles of her lecture hall was wildly *un*predictable.

The geneticist in her was categorizing, identifying racial lines and possible antecedents. Too dark to be Mediterranean, and the cheekbones were wrong for Middle Eastern. He could have been Israeli; Mossad, based on the arsenal he was packing. Her feminine side, however, purred with unexpected awareness. He was dark, and the hard planes of his face were the perfect foil for an even harder body. His hair was cropped too close to his head for her to tell what the natural texture was, but those cheekbones would have guaranteed him bookings at any Manhattan modeling agency until the booker took a good look at those eyes. Those eyes weren't human. The dark irises were a rich black color. And they glowed with heat and emotion. Forget the small scars that flirted with the edge of his cheeks as if life had tattooed a warning sign on his face for all to see. This male was dark. Feral. And damned if that wasn't a possessive gleam in his eyes.

He also wasn't human, and he was way out of her league, even if she did have one extra chromosome.

She ran her eyes over that face again. Yeah, that coloring, that bone structure, told her all she really needed to know. His genetics were right there on display.

"Goblin," she identified. "Fallen angel." So, he clearly wasn't here to listen to her lecture on introductory genetics or to discuss her recent paper on the Book of Numbers. Lines and patterns. Relationships. All neat and tidy on paper. Probably messier than hell in real life, not to mention vaguely incestuous. Of course, if you went by the glazed-over look of her students, not too many people found it interesting. At all. So, she was a freak in more ways than one. It still didn't explain why *he* was here or why he had an interest in manhandling her.

Her fingers curled around his wrists, tugging. He let her—probably because it amused him, the bastard. Her futile efforts only managed to dislodge the sleeves of his leather duster, revealing dark bands of ink around both those thick wrists. When a Goblin and a human bonded, that bond was literally imprinted on the skin of both, dark swirls of ink-like black markings on their wrists and forearms. Rumor claimed that the larger the favor, the thicker and darker those markings were. She didn't think Zer's marks were natural, which meant he wasn't bonded. He'd gotten the art for his own reasons.

He shifted on top of her, and she sucked in a much-needed breath before the weight returned. "Yeah. Like what you see, doc?"

She did, but she wasn't stupid, just having a really, really bad day. He'd traumatized her entire undergraduate seminar, pinned her to the floor, and, from the sounds coming from outside her hall, he wasn't alone. Still, the distant crackle and pop of gunfire indicated that campus security might finally be riding to the rescue.

Oh, God. Maybe she'd never woken up at all this morning. Maybe the nightmare of the dean's office and this unthinkable disruption of her lecture were all part of the same nightmare. Maybe, if she concentrated hard enough, she'd wake up. Unfortunately, she was desperate, not crazy, and the two hundred-plus pounds of male atop her was no dream.

"Get off me." She didn't think he'd budge, but that wasn't going to stop her from registering a protest. He had no right to just stride in here and manhandle her. He didn't own her soul and never would.

She refused to focus on the frisson of fear the sounds outside her lecture hall provoked. First, she needed to get free. Then, she could panic.

"You are the doc, aren't you?" His eyes examined her face, as if he expected to find a name and number stamped there for his convenience.

She considered refusing to answer his questions—after all, wasn't that what members of the military were trained to do? Provide only rank and number when they fell into hostile hands?—but one large thumb was now stroking slowly over her exposed collarbone in a little absentminded motion that could have been unconscious on his part. Except she didn't think so. His eyes didn't budge from her face.

He knew exactly what he was doing, and that unwilling little trickle of heat that shot straight to her groin was a warning. God, was she *stupid*? He'd chased her, pinned her. And yet she couldn't help noticing the delicious heat and weight of his too-large body.

"Tell me your name," he demanded, giving her more of his weight. Breathing became a concern again, as the air whooshed from her lungs. He wasn't hurting her, not yet, but the message was loud and clear. Her assailant was in charge here, and he planned to have her dancing to his tune.

Her eyes narrowed. Not if she had anything to say about it.

When he reached over her for her dropped laptop, however, she fought back panic. Had she backed up? What if the automatic software hadn't done its job? This bastard wasn't taking her data.

"Nessa St. James," she said quickly, breathing more easily when the large hand retreated from the titanium casing of her laptop. The backup software had a 99 percent accuracy rate, but she wasn't chancing that 1 percent. Outliers were a bitch.

"Nessa St. James."

"That's what I said," she snapped, because she wasn't going to let him know that she was scared. She was tired of being scared. Tired of running from her problems, even if today's current problem outweighed her at least two to one. From the feel of him, he was six-foot plus and a good two hundred pounds. "You want to let me up now, I'll get my purse. Show you some ID."

A hard, mean smile creased those sexy lips of his. "I'm not ready to let you *up*, baby," he said, making the innocuous words sound like the dirtiest of promises. Shamefully, she felt an unexpected dampness slick her sex. She couldn't possibly be attracted to this Neanderthal.

"The hell you're not." She focused on the noise outside. The snap-crackle-and-pop was louder now, but she didn't know if campus security was up to this job.

He rolled, taking her with him, tucking her into the protective shadow of his body as he rose smoothly to his feet in a half crouch. One large hand reached down toward her and stopped.

"Zer." That grunt must have counted as an introduction in

his book. No one had ever accused the Fallen of having manners. She didn't like lying flat on her back, staring up at him, so she sat up. He was watching her, and the look in his eye said she was prey.

"So, Zer, why are you here?" She waved a hand around the carnage of her lecture hall. "If you'd wanted to audit my course, you'd have come to my office hours." And she would have made him ask nicely. No. Scratch that. She would have made him beg. She suspected no one had the upper hand around this Zer, but she'd take whatever opportunities life handed her.

His eyes assessed the smashed-in door. "We need to get out of here."

For once, they were in agreement. She thought of her ruined lecture, the screaming students, and decided that she'd had enough of his alpha-male crap for one afternoon. He could kill her and get it over with, or he could damn well let her go.

"I agree," she said, ignoring his hand and shoving to her feet. "I'm done here. You're done here. I suggest you head on out that door you stove in and explain to campus security what was undoubtedly a very good reason for acting like a complete Neanderthal. In the meantime, I'm going to leave through the other door and see if there's anything salvageable of this day."

"No," he said in that low, raspy growl of a voice. "I can't let you do that, baby."

She'd play his game. "Why not?"

Explanations were clearly killing him. Not a big one for talking, she decided, or he just couldn't be bothered wasting words on her.

"Come with me," he demanded.

She ran through a list of possible reasons to walk out of there with him and came up blank. "No."

When he reached for her again, she scrambled backward.

"Listen to me," he said, and she got the impression that he would only explain once. He didn't strike her as the negotiating type of guy. No, he'd *take* what he wanted, and if she couldn't stop him, he'd figure he was right. "I need you to come with me. Right now."

Damn it, where was campus security? They were supposed to keep her *safe*. When she was finished here, she'd be having words with the dean about this situation.

When she flinched, the Fallen pulled back his hand, crossing his arms over that broad chest of his. The soft cotton of his black T-shirt pulled over impossibly large muscles. Her unwanted companion was seriously built.

"You know what I am, right?" the male asked her.

"Besides an unwelcome intrusion breaking up my afternoon lecture?" When he gave her that cold-eyed stare of his, she decided it might be wiser to humor him. "You're a Goblin." She shrugged and assessed the distance to the door. She wouldn't make it before he'd be on her. Unfortunately. "You're one of the Fallen."

He nodded, as if she was a particularly gifted student. Straining her senses, she listened intently. The sounds of panicked, fleeing students had faded, but she should have been hearing the heavy thud of booted feet as campus security came through the lobby.

Instead, she got dead silence, and that couldn't possibly be good.

"You know what the Goblin bond is?" He eyed her like a stranger offering candy. "You heard of the favor?"

Goblin favors were legend. One favor, any favor at all. The catch was, though, you had to be willing to rent your soul out to the bastard doing the favor. Nothing in this life was free. "You ever thought about it?" His voice was a dark, liquid rasp that promised straight-up sex and pleasure, and she had to remind herself that she had no interest in a Goblin bond. Ever. She'd worked damn hard to get where she was, without owing anyone. "What you might ask for if you had the chance?"

"Pass," she said when he stopped, clearly waiting for an answer. "I'm not interested in whatever you and the rest of your gang are selling."

"You come with me," he said, the words half dragged out of him, "and you can have that favor. Anything you want. You want this?" He waved a hand around the lecture hall. "It's all yours. Tenure. Department chair. Unlimited funding." He said the words as if he were waving an American Express black card and magic wand rolled into one. And maybe he was. He'd clearly done his research and maybe even knew what had transpired in the dean's office. Well, she had a new research partner on the hook—the ubiquitous Genecore—so she didn't need his damn money. Or anything else he had to offer.

"Fuck off," she spat. Could the day get any worse? "My soul isn't for sale."

"You know what's out there in your lobby?" he pressed. She just kept doing that subtle backward hitch that wasn't as subtle as she'd hoped because, clearly, he knew she was jonesing to make a break for it. "You got at least one dead human. Think my offer over."

Okay. So she'd been mistaken. The day clearly could get worse. "Did you kill him?"

Zer shook his head. "The security guard? No, I didn't. A rogue did, and if my boys and I hadn't killed *him,* he'd be in here gunning for you. You don't know what you're up against, my Nessa, and that shit's going to get you killed."

"Why would anyone be coming after me?" *He had,* a small voice whispered.

"The Fallen want to bond with you," he insisted without answering her questions, sliding one booted foot closer to her.

"All of you?"

"No." He shoved a hand through that so-short hair of his. "One of us."

"You?"

"Hell. No." He looked appalled, and *that* offended her in a way that all of his manhandling hadn't. "I'm going to take you back to G2's, introduce you to the brothers. One of them will bond with you."

Right. And apparently her free will didn't factor into this at all in his Neanderthal worldview. She was done playing his game, and she wasn't taking a field trip to one of the most notorious clubs in M City. Junior faculty who wanted to make tenure didn't spend time in those kinds of venues. "Pass. My life doesn't require the complication"—*the* added *complication,* that traitorous little voice whispered in her head—"of taking on a Goblin bond. Look elsewhere," she suggested sweetly. "Try the French lecture on Thursday afternoons. Maybe you can find a taker there."

She wasn't a sofa or a framed piece of artwork. Sure, he was sexy as hell, but clearly he saw her as little more than an object to be passed around among those like him, hung up on a wall until they found the place where she worked best. Her wishes didn't come in to it. He could damn well find someone else, someone who needed that Goblin favor. She was off the market as far as he was concerned.

"No good," he said, and he dropped his bombshell. "It has to be you."

She knew she wasn't that special. "Find someone else," she snapped. No way was she buying into his silver-tongued promises. "I don't want what you have to offer. I like my life as it is just fine. Anything that's missing, I'll get for myself. I don't want your handouts and—news flash—my soul's not for sale."

His business hand, the one that had never let go of a knife, came up, and she felt her heart stutter. She didn't want, she realized, to die.

The knife flashed, but that hard edge wasn't headed her way. No, it was moving toward the muscle-bound male loping through the shattered doorway. A big, hard, mean fighter with the cold eyes of a stone-cold killer. Not half as bad, however, as what he chased into her auditorium.

The noise should have been her first clue, the inhuman growling of a predator who'd scented prey. The second was the darkened face and twisted, brutal jut of the male's jaw. Her mind was cataloging the features, tracking the male's bloodline, even as the words came out of her mouth. "Oh, my God," she said. "He's one of you."

"Not anymore," her strange protector said. "Now, he's rogue."

Any killing done here in this room, Zer was doing it.

Primitive instincts he hadn't known he possessed roared for him to protect her. She wasn't safe, and that made him unexpectedly angry. He was going to make things safe for Nessa St. James, and killing this rogue was just the first step.

"No worries, darling." Palming his blades, Zer threw. "Time to break up this party."

Before Zer was halfway up the aisle, the rogue launched his counterattack, snarling as he pulled a fyreblade. Only Dominions, first-line angelic defenders of the Celestial throne, were supposed to carry those blades—and only in the Heavens. This was the second fyreblade Zer had seen in as many months. Someone who clearly hadn't gotten the memo had boosted a load of forbidden weapons—and distributed them to the lowest of the low. The rogues.

The blade landed and bit at his flesh, the angelfyre leaping from blade to wound, burrowing through the thick leather of his duster. Blocking the pain, Zer reached for the cold discipline he'd mastered in another lifetime when he'd fought for what was right and what was good. Pain didn't matter, only defeating his opponent. No way this motherfucker was leaving the auditorium. One quick glance upward showed that that direction was no option, even if the rogue had himself a pair of wings. No windows, just too-narrow skylights.

The rogue slashed down again with the blade, forcing Zer to feint. "My soul, Fallen," it hissed. "Nessa St. James comes with me."

Yeah, well, Zer wasn't in the market for leftovers, and he sure as hell wasn't sharing this new female. He'd always hunted for himself. *Before,* a little voice mocked in his head. Flowing smoothly from one defensive position to the next, he brought his own blade up to block the next lethal downward stroke. That blade hit deep—hell, if it hit the leather of his duster one too many times, he was toast. Eventually, those blades cut straight to the soul.

He countered smoothly, pushing the rogue backward with sheer, brute force. This time, the rogue's fyreblade sliced cleanly through the expensive leather coat. For the second time. Fuck it. He was done playing. He'd liked that coat.

Vaulting over the rogue's head, he positioned himself between the rogue and the professor. She swore and wisely backtracked behind the lectern.

Zer slashed left and right, blades dancing in his hands. Circling, he waited for his opening.

His own inner rogue too close to the surface, he could feel his features growing darker, more savage. Michael's curse threatened to devour the Fallen angel and leave only the rogue. No more squeaks from his human companion now. Instead, she was staring, and she wasn't watching the rogue charging back up the aisle.

No, she was staring straight at Zer.

Zer knew what she was seeing, and he scared the shit out of himself, too.

"Head for the door, baby," he growled, scooping up her

laptop and throwing it to her. She caught it like he'd thrown her some sort of bizarre lifeline, then took off in a staggering run in those impractical little heels of hers. Yeah, she was good to go. Nael was already moving effortlessly to intercept her if need be.

Zer glided in smoothly. The rogue didn't understand that Zer was the deadlier predator. Or that, this close, Zer's steel blade would be just as effective as a fyreblade. No, instead the rogue launched himself in a running line, making straight for Zer, fyreblade out like a damned battering ram.

Surging forward, Zer delivered a powerful kick to the rogue's chest. Jerked sharply down on the unprotected blade arm. There was a crack as bone gave and then the rogue's high-pitched whine of pain, but Zer's blade was already sliding through leather and skin, along the ribs and home.

The blade shut the rogue up, but the doubts remained.

"We've got more company coming," Nael warned. "Rogue in the lobby, he's out for the count. But there's more of his kind blazing a path across campus. The sooner we're out of here, the better."

"Options?"

"We take her out the side door." Nael shrugged. "Or we go up, across the roof. If the bastards have their wings back, though, we might as well paint a bull's eye on her back now if we go that way."

No concealment had him opting for the side door. "Transport's waiting?"

"Outside." Vkhin spoke. His cold, precise accent clipped the word to the bare minimum. "She ready to roll?"

Nessa was almost to the door, but she went nowhere now without his say-so. Of course, she was under the mistaken impression that she had a vote here. He needed her to bond with one of his brothers because she was someone's soul mate. It didn't matter if he didn't know which male yet. She'd belong to one of them, and the details could come later.

Zer figured he could reason with her.

Or, he could just kidnap her.

Since B was the quicker route to his goal, he went with B.

Effortlessly catching up with her, he tossed her ass over his shoulder and made for the door.

CHAPTER THREE

Zer bundled the professor, kicking and screaming, into the waiting SUV. The tinted windows and the slick black paint job seemed bad gangster wannabe, but the car was built to take a direct mortar hit. He didn't know how it would stand up to a fyreblade, but he wasn't planning on waiting around to find out. He wanted a smooth ride and a clear shot. Traffic congestion was a danger he couldn't predict, but there was a nice, straight piece of asphalt between here and the club. No curves and a limited number of side streets. He'd have her secured in ten.

With a curse, he tossed the female onto the seat and followed her down. Good thing, too, because she immediately surged up from the seat, fighting like a wildcat. Hell, he didn't want to hurt her, but she clearly planned to be difficult.

Nael shot him a hard glance, sliding into the front seat to ride shotgun. He said something to the driver in a low, hard voice, and the car slid rapidly away from the curb. Vkhin sprawled in the back, weapons out.

"Last chance to play nice, baby," Zer growled. He could almost taste her soul, the hunger riding him mercilessly. Nael's blonde amusement at G2's had been merely an appetizer. A diversion.

"Maybe she likes it rough," Vkhin said from the rear seat.

The Fallen's eyes methodically quartered the streets sliding past the tinted windows of the SUV.

Nessa's pupils dilated, her breath catching in a little hiss of uncertainty that he shouldn't have found so arousing. Deliberately, he dropped his gaze, letting his eyes wander over the stretched white fabric of her blouse. Her nipples were hard little nubs, but he didn't know whether that reaction was fear or desire. The uncertainty bothered him and shouldn't have. He needed her to listen to him. He needed her to obey.

Fortunately for them both, he was very, very good at making humans do what he needed them to do.

Deliberately, he crowded her with his larger body, trapping her against the expensive leather of the seats. Immediately, she tried to slide away from him, but he wasn't having that. Inexplicably, he wanted her—he needed her—just as close as he could get her. This close, he could taste the delicious heat and scent of her skin. He didn't want her to be afraid of him. No, what he wanted was to stroke his thumbs along the sweat-slicked line of her collarbone. Follow that feminine shadow with his tongue. His teeth.

Christ. What was wrong with him? She was a weapon in his fight with Cuthah and making this personal was a disaster waiting to happen.

"This is kidnapping," she hissed up at him. "Kidnapping. Do you know what the penalty is for that?"

"Ten years," Nael tossed over the seat. Brother had a mistimed sense of humor, as always. "If you're human. Your kind haven't built prisons that can hold *our* kind, love. There's no point in making useless threats."

"Is that true?" Her glare drilled into Zer as if he was honor-bound to tell her the truth. Clearly, she hadn't gotten the memo that the Fallen were no longer members of the choir. "You think you're above the law? That you don't have to play by the same rules the rest of us play by?"

He eyed her.

"You want to kidnap me, feel free to try."

She was absurdly feminine, lying there sprawled on the seat. Her careful chignon was lopsided, sliding out of its pins. He reached out and pulled the last survivor free, ignoring her hands as she batted at him. The heavy locks spilled around her shoulders, all waves and gentle curves. He wanted to bury his fingers in those sweet strands, run them through his fingers.

No. He didn't want a lover—and he certainly didn't want a vulnerable, fragile human lover. It didn't matter that she was the prettiest thing he'd seen in months, startlingly alive and achingly vulnerable. Someone had to seduce her, coax her into falling in line with the plan. That someone could be him.

His cock's violent reaction warned him that his body was so on board with that plan. He'd been hard since he'd laid eyes on the professor.

Not happening, though. He'd learned millennia ago, hadn't he, that lovers made a male vulnerable? The minute he let her into his bed—the minute he saw her as anything but a tactical advantage, a pawn to be sacrificed in the game he was playing with Cuthah and the Archangel Michael—he knew what could happen. Once he'd sunk himself deep inside her, he might not remember that, in the end, she was a weapon. A game piece to be played.

Forget about seeing her as a female—as a person. He'd learned three millennia ago, hadn't he, that making emotional choices only ended in disaster.

She wasn't his. He had to remember that.

He was going to play her in Cuthah's damn chess game and nothing more.

Still, the glare she shot at Nael should have frozen the brother in his tracks. Nael, of course, merely smiled, a slow, heated warning of a smile. If his Nessa wasn't careful, Nael might be doing some claiming of his own.

"No," she said, and someone should have warned her that no one said no to the Fallen. "You stop this car," she ordered, "and you let me out right now. This is ridiculous. This is the twenty-first century, not the Dark Ages. I don't know where you get off, manhandling me like this, but you're breaking a half dozen laws, and I'm going on record right now. Stop."

His cock hardened, thickened with pleasure at that feminine defiance. Someone should have warned her what happened when saucy females baited dominants.

"No," he repeated, his voice low and hard. "You don't get to say no to me, baby." Fuck the hands-off shit. It was time to engage.

"Zer—" someone warned from the front seat. Nael. "Let me take care of this." Leather rustled as his brother shifted. Beside him, Nessa froze.

"No," he said again. "Professor here issued a challenge. I'm taking her up on it."

Nael spat a low, masculine curse, and the female flinched but didn't back down. Instead, her hands came up between them and shoved.

"That's not a challenge, you idiot," she hissed. "That's legal fact. Stop the damn car right now."

He savored the warmth of those small hands. No rings, he noted. Good. A permanent lover would merely be another obstacle to overcome. The possessive swell of emotion that thought aroused was unfamiliar, so he brought the conversation back to known territory.

Deliberately, he wrapped a hand around her thigh. The too-thin, soft fabric of her nylons slid along his palm in an erotic tease. The woman pinned beneath him had dedicated a lifetime to genetic profiling. Her research had been brilliant, identifying paranormals as if they were some kind of disease, handing Zer's enemies an easy means for uncovering the Fallen's vulnerability. He didn't like her. Didn't like what she'd chosen to do. He damn sure wouldn't underestimate what that clever mind of hers was capable of imagining. How did she like it, he wondered, now that the shoe was on the other foot? Oh, she'd never spoken out publicly about the paranormals, had never joined in the public debates about what rights non-humans should—or should not—be granted. Of course, he'd never waited around for anyone to grant *him* anything. He'd taken what he needed, what he wanted, and he'd never questioned that decision.

"Don't touch me," she ordered, but not before he caught the hesitation. Scented sweet, heated welcome. His professor was curious.

"No," he repeated in a soft rasp. "I don't think you mean no at all, baby."

"I do." He didn't miss her continuing hesitation. His female hadn't moved. Was frozen on his leather seat while her fingers fluttered against his chest, over his heart. He lowered his head slowly, giving her time to protest, but all she did was chew on that too-delectable lower lip, so he closed the distance, bracing her between the soft cushion of leather and his body. Surrounding her with his heat and hardness.

What would she taste like? Would she push him away—or pull him closer? His lips met hers, and he was lost.

Her hard-eyed dom had her pinned to the seat of a car that cost more than she made in a year. She should have been shrieking protests. Kicking. Clawing at him. So why were her fingers curling into the butter-soft leather of his coat, stroking the fabric as if it was his bare skin and he was her lover?

Stockholm syndrome, Nessa decided. Stockholm syndrome was the only logical answer.

Because it had nothing to do with curiosity. Or the hot, needy aching spreading through her, until her pussy wept with *desire*.

Desire was a chemical reaction. She didn't truly want the Goblin slowly wrapping her in his arms and lowering the hot weight of his large body onto hers. She definitely didn't want the delicious press of skin against skin, pinning her into the luscious depths of the seat.

God, she didn't want any of this.

And yet it was happening, and she wasn't doing anything to stop it.

Closing her eyes, she dragged his scent deep into her lungs. Bayberry and cedar, smoky, woody notes as rugged and wild as the man himself. He pulled her closer, his growl of masculine approval sending goose bumps skittering over her exposed skin as the thick, delicious heat of his large body surrounded her. The car swayed gently, taking a corner faster than it should have, rocking her body against his. The reason for the speed was lost in the sudden, erotic silence of the car, the hard breathing of its occupants.

"Is your answer still no?" He growled the challenge against her mouth.

"Yes," she whispered, because she didn't know what she meant, and, God, she was tired of thinking. She deserved something after her hellish day, and he was far sweeter than the pint of ice cream she'd planned on for dinner.

"Close enough."

His mouth closed over hers, and, yes, he tasted as good as he smelled. The dark spice and bay taste of him teased her, a throaty, rich scent that had her fingers curling against his skin. She forgot why she was supposed to be resisting. Why she'd ever wanted to say no to him.

Hard lips pressed hers apart. Ruthless. Male. For a moment, she panicked. What if she couldn't do this? It had been so long since she'd kissed a lover. Maybe he wanted someone more experienced. Someone *better* at this. She jerked her head back, but he had his hands anchored in her hair now, and he wasn't letting go. And that tongue—God, that wicked tongue—stroked a damp, heated path along the seam of her lips.

"Let me in, baby," he growled, and, God help her, it didn't matter anymore. She wanted to know what he'd feel like. What he'd *do* next. She opened up for him, and he swept inside. Took her mouth, his tongue stroking wickedly along hers. He was making her wet, and he wouldn't let her hide from what he was making her feel. She hummed a little note of pleasure and happiness, relaxing into his touch.

He groaned into her mouth, eating at her like a starving man, and she was lost. His hands tangled deeper in her hair, angling her head for his possessive kiss. Massaging her scalp as one heavy leg pressed between hers, tangled in the fabric of her pencil skirt.

Her moan was shockingly loud in the sudden silence of the car. Oh, God. What was he doing to her? She never moaned. She chose what she showed her lovers—or not. And yet here she was, coming undone in his arms. Underneath him, and all she wanted to do was to pull him closer still.

The sweet pulse of desire had her hands curling into his jacket, making demands, and, God help her, he was going to give her exactly what she asked for.

Zer figured if he kept kissing his professor, she might finally shut the hell up. Nessa St. James needed to stop fighting him, had to get with the program and do business with him. The unbelievable taste of her mouth, however, had Zer stiffening against her heated little body, his hands dragging her closer still. That kiss, her tentative touch, was a revelation. He was driving home his point that he was larger, meaner, more dangerous, yet he wished he hadn't. When she kissed him back, her tongue pushing shyly against his as if she hadn't kissed a male in years and wasn't quite sure she remembered the hang of it, he was lost.

He drank her in, the sweet, wild, shy taste of her pumping

through his veins and filling up that empty space inside him where his soul should have been if he wasn't such a heartless bastard. God, she tasted good. He couldn't get enough of her, and she, well, she was melting beneath him, arching up into his touch like just maybe she couldn't get enough of *him*, either. He deepened the kiss, his mouth moving over hers with hard urgency as he drank her down.

Nael's hand fisting in his collar was an unwelcome intrusion. The brother's eyes were cold. Determined. "Let her go now. Back off." Nael's hand twisted in the leather and yanked hard. "Back off *now*."

Zer snarled and wished he hadn't.

Nessa was staring up at him wide-eyed. Dazed. Pale.

Too pale. Now that he was clear of her mouth, he could see the too-white color of her face, and he wanted to say something but didn't know what. He'd been drinking her dry like the worst rogue out there. Instead of mouthing useless apologies, however, he shot off her as if she was something contagious.

He inhaled sharply, acknowledging the thick, hot swirl of pheromones filling the car. Brothers could scent her, too. Hell.

Nessa St. James was meant for one of *them*. Not him. He didn't want a bond mate, couldn't guarantee he wouldn't kill her if he took her. And there was no way in hell he merited a soul mate.

Taking one last, deep breath, he put the seat's length between them and stared out the window at the streets sliding past. Hurting Nessa St. James wasn't part of the plan.

Not yet.

CHAPTER FOUR

Zer tapped the leather-duster-wrapped bundle tossed over his shoulder. Not a particularly elegant mode of transport, but Nessa had made her choice when she'd refused to get out of the SUV. From the muffled squeak of outrage, he'd been patting her ass. Too damned bad. Deliberately, he stroked a hand over those smooth curves. Yeah, definitely ass. Smooth. Warm. Deliciously feminine. The unknown brother who took her would be a damn lucky male.

The bouncer guarding G2's door let them in without hesitation, but there was no missing the spark of curiosity or the lazy, sensual appreciation in the male's eyes as he got with the program. He acknowledged Zer's entrance with a hard nod of his head and then turned his eyes straight back to the street. Good male. There shouldn't be any trouble here, in the heart of Goblin territory, but no one survived three millennia by being careless.

He took the stairs two at a time, deliberately tightening his arm when Nessa St. James picked up the pace of her struggles. She wasn't stupid. She knew she was good and trapped. Plus, Nael and Vkhin were hard on his heels, the brothers flanking him. Even if she got free of Zer, she wasn't going anywhere.

Keying the combo on the access pad outside his door, he pushed open the door with a booted foot when the light glowed green. Zer had kept a suite of rooms above G2's for the last decade. Most of his brothers had their own lairs scattered around M City, and the suite here was one of several he maintained. Not a home—just a place to lay his head when he was done hunting. He'd never let himself forget that this place, this world, was temporary. Somehow, he was getting them all back home.

He stroked his leather-wrapped bundle again. He had the means to win now.

He'd forgotten what it felt like to succeed, damn it. The slow, hot curl of satisfaction unfolding in his gut. It was a shame that Nessa St. James was going to be the one to pay the price for that success, but he'd make it up to her. She'd have the favor to look forward to, and that had to be a powerful incentive.

He moved swiftly through the suite, past the unused cozy grouping of sofas—because none of the Fallen were given to sitting around and chatting—and dropped her onto his bed. The bed wasn't the black leather and sleek chrome Nael favored—minimalist crap picked out from a magazine spread. No, Zer had chosen Russian antiques, the really old ones that belonged in a damn museum, because they reminded him of the country estates and hunting lodges he'd favored four hundred years ago. Estate-sale relics that smelled of lemon polish and age. Downright feudal, as one of his brothers had pointed out, but he was no interior decorator—he was the sire. He *was* feudal.

The duster wriggled with feminine indignation, and he sprawled in a large leather armchair beside the bed, watching. Hunting dogs had scratched deep gouges into the surface.

"Out," he said softly, and, behind him, Nael and Vkhin

took their cue, vanishing swiftly. The door clicked quietly behind them as *she* scrambled out of his coat, her eyes shooting daggers across the thick velvet counterpane at him.

"You killed someone. You killed that . . . that man in the lecture hall."

He laughed. "I did, baby, but he and his pals had to die. They came after you." He could read the truth on her face. She wasn't used to viewing her life as a battlefield, but he was. Every choice, every move he made was another move in the chess game he was playing with the Archangel Michael. "And he wasn't a man. He was a rogue." She frowned, so he plowed on with the explanation. "A rogue is a Fallen angel who's gone that one extra step. He's drunk a few souls dry, and he's addicted to the taste. He'll keep on killing to satisfy that thirst. There's no rehab for that kind of sickness."

"So you just killed him." She didn't look as if she found his explanation particularly convincing, but that was her problem. Not his.

"There will be more rogues. There always are." He shrugged. And he'd kill each and every one of them. That was truth she could take to the bank.

Instead of looking grateful, however, she looked even more horrified. He should have expected her reaction. She was human. Until today, she'd gone about her life ignorant of the role she was about to play.

Ignorant of one inescapable fact: she was a pawn.

And, since he could not allow Cuthah to control or destroy her, he would put her into play. He would match her with one of his brothers.

"You can't go around killing people."

He crossed his arms over his chest, deliberately playing with her.

"Rogues don't count."

Her face froze. It was too bad, really. Her smile would

have lit the room, but she wouldn't smile for him. So, fine. Fortunately, he didn't need her smiles. All he needed was her body. Her soul. And a few words.

It didn't take her long to battle back, though. "Call MVD," she ordered, sitting up straighter. "Let them handle it."

"There is nothing they can do." He didn't even have to lie, because that was the honest truth. There was nothing M City's paranormal police division, MVD, could do here. The fact was that MVD was outmanned and outgunned. Good for picking up the bodies, but not so good for putting them down. Fortunately, she had him and the Fallen to see to her protection. "You stay here. With us."

"You bastard." Her fingers curled into the pillows on top of the bed, and he wondered if she was going to throw a pillow at him, because he could see her visibly reaching for control. He liked seeing her on his bed. "Take me back. Now."

She stayed on the bed, though, and he figured that was telling. Her body accepted that she wasn't getting past him, even if her mind was having a hard time playing catch-up.

He shook his head, crossing his arms over his chest. Eyed her slowly. Even all mussed up and heated, she was lovely. Her hair had uncurled completely from its disciplined chignon, delicate wisps caught along her jaw. She was beautiful, right down to the pink flush on her cheekbones as she glared at him.

"I told you." He didn't usually have to repeat himself, but somehow he didn't mind making an exception for her. Because it riled her up. He was a bastard, but he found that feminine resistance damn sexy. Since she wasn't going to be his, he figured he was entitled to a little payback for the work he'd done to get her here. So he'd enjoy all the outrage she wanted to throw his way and drink it in, just a little. He had to wonder, though, what she would think if she knew that he could taste her anger, and it was ambrosia. "You stay here."

Her eyes flared, and he drank more deeply. Feminine outrage. A flicker of—not fear, but discomfort. Something had changed between them during the car ride. Curiosity. Heat. He leaned forward. "You're going to bond with one of my brothers. All you have to do is choose."

Zer slid the little white lie in without blinking. Humans knew about the bond mates. Hell, they lined up and volunteered to *become* bond mates. The soul mates, however, were a carefully kept secret. Almost no one in the human world knew about soul mates because the Fallen didn't advertise that possibility. That knowledge was a dangerous liability— and the mother of all bargaining chips.

Plus, soul mates were forever. Nessa St. James was already reluctant—so how much more reluctant would she be if she knew she was trading away her life and not just a handful of days, weeks, or months? She'd find out when she found out—and it would be her mate's problem. Not Zer's.

"You realize," she said, laying out her objections in those cool, measured tones that didn't match her rumpled appearance and that had him wondering what she'd sound like when she came, "that I have research. A laboratory to run. You keep me here, and you destroy months' worth of my work." She huffed out a breath, her hands reaching up automatically to fix her hopeless chignon. "I'd be likelier to smuggle nuclear warheads into the heart of the White House. And last time the Russian legislature tried to do that, they failed."

Yeah, he remembered that particular bloodbath. Not as if his kind hadn't had a hand in it. One of those damn Goblin favors, but having the politicians in your pocket was a useful thing.

He crossed his arms over his chest and glared at her.

"Yeah. Like I said, not something I'm interested in. You want to use it for pillow talk, you go right ahead—after you choose one of my brothers."

She spat like a cat hitting water. "Look. I've dealt with your type before. My dean is a dick, pure and simple. He has no interest in answering academic questions—only thing he wants to hear from me is how he can line his pockets with as many research dollars as he can grab. I show him once and for all the commercial potential of my research, I've got him. Conversely, if he can't see his way to making a buck, I'm dead in the water. No support. No lab. Nada. And your pulling me out of my lab right now isn't helping me sell my case. Private backers—they're going to hold me to the same standard."

"You want money, we can give you money." Everyone—everything—had a price tag. He knew that better than most.

She ignored him as if he was offering her a dead fish. "You know how long I've spent working on my research? I've tested the waters. Given papers. Sat on panels. I'm on to something, and I know it."

Right. He settled back, because he didn't think she was going to stop anytime soon. No, she was just getting warmed up, and it seemed a shame to spoil her rant.

"I'm not some consultant you can 'borrow,' Zer." Hearing her say his name sent a little curl of satisfaction zinging through him, even if her next words were an unpleasant surprise. "I don't want your checks. And I certainly didn't want your interference. You think I don't know precisely what would happen?" Those magnificent eyes narrowed. "You'll take control. I'll lose control. Money always ensures that equation."

Damn right he was taking control. And it had absolutely nothing to do with money.

"Opening the funding tap?" she continued explaining in

those low, modulated, *sexy* tones, her hands efficiently weaving and plaiting, restoring order. "That's the same futile kettle of fish. You fucked this up. You brought me here." Her hands dropped from the now-perfect-again hair, crossing over her chest. Yeah, if looks could kill, he'd have been well planted, because those eyes were measuring him for a coffin.

"You fix it," she demanded.

"I could, baby—" He stretched slowly. "But I don't want to." He smiled, slow and hard. He decided he didn't care if he scared the fuck out of her or not. "Make me."

Yeah, he was done negotiating. His professor needed to accept some cold, hard facts, no matter how unpalatable she found them. He came down over her, covering her on the bed to keep her in place. Of course, she bucked against him, as if she were big enough to throw him off. No chance of that. Threading his fingers through hers, he slowly drew her hands up over her head.

"You listen to me now." The perfect chignon was unraveling again, he noted with satisfaction. "You're not in charge here. I am. And I think you like being kidnapped. Do you like to play sexy little games with your lovers, baby?"

"No." She glared up at him, shaking her head, so he captured both her wrists in one hand and threaded his free hand through that hair of hers. Checkmate, he thought with savage satisfaction. Just to prove his point, he lowered his mouth to hers, nipping at that naughty bottom lip of hers with a sharp, hot kiss. Her breathy little inhalation had him wondering if he was going to be able to stop.

God, she tasted so *good*. The females Nael chose had always been older, if not in biological years, then in experience. They'd seen it all, done it all, and they'd made their price tag perfectly clear. Nessa St. James was all fear and indignation, a sweet, feminine anger—coupled with a deliciously unwanted erotic thrill. She didn't want to want him, but she did, and he could taste it as clearly in her soul as he could feel the sweet, hot warmth of her body curling toward his.

He wasn't sure which emotion tasted sweeter. Fear or desire.

Wrapping one large hand around her waist, he pulled her closer. She was too important to risk. And that wild, feral part of himself wouldn't let him lose her. He was going to keep her safe.

For someone else.

She shoved against his body with her own, demanding space, and he bit back a groan. "It's not safe around you," she accused.

"No." He shook his head slowly. He'd give her that much of the truth. "But we're not the problem. You are."

She shot him another glare. "No one wants to kill me. On the other hand, someone clearly has it out for you. I'd like to be left out of this."

"You think it was an accident that rogue ended up in your lecture hall?"

"Yes. Yes, I do." She was connecting the dots, though, even if she didn't want to.

The rogue in Nessa's lecture hall had long since stopped fighting.

"He came for *you*, baby. He's an assassin, and he was sent to kill you."

"Prove it." The professor was back.

There was no way she hadn't heard about the murders that had plagued M City in recent months. No one was that isolated. "Three months ago," he began, "there was a series of murders. A recent immigrant. A stockbroker's wife."

"They found her in a red negligee." Nessa nodded.

Yeah, she'd heard the story. Good. Made his job here easier.

"Dead on the Arbat and covered in blood," she said grimly.

"Cracked wide open," he corrected, "from pelvis to sternum." If the negligee hadn't been red to begin with, the blood would have dyed it crimson. Wrong time, wrong place—that was MVD's conclusion. Zer and his brothers had known better than the human policing unit. "Two more after that, that MVD found."

"Were there others?" She looked at him and clearly drew her own conclusions. "*You're* dangerous," she said. "*You're* a killer."

He didn't deny it. He didn't want her brand of redemption for himself; it was a luxury he couldn't afford, and didn't deserve. Besides, he was beyond all that touchy-feely, come-into-the-light-my-son bullshit anyhow. When Michael had kicked his ass out of the Heavens, he'd thrown away the key, and Zer almost didn't give a fuck anymore. He'd stood on his own two feet long enough to get used to it. But his brothers deserved whatever chance he could give them.

"You are telling me this for a reason, right?" she insisted.

"They were all on a list," he said, careful not to share too much. "A list your name is on, too." Christ, that sounded lame. The yellow pages had lists of names, but he hadn't gone hunting there.

Clearly, she agreed with him. "You kidnapped me because my name is on some hit list? That makes this a job for MVD," she scoffed. "This has absolutely nothing to do with me, and you have nothing I want."

That's where she was wrong. It had everything to do with her, but he couldn't afford to tell her that. He needed her to agree—now—and if she knew what she was agreeing to, she'd ask for sun, moon, and stars. And he'd have to do his damnedest to provide. No way.

"The murdered women were bond mates," she guessed.

"Yes." And would have been soul mates, if the Fallen had

gotten to them first. If the Fallen had known. They'd been potential *soul mates*.

"Goblin junkies?" She hunched her shoulders as if she abhorred the very idea of women who would hook up, quick and easy, with one of the Fallen. He didn't think she was the kind of woman who condemned others for their sexual choices, so he had to ask himself: what was it about the idea of a brief, hot, sexual affair in exchange for an enormous favor that made her so uncomfortable?

"No, mates. They were special." Women liked romance. He needed to spin this carefully. He didn't want to tip his hand and tell her about soul mates. Not yet. "Whatever they wanted, it could have been theirs. All they had to do was ask."

"There's more to life than favors and sex, Zer."

Damned if it didn't make him hard as stone, just that simple little thing of her calling him by name.

"Maybe." When you lived as long as the Fallen had, you didn't dismiss sensual pleasures so lightly. You took what you could, where you could, just to feel a little more alive than dead. "Imagine a lover who knows what you want before you know it yourself. Who exists to give you pleasure."

"It's no gift."

It was and it wasn't. He wasn't so far gone that he didn't recognize the truth of her statement, even as he wanted nothing more than to deny it. "All relationships are give and take," he said. "Our females give us what we need—and we always give them what they need." His brothers were consummate seducers. She didn't stand a chance. She was stuck with him, with *them*, and the sooner she accepted her role, the sooner she stopped fighting him, the sooner he could get on with the important business.

"Do you know what the bond mates are?"

"Women," she said. "Women who trade their souls for favors."

She made it sound sordid. Cold. And it was anything but that. No, it was the hot, heated lick of lust. The lush scent of aroused female flesh. There was nothing cold about it at all, and she'd learn that truth soon enough. "We don't choose just anyone," he warned.

"Right. You choose. The woman doesn't do anything?"

Oh, she did. Nessa St. James would. "She chooses, too," he whispered darkly. "She chooses what she wants. She chooses her pleasure."

"Why?" she surprised him by asking. Most got that glazed look in their eyes thinking about the favor and its potential. "Anything" was a powerful promise, and he didn't believe for one minute that Nessa St. James lacked an imagination. No, she might discipline that imagination, keep it under tight lock and key, but she'd thought about the bond. And the favor.

Even if she wasn't going to admit it to him.

"Terms of our parole," he said lightly. "When our asses were booted out of the Heavens, we were sentenced to play seducer down here in this world of yours. We seduce, and your kind likes it, baby."

"So you were condemned to an eternity of illustrating the pitfalls of giving in to temptation—and you think I should just agree to join you in that Fall?"

She was dangerously quick. "There's always a price for pleasure, baby. But we make it worth your while. You'll enjoy every minute of it." His voice was wicked, liquid promise. "You're enjoying it now."

"Am not."

"You are." He smiled deliberately, a slow, masculine smile he knew would irritate the hell out of her—and stoke the fires. "I can smell your arousal, baby. Hot, sweet welcome. I touch you right now, you're coming on my bed. For me."

She shook her head. There was a dazed look in her eyes that he liked. That look was for him.

"If that's what you want." All she had to do was tell him what she wanted, and he'd find a brother to deliver it.

"I don't believe in romance." She didn't bother yelling this time, just laid out her words, calm and slow. "I'm not going to be a bond mate. This isn't something you can make me do, Zer, and we both know it."

"You have to do it," he countered.

"Make me," she breathed, and he knew that she was remembering his kiss. In the SUV. Hell, it wasn't as if he could forget it. He'd been two seconds from shoving up that sexy little skirt of hers and getting inside her.

"You don't leave," he decreed. "Not until you've chosen."

"You can't make me pick one of you." She shook her head, and the thick coil of her hair bounced around her shoulders. He wanted to wrap his hands in that hair and pull her toward him. She didn't know what kind of creature she was baiting. He was a monster, and he had no business staying with her.

"You will," he warned, striding toward the door. She shot off the bed, coming after him. "You want your life back, you give me what I want. It won't be so bad, baby." She'd liked him just fine in the SUV; she'd like one of his brothers even more. "Think about it. All your fantasies, come true."

"I don't need a man."

"No." He stopped short of the door and gave her the meanest, hardest smile he had in him, because he knew the truth. "You need money. And a lab. University backing and pages in a peer-reviewed journal."

"You," she said coldly, "are not my peer."

"No, sweetheart, I'm not." He folded his arms over his chest, the leather duster stretching over his shoulders. "I'm one better. I'm your new boss. I own your lab. Your university." He smiled again. "Your life, I believe you called it. You give me what I want, and you can have it all back and more.

You want an endowed chair, unlimited lab funding? It can all be yours."

She shook her head. "It's not the same."

"Excuse me?" Money was money, and it spent the same no matter where it came from. "It is the same."

"No," she snapped. "It's not. I worked damn hard to get where I am."

Yeah. And it was fabulous. He'd gotten an eyeful of the dingy lecture hall, the stack of dusty books and dustier surfaces. Precisely where he'd want to spend the rest of his life. His skin had itched just being there.

"I don't take handouts, Zer."

"But will you take a paycheck?" He reached out, his coaxing, stroking finger tracing a naughty pattern down her throat, along her collarbone. "Tell me what you want, baby."

She'd run if he gave her the chance, so he made it damn clear that there was nowhere for her to go. It wasn't gentlemanly, but he was no gentleman. After he'd been all over her in the SUV, they both knew that.

He didn't know why that bothered him. Maybe because she deserved more. Deserved better. If the brother she chose hurt her, he'd kill the bastard.

He strong-armed the door open, ignoring her flinch when the door slammed loudly against the wall.

"Come here," he said, because he was only saying this once. Threading his fingers through her smaller ones, he tugged. She came, but then, he hadn't given her a choice, had he? She probably thought he'd treat her like the door. Slam her around a little if she gave him any more lip.

That thought shamed him, so he did what he needed to do so he could leave.

"Nael and Vkhin." He indicated the brothers standing on the other side of the door with a quick jerk of his head as he named them. "They stand here, and they keep an eye on my door. You need to go somewhere in this club, they're your shadows."

"My jailers. If they're going to stop me from walking out that door," she bit out. "Let's call it what it is. They're not here for me. They're here for you."

She didn't understand that her life was at risk, had been from the minute Cuthah had put her name on his list. She went nowhere alone, even inside the comparative safety of G2's. She was too important for him to be taking chances.

Nael stepped up to the plate, examining her with familiar, playboy sensuality. "You might like us, baby." Those dark, sleepy eyes examined her from the frame of his waist-length hair. Brother left it loose until it was fighting time. All those smooth, silky strands pouring arrow-straight down his back and moving with the bunching of powerful muscles. Even though Nael had the same hard face they all had, that hair got the females every time, made them want to stroke the brother like he was some feral cat they could gentle. That hair was as seductive as the male. Females didn't notice the danger lurking in those black eyes until it was too late. Nael was rapier sharp and every bit as lethal. "We're not so bad."

"Dream on," she said, shutting him out and slamming the door. Zer allowed her the little fit of feminine pique because he'd already taken so much away from her and he wasn't done yet.

"She know?" Vkhin leaned silently against the wall. A good male and a fierce protector. But there was nothing soft about him at all. If she ran, Vkhin would be all over her. Nowhere she could hide from him, and that was why Zer had chosen him. Vkhin was all close-cropped hair and ice eyes. Cold and hard, the brother didn't display emotions because he had none left. He was 100 percent killer, with the brutal build of the meanest street fighter. On a good day, he merely stood in the shadows, watching with those eyes that didn't seem to move but that saw everything. Those ancient eyes that stripped away all the pretty pretenses and went bare knuckle on the truth. Brother didn't lie, and he never pulled his punches.

"Not all of it." He thought about Vkhin's question and shook his head. "Enough, though. She'll do what we need her to do."

"Bond with us." A slow, sensual smile split Nael's face.

"Yeah." The twinge of emotion was unexpected. And why the hell was that? She was an advantage he could exploit. He had himself a corrupt Archangel to kill, and, unfortunately, he couldn't make that kill. Because his ass was exiled to this misbegotten planet. Without wings, he couldn't make the return journey to the Heavens and take down the Archangel Michael who had framed him and his kind. He'd been left hanging out to dry. Worse, he'd handed the Archangel the tools to do the job. He'd made that mistake once. Now, when Cuthah, the Archangel's left-hand man, came back for Nessa St. James, Zer was going to be ready. He'd stick closer than glue to her, and he'd have the drop on Cuthah when that bastard finally made his move. Wait, and his enemy would drop right into his lap. She was bait in his trap—nothing more.

"She might not be so keen on bonding with one of us," Nael pointed out.

Whether or not she liked the choices laid out for her was irrelevant. Too bad. So sad.

"We need her." It was as simple as that.

"Yeah." Nael sprawled languidly against the wall. "But if she doesn't need us?"

Nessa was the tactical advantage he needed, so her wishes didn't count for shit. Besides, he'd never met a human who didn't come with a price tag. "She'll be ready to bond."

"With one of us," Vkhin added in his slow, deep rasp, folding himself deeper into the shadows.

"One of you," Zer agreed. Maybe she'd mate with Nael or

Vkhin. Both were more than worthy. They'd fought side by side for millennia, and he couldn't think of anyone more deserving.

She was in good hands, so he turned and walked away. She wasn't someone he should be thinking of, anyway.

She wasn't for him.

CHAPTER FIVE

Gritting his teeth, Cuthah dragged his thumb over the edge of the blade.

"You lost her," he said. "I gave you her name. Her address. Her place of business. And yet none of you could retrieve Nessa St. James before the Fallen discovered her whereabouts?"

He wanted these women. He *needed* them. Kill them, and he cut off the Fallen's last hope. He'd never forgotten the Fallen were still Dominions at heart. They'd been bred to defend. To kill. To do whatever it took. Once they learned about the existence of these women, nothing would keep the former Dominions from finding them.

He knew he was grinding his teeth, but maybe the stupid fucks standing in front of him would finally get the message. He wanted these women. It was their job to deliver.

When he'd cast the Dominions from the Heavens, Michael had made sure his Fallen would have precisely what they needed to earn their redemption. He'd seeded the thirteenth tribe of Israel with these women, and each daughter's daughter had carried her mother's legacy. Each one had been a potential soul mate for a Fallen.

Emphasis on *had been*.

Michael had scattered the tribe across the face of the earth, a little shake-up so the former Dominions didn't find their soul mates *too* easily. Cuthah had simply made sure of it. He'd stolen the information he needed, and then he'd killed as many of the women as he could after Michael had disappeared into seclusion.

But Michael's little diaspora had worked too well. Cuthah had lost sight of a handful of humans because he'd still been cementing his own place in the Heavens. He'd spent millennia hunting down those remnants. Until he'd discovered Nessa St. James.

When his cell had rung earlier with Nessa St. James on the other end of the line, he'd known it was a sign. She'd gone for his lure, told him she wanted to work on the research project he'd offered her. Her kidnapping was a good thing, now that he thought about it. She was vulnerable. And she had access to precisely the kind of sample set she needed. Once she'd wrapped up his little research project, she'd be dialing him for an extraction—and would waltz right into his hands. The irony of it all was delicious.

Perfect.

The four rogues standing before him stiffened silently under his icy regard but didn't move. Good. He'd kill the first one who flinched, kill them all for failing him. He'd have taken care of this business himself if he hadn't believed that an extended absence right now from the Heavens would have drawn unwelcome notice. He was walking a fine line, and one misstep would mean the end of everything. So, even though their screw-up had worked out to his advantage, he had to make his point.

Striding over to the wide plate glass window, he stared down at the barren mountain slope. "I gave you this female on a silver platter," he snapped, "and you still lost her. Tell me why I shouldn't cut those wings off your backs now."

"Shallum is dead." The rogue Goblin nearest the door made the observation emotionlessly. His black eyes never blinked. "Hasrah, as well." Chalk one up for the Fallen. If his emissaries hadn't been dead already, he'd have killed them now for their failure.

"Excuses," he growled. Shallum and Hasrah were pawns, sacrifices in the larger game. Fortunately, the Dominions' endless thirst guaranteed Cuthah a bottomless well of replacement rogues. "You were forewarned. You have wings and fyreblades. Instead, you pissed away your advantages and allowed the Fallen to take Nessa St. James away."

"We'll retrieve her." The first rogue spoke again.

"Damn right." When he was ready. Cuthah rested a hand against the window.

The glass was cold from the ruthless temperature of their surroundings. Night was coming quickly now, dark shadows sliding along the ground as the sun slipped weakly down behind the mountain peaks. The mountain fortress deep inside the rogue Preserves pleased Cuthah. Even the landscape here had given up all hope. The stark outcroppings of stone were a visible reminder of just how bleak life could become without the promise of redemption. A century ago, the place had been the playground for decadent Russian noblemen more interested in fucking serfs and killing game than keeping their fingers on the pulse of Russian politics. Cuthah had never made that mistake. He had his pleasures, yes. He eyed the four-poster bed and the prey staked out there. The delicate female had lasted for a surprisingly long time. She might even last out the night—but he'd never let pleasure interfere with business.

Matters were heating up in the Heavens.

He'd set the pieces in motion, and then he'd waited; now, the moment of victory had almost arrived.

If the Fallen wanted to push back, wanted to make this

personal, Cuthah would. For three thousand years, he'd methodically searched for and destroyed every potential soul mate. Until one had slipped through his nets and his fingers, landing in the arms of her destined lover. Mischka Baran was the other half of Brends Duranov's soul, all that was light and good. The bastard had held on tight to what fate had handed him, and the damage had been done.

Now, the Fallen knew. The Fallen were searching, and it was a race to identify and take the few soul mates left in this world. Once the soul mates were gone, so, too, was the last hope the Fallen had for redemption. Cuthah looked forward to slamming the door of the Heavens square in their arrogant faces.

Nessa St. James, however, was taking the game to a whole new level.

She might be able to unlock their genetic code.

That made her the Fallen's last hope, but also their weakness, even if they hadn't realized it yet. He'd studied Nessa St. James for a year. He knew how she'd react and that she wouldn't be able to curb that delicious curiosity of hers. No, Nessa St. James would ask questions—and find answers. Once she had those answers, he'd retrieve her—and he'd know precisely how to track down the remaining soul mates.

Science was really a beautiful thing.

The middle male took a step forward. "It wasn't my fault," he argued. "Give me the name of another bitch, and I'll bring her to you."

The rogue was as good as dead, because Cuthah never tolerated excuses, but the asshole standing there so confidently didn't know his words had sealed the death sentence. Cuthah figured he'd make that point right now. Whipping around from the window, he drove his blade deep into the other male's gut. The scream was satisfying.

He kicked the male curled on the floor with a booted foot.

"No excuses." He made eye contact with the two remaining rogues. The gut wound wouldn't kill, but it sure as hell was going to hurt.

Reaching down, he delicately ran a finger down the side of the male's face and considered the blood on his fingertips. If he killed this one and made an example of him, he'd need to recruit another one to his cause. He shrugged. The benefits outweighed the cost. This one had failed. This one was flawed.

There was no room in his Heavens for the flawed.

The fyreblade hummed to lethal life in his right hand, the smooth arc of the blade cutting through the waiting air. The head toppled from the rogue's body. Yeah. That wound would kill.

Behind him, he heard a sharp indrawn breath from the female. How delicious that she'd—finally—learned not to scream.

Screaming bought her nothing, and they both knew it.

The eyes of the other rogues didn't flicker. The bastards were just as cold and reptilian as any predator. Neither blinked at the violence, but Cuthah knew his message was clear. "Fail me again," he said, "and Eilor's fate will be yours. I want the other three females on the list." He'd leave Nessa St. James where she was for now. He'd watch her, wait for her to give him what he needed.

He turned away from the body. He needed those females, and he needed them now. The time was perfect for him to take the next step in his campaign, but he couldn't do so until he had the girls. "Go," he ordered. "Two weeks. Find them within the next two weeks."

The first rogue paused at the door, booted foot on the threshold.

"Dead or alive?"

Dead was safer, but alive could be useful. Cuthah's eyes narrowed. There were possibilities. "Preferably alive." He shrugged. "If you can. If not, dead."

"Now, darling," he purred, striding back to the bed and its terrified occupant. She scrambled against the sheets as if the linen could hide her. "Why don't you show me just how much you've missed me?"

Her shattered cry was music to his ears.

CHAPTER SIX

Zer needed a fight. No, scratch that. Make it plural. He wanted to move, wanted to pound his fists into someone until they bled—and the rogues would make a damned fine punching bag. The pounding rhythm of the house music vibrated in his bones until he was itching to move out. There were too many damn humans too damn close for his taste. Business was good, and the dance floor was filled. Brothers prowled through the crowd, making their choices. Taking what they needed.

Until they saw him come back down those damn stairs. Then they converged on him as if he'd come to announce the second coming. So much for not engaging and for taking his aggression outside.

"Is it true?" The brother closest to him muttered the words as if he couldn't quite bring himself to believe them. "Did you find another soul mate?" That was the question they all wanted the answer to. Any human could be a bond mate. But a soul mate? She was one in a million. Literally.

Picking up his pace, he arrowed directly at the club's exterior door. He'd secured the first female, and his brothers wanted to hear the deets. "Yeah," he drawled. "She's upstairs." Safe.

"She meant for you?" A hint of something Zer didn't recognize entered the male's eyes. Fear. Hope. And, yeah, a whole lot of desperation. Going without had been marginally easier when they'd all believed that there were no soul mates.

"She chooses."

"Straight up?"

"Yeah." He wasn't going to take her, even if he knew that most of the brothers watching this little exchange believed that was his right. He was their sire. Their leader. He was first in line for everything, whether it was Heavens' smackdown all those millennia ago or the sweet, hot promise of redemption he'd just hauled into the club like a berserk caveman. And if he'd enjoyed that atavistic behavior, well, he wasn't going to make any excuses. He was who he was.

"So, what's the plan? What are you going to do with her? You guarantee she's choosing?"

"Yes," he said, and he made eye contact with each male in the hard press of bodies. "Yeah, I am." All eyes turned to him, and, beyond the edge of the crowd of armed males, there was Brends making his way over. Figured. Just once Zer wanted to act first and think later. He'd retrieved the female, and he'd stashed her here. That was the critical point. Now, he'd do a little wait-and-see. Maybe, her presence in G2's would be enough to draw Cuthah out. If not, he'd still be up one soul mate, and he'd use that advantage.

"We let her choose," he repeated, letting his hand rest on his blade just in case anyone got any other ideas about the female waiting upstairs. "That rave G2's is holding night after tomorrow—we bring her downstairs then. Anyone who wants a shot can come and do their asking then. She'll listen, and then she'll decide."

The group parted to let Brends through, but that was no surprise. What was surprising was that Brends didn't have his soul mate wrapped around his arm, but Zer figured she couldn't be far behind. She didn't like the club, didn't like what they hunted here, and so she'd be close at hand, eager to pry Brends free. God help them all if Mischka learned about the female upstairs.

"Keep this on the down low," he cautioned, and Brends's eyes flashed. Yeah, he knew his mate wasn't going to care for this particular secret. At all.

"You found one of the four." Brends didn't bother with making nice.

"Her name was on the list. Face and ID match." He spoke lightly, but they both knew the words meant the world. Brends had his soul mate, but the others didn't. The others were still lost. "She's a match."

"You think it matters which one of the brothers she chooses?" Brends's eyes narrowed, as if he didn't appreciate the idea that maybe his beloved mate hadn't chosen him because he was best but merely because he was first. Yeah, Zer bet that stung. Still, he could refute the whole first-in-line argument, right? Nessa St. James hadn't gone for *his* sorry ass. Hell, she'd have kicked him straight to the curb if she could.

"It's not first come, first served."

Brends looked like he wanted to disagree. "She's not a weapon," he pointed out.

And that was where his brother was wrong. That's precisely what Nessa St. James was.

"We can't keep this war up." Vkhin's voice slid out of the darkness behind Zer. The male made a habit of forgetting Zer's orders—he was supposed to be guarding Nessa with Nael. Vkhin had been the other candidate for sire. Maybe the powers-that-be hadn't chosen him because he was *too* strong. Certainly, he was older that Zer. Much older. Pure, emotionless control, a deep, still pool of a male.

Unfortunately, Vkhin spoke only the truth. The Fallen couldn't keep up this war. Couldn't win. Didn't mean Zer liked hearing it, though. Shoving off the wall where he'd parked his sorry ass, he headed for the door, running a mental inventory of his weapons. Weapons, he understood. Draw.

Stab. Kill. He'd had millennia to perfect that skill. Most of the time, he didn't even have to think about it, fighting being even more natural than breathing. Unlike that last time in the Heavens, with Michael's dark, cold eyes taunting him. He shook off the memory. No point going back down that road. Much as he wanted a do-over, all he had now was the present. The past was gone.

Christ, he needed a fight. The rogue within was riding him hard, the creature struggling to punch through the surface. When he caught sight of his face in one of the mirrors some sick fuck had walled G2's with, he recognized the cold-eyed bastard all too well. He looked like death prowling across the floor. Walking, breathing sin incarnate, that was him. "I'm out of here," he growled.

His brothers let him lay in a course for the door, but they came right along.

"You in?" he growled. If he had to pick up a posse, they could damn well fight for him.

"I'll fight," one of the Fallen said cheerfully. Male sounded as if Zer had brought him flowers. Damn hothead would get himself killed long before the soul thirst ate him alive, but that was part of Keros's charm. He didn't think. He just *did*. Brends claimed Keros was working his way through the penal code, one act at a time, and Zer didn't disbelieve him. Last he'd heard, Keros had been running arms for some of the hotter-headed human tribes on Russia's southern border. Male probably had his reasons—and Zer didn't care what they were—but he made an order of Uzis sound like take-out pizza. Eventually, Zer would have to step in before Keros made a mess too large to clean up.

Not tonight, though. Tonight, all Zer wanted was a fight.

He strong-armed the outer door open, sucking down the cold night air. The weather was an icy wake-up call to all his senses. When he looked up, he could see the watery silver light from the moon overhead and the dying glow of the mazhlights. Almost dawn, but still more than enough time to do some hunting. Take out his frustrations on M City's rogue population. Left or right. His direction didn't matter.

"Do me a favor. Let's roll," he said to the pair closest to him. Keros and another tough male named Tarq. They'd do. "I'm feeling restless tonight."

Tarq's smile was slow in coming and frightening when it finally cracked his face. Only the promise of blood woke the brother up. "Fighting or fucking?"

"Fighting."

Fighting, he understood.

The weather still screamed winter, cold and bleak. An almost arctic wind trickled down the dark street as he strode along. Humans, he couldn't help noticing, gave him a wide berth. They were smarter than they looked. That, or the leather duster billowing around him and the steel-toed shit-kickers eating up the pavement were ample warning. He dressed like a badass, and his clothes were a warning label.

"You sure about this?" Vkhin's expressionless face examined his.

"Yeah." He was more than sure. He didn't really care about protecting the humans in M City from rogues, but fighting was a habit now that he couldn't shake. He'd fought for the Heavens, had served as a Dominion for centuries before the Fall. Laying it down was second nature.

"You going to tell me where you're headed?"

It didn't matter. "Left," he said. If possible, Vkhin's face grew even emptier. Not like Zer hadn't disappointed him before. Whatever Vkhin felt about his sire's decision, Zer reminded himself savagely, it wasn't *new*. Nothing was new anymore. "You want me to march right on up to the Heavens? Leading an army of three? Hell, Vkhin, I can't even go myself."

Vkhin slid his hands into his pockets. "Maybe you could. Maybe that female up there is your soul mate."

Zer shook his head. Left, it was. He was so done with this shit. "You got to feel, Vkhin, to have a soul mate. Me, I don't have anything left." Just the rogue inside and the never-ending urge to kill. To finally, finally drink his fill. A tendril of something snaking out from the left had his senses going on high alert, the beast sitting up at attention.

Vkhin just looked at him. "You got to try first."

"I spent the first two millennia trying. Now, I'm going to settle for a little ass-kicking. Piss off if you don't want to play."

CHAPTER SEVEN

The handbag-jacking motherfucker in the alley needed to stop.

The handbag in question was impossibly feminine—hot pink vinyl with a cheery little sequined flower stitched to the zipper. Flowers like that didn't exist in nature, any more than the monster putting the handbag's owner in a lip-lock did.

Zer palmed his blades and assessed the situation. Vkhin had melted into the darkness, making it clear that if any killing was done in this alley, Zer was doing it.

It was night, but it was almost always night in M City now. The days were shorter than normal, and there was way less light. Some of M City's residents—the ones who were still human—blamed the Fallen for the darker days, and maybe they were right. The former angels had been thrown out of the Heavens for gross acts of rebellion, and they'd brought their vices with them. Zer's kind were sinners and killers, and they made no bones about it. The hulking shape at the far end of the alley, however, didn't belong to one of his fellow Fallen.

Not anymore.

The noise was the first clue, the inhuman growling of a rogue who'd scented prey. A thick blanket of midnight had settled on the street. The gray sidewalk disappeared into the cavernous entrance to the underground Metro. The news kiosks were metal-shuttered for the night, although those vendors moved few papers during the daylight hours. Papers had been replaced by packets of condoms and serving-sized bottles of alcohol, the kind with a non-reusable screw top. Drink it or dump it, but no planning for tomorrow. This late at night, no one was in sight. The human residents had abandoned the premises to the night.

Somewhere, however, the rogue had found himself a girl. A little hooker in a too-short vinyl skirt and faux-fur-lined boots. He'd already done the business he'd paid her for, because the thick, hot smell of sex and semen mixed with the too-crisp night air. He'd pinned the human female way up the alley, clearly counting on either the shadows or the noxious smell of days-old trash to keep his business private. The darkened face and twisted, brutal jut of the male's jaw identified the predator as rogue.

No rogue hunted for souls in M City. M City was Zer's territory.

The rogue clearly scented Zer's approach, not that Zer was going for subtlety. He was no damn knight-errant, but he was the enforcer of his kind's laws. What the rogue was doing to his human companion was an act of psychic vampirism that wouldn't end well for anyone. Zer figured if he'd managed to refrain from draining a human soul so far, this bastard could, as well. So, he took it as a personal insult that the rogue was drinking her dry, the psychic stench growing fouler with each deep swallow, dark ribbons of aura peeling off the girl.

"Hello, darling." Palming his first set of blades, Zer threw. "Time to break up your party."

For a moment, Zer was backlit, silhouetted against the mouth of the alley. The blade sliced the rogue's arm, forcing him to drop the girl. She was almost gone; she didn't so much as budge from her awkward sprawl. *Christ.* He was going to have to move her before he could get down to business.

Behind him, Tarq and Keros had his back in the usual fighting triad. Vkhin had vanished to do some reconnoitering of his own. Motioning sharply, Zer indicated they should fan out, welcoming the soft hiss of blades being pulled. Tarq took the shadows; Keros moved in for the girl, then hesitated.

"Let me," Keros said.

Yeah, Keros thought there was a good chance Zer would merely take the rogue's place. He wasn't wrong.

Zer nodded once about the girl but not the rogue.

He wanted to do this. He needed to do this. "This one's mine, Ker."

The rogue charged, fyreblade flashing.

Zer evaded smoothly, ducking under the blow. Coming up, he pulled his own blades and caught the bastard right in the gut. Not a kill wound for their kind but enough to slow the rogue down. Make him clumsy. No one regenerated that fast. Right on cue, the fyreblade wobbled.

The rogue cursed in a harsh, inhuman stream of syllables. Turning, he came back for Zer with the persistence of the newly damned, because, fuck, there was no walking away now. Not that Zer had ever seen one of them back down from a fight. Mindless beasts. This one couldn't keep his eyes from sliding over to the human female. He was still thinking dinner, even when it was his immortal soul on the line.

The fight wasn't going to be long enough to work off all the aggression Zer had trapped inside him, and that pissed him off. This time, when the rogue attacked, Zer brought the blade up, slicing it across the rogue's neck in a lethal swipe. Blood spurted, and the look of unexpected surprise crossing the rogue's face let Zer know the bastard hadn't really believed he could lose.

"Yeah, you got that right."

The fyreblade clattered to the ground. Keros moved in to pick it up. "Might be useful." His voice didn't change, as if Zer had simply taken out the trash.

Blade might be useful, but already the fyre was flickering, dying, and, sure enough, it winked out altogether as Zer stepped up to the crumpled pile of rogue and finished the job he'd started. Head separated from neck. Too young, too recent a convert, to have gotten the hang of his new strength or even to remember what to do with the fyreblade. Now he *was* simply trash.

Flipping the body onto its stomach, he anchored it in place with a booted foot. Before he could second-guess his instincts, he drew the sharp edge of his blade down the dead male's back, the fabric of his clothing parting easily on either side. Dark skin. A few battle scars framed by the desecrated fabric. In other words, nothing he hadn't expected to see. The Dominions had lost their ability to heal effortlessly when they'd lost their wings and their place in the Heavens. Still, something wasn't quite right.

"Light," he snapped, still staring down at the smooth, dark skin. What he *didn't* see were the souvenir ridges of scar tissue, Michael's little parting gift. Where he *should* have seen the evidence of former wings, there was nothing but a tattoo. The red edges of the ink faded even as he watched, filling the air with the stink of mazhyk.

"Who'd you make a deal with?" He muttered a curse when he spotted the female victim lying on the ground behind the rogue, where she'd been tossed like so much garbage.

His damn mind took him straight back to that last night in the Heavens. The night he'd learned precisely what an Archangel could do to a female body. When Esrene had fought off her attacker—an attacker who outweighed her by more than a hundred pounds—he'd snapped her legs so she couldn't run. And then he'd played with her. Mentally, Zer reigned in his thoughts. He didn't want to go there. Not again.

Bastard had gutted the female Dominion like so much prey, sliding his blade into the soft, vulnerable curve of her belly and ruthlessly drawing the blade upward, splitting her chest open the way he'd too clearly split her open lower with his own body. Zer thought of Esrene and admitted that she'd been, in the end, reduced to a catalyst. Michael had sacrificed her without hesitating. He'd known Esrene's death would infuriate the Dominions, and Zer had fallen right into his trap.

He'd incited a rebellion.

A rebellion he'd lost.

Behind him, Vkhin had reappeared and was phoning in for a cleanup. Although they could have left the body there, Zer knew the limits of the humans living in his territory. There would be full-blown panic, and panic was never good.

None of his people were dead or injured. That was a good night.

What wasn't good was the truth lying at their feet. That rogue could have been them. Would someday *be* them, unless they found soul mates. This one had simply given up sooner, slid faster.

Zer was hanging on by his fingernails, and they all knew it. He looked at Vkhin. "You don't hesitate," he warned and he knew he didn't have to explain. Vkhin knew. After all, he fought with the same inner rogue Zer did, and that was just one of the many reasons Zer trusted his brother with his back. "You pull the blade the instant I step out of line, and you do it fast."

"I promise."

Zer hadn't earned a quick death, but the simple truth was: he was too dangerous for anything else. Right now, however, he needed to feed. Fast.

*   *   *

Zer charged the doors of G2's for the second time that day and made for the stairs. What he wanted—who he wanted—was so very close. When, in response to an unspoken signal, the guards stepped in front of him, blocking his path, he growled.

Fighting the urge to draw his blades and carve his own goddamn path to the elevator, he realized the Change was flickering over his features. He could feel the darkness in him fighting, clawing for release.

Christ, he was in trouble.

He wanted to bound up the stairs. Take her. Drink her. She was waiting for him, damn near gift-wrapped—and he was going to take care of this damn thirst that was riding him.

Nael's hands curling around his forearms were an unwelcome surprise. Those hands were loose, but they could and would tighten. "You don't want to do this."

Oh, he did. "You aren't going to stop me, Nael. Don't make this into a fight you'll lose."

He was the damn sire, and he had battle lust pounding through him. The soul thirst was a painful hunger raging through his body, and G2's looked like a banquet of souls. The sweet, luscious psychic strands called out to him, teased raw nerve endings with false promises of pleasure. Relief. Unfortunately, he didn't want what was for sale down here. No, he wanted *her*.

Nael bowed his head, but the bastard didn't move. His hands were still resting loosely on Zer's own damn sleeves.

"I'll take you there if you need to go." Nael's dark eyes watched him. Didn't blink. "But what you need is down here, sire."

"No, it's not." What he needed was up there, waiting for him in his suite. Part of his mind was trying to remind him of something, that there might be a reason he didn't want to do this.

Nael reached behind him, beckoning without looking. A female sauntered from the dance floor. Another random stranger. Something flashed in Nael's eyes and was gone. "You let me do this for you, and then you go to her. Take a breather first."

The air was ripe with the heady scent of the female. She was all lush promise, wide open, her gazing sliding from Nael to Zer and back again.

"This will make you feel better," Nael murmured. "Trust me."

She wasn't the right female, but the thirst was taking over, and Zer was just man enough to mourn the loss of those brain cells. Yeah, he wasn't right in the head. The wall of males sliding between him and the elevator made that clear. Part of him was just sane enough to be grateful. His brothers had his back and wouldn't let him jack this up too badly.

Male hands pressed him down into a seat.

"Trust me," Nael said again, and, this time, Zer didn't know to whom Nael spoke. The female was nodding, though, and Zer recognized that covetous look. She wanted whatever she could get, and she'd come to the right damn place.

"Time to fall, love," Nael whispered, swinging her up onto Zer's lap. She settled in like she was coming home, curling her fingers in his leathers.

A lapful of sweet, warm female. The wrong one, but fuck that. He couldn't have the one he wanted. He was too far gone, and *she* deserved better than a beast.

CHAPTER EIGHT

What the hell had she gotten herself into?

Firing up her laptop, Nessa held her breath for long seconds. Without Net access, she was dead in the water. If the Fallen had overlooked the wireless card on her laptop, she figured that negligence wouldn't last long.

Not if they were serious in this kidnapping attempt of theirs.

She had to get out of here. Her reaction to the Fallen's leader was humiliating. What kind of woman lusted after her kidnapper?

Fingers trembling, she launched a chat application, tapping in her access code. When she placed the call to Genecore, knowing she probably only had minutes before the Fallen would pick up on her access, the foundation's president picked up right away.

As if he'd been waiting for her call.

"You're in," he said, not waiting for her to launch into explanations. "Good."

"Excuse me?"

"The Fallen picked you up. You have access to them and to their DNA. Everything you said you needed."

This conversation wasn't going the way she'd intended it

to go. "You told me *you* had DNA samples. I intended to use those samples. I never agreed to go undercover and live with Goblins." Unstable, psychotic, sexy Goblins.

"Details." His cold voice rode roughshod over her objections. "Fresh samples are better. You agreed to work for me. I simply arranged for you to have the access you need."

"You arranged to have me kidnapped." She was supposed to ignore that? Work through it? He made her kidnapping sound like a brilliant career move. Like hell it was. She was a prisoner.

"I never agreed to this, and I could have been killed," she snapped.

"No," he said. "My team had their orders."

Maybe, he just wanted her to finish her research. Maybe, his arranging her kidnapping was some sort of twisted version of grant funding. She didn't think so, though. He'd set her up for something.

"This is not what I signed on for. The Fallen who headed up the search-and-retrieval was none other than the damn leader of the lot. He has no intention of seeing his plans head south." And that was putting it mildly. "What you've landed me in is a mess. Of titanic proportions."

The man on the other end didn't hesitate. "This is the opportunity you need. Take it. Although I strongly suggest you avoid bonding with any of them."

"No problem. I don't do sexual bondage. Any more than I do forcible captivity."

His cold voice cut her off. "If you do bond with one of them, I should point out that your mate would have unlimited access to your mind. If he took the time to look, he would know at once that you were a plant. You would not enjoy that discovery."

Hell. This just got better and better, didn't it? "I'm leaving. You can consider our partnership finished." Partners did not

conceal critical information—and they certainly did not or-
chestrate kidnappings. Nothing—not even her career and her
research—was worth that. She didn't do ethical gray areas.

There was a moment of silence on the other end, and she
considered—and discarded—the idea of hanging up on her
erstwhile partner. Too unprofessional. Too damn tempting.
But she'd given in to temptation once already.

"Good luck," he offered finally. "I suggest you focus on
completing your research. When it is done and has been delivered, I will retrieve you." Which meant he could retrieve
her now, damn it. There had to be a way to negotiate an exit
from this nightmare. "I think you will find it extremely difficult to walk out that door right now. The Fallen take their
mates rather seriously. You will find that you go nowhere
until you have satisfied them—or me."

Ultimatums weren't her favorite form of communication.
Plus, the kind of marching orders Genecore had just laid on
her made her want to do the exact opposite. Whether she got
with the program or not, learning more about her captors
was smart. A little informal observation was the logical
course of action. So, the question really was, why wasn't she
observing the vidscreen for entrances and exits? Different
views of the club were on full display in the bank of vidscreens occupying the west wall of Zer's palatial personal
suite.

Idly, she watched the comings and goings on the vidscreens, mentally jotting down times and players, cataloging
features. Now, mentally, she ran down the probable ancestry
of the dancers. Deciphering someone's ancestry was impossible by looks alone. Hell, she was living proof of that. But the
idle speculation kept her from screaming.

Her fingers itched to note her observations. There had to
be paper in here somewhere. Place was like a damn hotel on
some levels, so there should be a drawer with cheap-ass sta-

tionery and ballpoint pens. Sure enough, a quick rifle of the bedside drawer—she squelched the frisson of guilt for pawing through *his* things—and she was equipped. Nothing beat the sensual glide of black ink over paper—certainly not the frantic tapping of keys. Later, when she was writing everything up, putting her new knowledge into print-worthy form for a scientific journal, she'd use the laptop. But not until then.

Old-fashioned observation and recording—that was her thing.

The club was busy, even for a Friday night, packed to capacity with gyrating, drinking, pleasure-seeking patrons. The cameras afforded her an unparalleled view. She estimated fifty-plus in the mirrored lobby alone, all fighting to make it inside to the dance floor.

All human.

The Fallen were inside, waiting for their prey. Yeah, the humans jostling one another in the lobby had another think coming to them if they really believed they had the upper hand here.

Two Fallen by the first bar, their intense gazes focused on their female partners. No visible bonding marks, so, clearly, a hookup was in progress there. The human behind the bar kept up a steady stream of full glasses, sliding slim flutes and squat bourbon tumblers over the counter. A dark male hand reached out and stroked a feminine thigh, gliding higher. A drink spilled onto the bar, unnoticed.

Yeah, next.

She knew better than to look, but the sensual tableau of the club was better than a train wreck. Each new camera pan revealed more Fallen and the human women they were hell-bent on seducing. The numbers didn't lie. Numerical data never did, but she wouldn't have estimated the damage to be this high. Did none of them say no? Was the one constant that no woman could resist? There had to be some human capable of saying no.

Who was she kidding? She was looking for something—someone—in particular. Two screens over, she found him.

Zer.

The visceral jolt of pleasure that shot through her was baffling. Unexpected. There was no logical reason for her to react so strongly to *him* and not to his equally striking brothers. And yet here she was, leaning forward in her chair so that she could follow his face on the screen. When the pen dropped from her fingers, rolling silently away, she admitted the truth.

She was lost.

On Zer's lap sat a tall, pale, and beautiful woman, apparently deposited there by Nael, who was still standing nearby. All too obviously, Nael had the caviar-and-champagne tastes his sensual smile promised. That was a Versace cocktail dress if Nessa didn't miss her guess—and nothing like Nessa's own practical business attire.

Hell . . . Nessa didn't like the spike of emotion the woman's presence in Zer's lap aroused. Nael's strong hands meant his female companion wasn't going anywhere he didn't allow, but, judging by the look on her face, she had no desire to go anywhere. Yeah, go figure.

The female pretty much looked like she'd just found heaven and it would take a nuclear holocaust to dislodge her. That shouldn't have bothered Nessa, but she still swallowed—hard—when Zer buried his face in the girl's hair, wrapping that large, hot body of his around her.

The same body that had held her, first in the car and then in his suite. *Get over him*, she ordered herself. So what if she wanted him? He was light-years out of her league and came with a price tag she had no intention of paying. But that didn't prevent her hormones from kicking into overdrive when she spotted him there on the vidscreen. Just hormones and a chemical reaction. That was all it was. But, God, it was a potent one. He was beautiful.

Nael threaded his fingers through the blonde's hair. His fingers tangled with Zer's. Oh, God, the erotic image was burned into her mind. Sharing. These two had shared women before, were confident in their sensuality, their ability to make the woman in their arms see fireworks.

Nael slid down the woman's body, unwrapping her like she was his Christmas present. Male fingers tugged at the zipper, and his hands stroked over the skin he'd uncovered. Followed the sensual path with his tongue. Nessa could all too easily imagine that tongue discovering her, tracing an erotic path over her breasts. No, not Nael. Zer. She shifted restlessly. She shouldn't watch this.

Shouldn't want those soft strokes for herself.

But, God, they were tempting. *He* was tempting.

So, there was a kink in her brain that couldn't deny the voyeuristic pleasure of watching Nael with his partner. Didn't want to, because it felt so damn good and it wasn't hurting anyone. Soon, though, she was watching Zer's face. The way his cock thrust against his black leather pants and the look of intense concentration and fierce hunger that lit his face.

To hell with it. Sliding a button free on her blouse, she stroked her own fingers along the smooth slope of her breasts. Heat crawled over her skin in a hot flush of desire. She was suddenly aware of the silky fabric of her bra cupping her breasts, her blouse clinging to her ribs.

On the vidscreen, Nael slid farther down the woman, eating at her through a wicked scrap of a thong. There was no sound, but the woman's head fell back against Zer's shoulder, her mouth opening on a soundless moan.

Of pleasure. Only pleasure.

Zer leaned forward, the muscles of his back bunching beneath the thin silk of his shirt. The woman perched on Zer's lap like she damn well belonged there drove her fingers through his close-cropped hair. Nessa wanted to trade places with her and run as far and fast as she could at the same time. What would it be like to have all that fierce masculine sensuality trained on *her*?

Her breath caught, and, damn it, she was wet. For *him*.

The butter-soft leather of her chair was a sensual caress against her bared skin, a substitute kiss for the lover she couldn't afford to take. She shouldn't do this. She was supposed to be escaping, but, instead, she was spying on the most intensely erotic scene she'd ever witnessed. But she couldn't stop watching.

On the vidscreen, Nael slid gently down his companion, his fingers spreading her ass. Dark pleasure spilled across her face and had Nessa's own mind superimposing an image of Zer doing the same to her.

Zer's eyes snapped up, that fierce, hooded gaze focusing on the security camera.

Oh, God.

He knew she was watching.

This time, his boys didn't make a scene. The guards let Zer enter the elevator and punch the buttons for his private floor without so much as a word of protest. He ached, his cock a hard, needy weight, but the hunger was less now. The beast locked up inside him had drained enough from Nael's newest find that it was unable to get out now. He knew he could walk through that door and not lay hands on Nessa. She'd be safe for tonight.

He considered knocking and dismissed the idea. This was his suite, and she needed to know that. Any rights to privacy she had, she had because he gifted her with them. That might make him an arrogant bastard, but he was the arrogant bastard who was going to keep her alive. Opening the door, he went in.

She sprang away from the vidbank as if she'd been burned. The pink flush spreading across her cheeks intrigued him, making his cock throb in hungry empathy. Christ, he could scent her arousal from across the room. Nael was on vidscreen, doing his thing. And Nessa St. James had been watching. How delicious was that?

"You're a watcher."

"No." Her denial was two shades of uncertain. Maybe she hadn't known she was a voyeur at heart, but she did now. Watching aroused her.

"Yes." Closing the distance between them, he examined her face. "You like to watch. I like to watch."

He'd never been anything but blunt in his sexual demands, and he wasn't going to let her hide from how she felt tonight. She wanted him. He didn't make mistakes about these things. Hell, he didn't make mistakes. Other than one corker of a mistake three millennia ago, his inner voice mocked him. Yeah, that had been the mistake to end all mistakes. But he'd learned from it.

So, he stalked her, backing her up against the vid console. "A gift." No strings, and he meant it.

He held out one large, male hand, and, God, was she tempted. She shouldn't. Oh, she really shouldn't. But it had been so long since she'd done something just for her. She knew it didn't mean anything, couldn't mean anything, so she wouldn't get hurt. She wasn't in the market for happily-ever-after, and, even if she had been, he wasn't selling, anyhow.

"No strings," she warned, and she put her hand in his. His fingers closed over hers. Strong. Warm. She couldn't tear her eyes from the fit. The teasing sensation of skin against skin wouldn't let her forget how rough he was, how masculine, how hard.

Not quite human.

He murmured a command, and the lights dimmed, wrapping them in a dark cocoon. Just the two of them. Maybe this wasn't such a good idea.

"Come with me." His voice was a dark promise. "Don't renege on me now. I'll make you feel good, baby."

"This doesn't mean anything," she warned again. She almost didn't recognize her voice. The tone was raw, husky with unfamiliar need.

"Understood. Just pleasure," he coaxed.

He drew her back to the vidscreens. Settled into the large leather armchair, pulling her down onto his lap.

"Watch," he breathed against her skin. One hand moved confidently over the bank of controls, punching in codes. The camera zoomed in, and Nael filled the small screen, still wrapped around his blonde.

Nessa was stiff in Zer's arms at first. "Relax, baby," he breathed against her ear. "We're just going to figure out what you like."

Her notes were spread out on the too-delicate little credenza, thick swirls of inky black on the bland white paper the club stocked. Observations. Numbers. His little scientist had an eye for detail that didn't surprise him. The question was: did she like what she'd seen?

He figured they could try each variant.

He was going to teach her exactly what she liked.

"Pleasure," he promised. "Only pleasure."

He drew one of her legs over his thighs and noticed that she'd removed the nylons she'd sported earlier. He made a mental note to order up a new wardrobe for her. She wouldn't go without, not on his watch.

"Zer," she said, and he drank in the soft, warm weight of her. Tentative. Tense. God, she was poised to run, as if she truly believed he'd let her out that door now that he had his hands on her.

As if he could.

Burying his face against her neck, he inhaled. Her scent was indescribable, that tormenting sugar-sweet smell of female. The soft strands of her hair clung to his jaw, to him. So much to explore, to learn.

He'd start with her skin, he decided. Learn the taste of her there. He stroked her lightly with his mouth, and her pulse jumped sharply beneath his tongue. She inhaled. Opened her mouth.

"Watch the vidscreen, baby."

On the screen, Nael's fingers were busy pulling up the too-short skirt of his companion's cocktail dress even farther. The fabric bunched, slid, revealing a wicked black lace garter belt.

"You want me to do that?" He growled the words against her skin, his fingers stroking softly over the curve of her thigh. "You want to give me that?"

"Yes," she said. Uncertain, then more sure. "Yes." As if she didn't know what she liked. An experiment.

He'd buy her a garter belt, he decided, removing his mouth from her throat. "You'll wear one of those for me. Wicked," he promised. "Little scrap of black silk to frame this pussy of yours. Lick you everywhere the lace doesn't go. Would you like that?"

"Maybe." Her eyes didn't move from the vidscreen.

On the screen, Nael stroked confidently between his companion's thighs, dark fingers sliding over the silk-covered mound.

Zer knew he couldn't wait any longer, could feel his beast pushing to get out. "My turn." Deliberately, he touched her, feeling her jump beneath his fingers. "Here, baby, where you're wet and swollen."

God, he was truly damned. He felt the plump, wet folds beneath his fingertips and wanted to rip off her panties and lick his way straight to the core of her. She tensed at the first light brush of his fingertips and then arched into his hand. God, yeah.

He let his hand rest there, drinking her in. Not the soul thirst, not yet, just delicious little tendrils of her psychic aura. Pleasure. Heat. Curiosity. God, that curiosity would be the death of him.

"Move," she ordered. "I want to know what that feels like."

Her wish was his command. He stroked softly, gently over the warm heat of her. Her curiosity intrigued him. What he felt from her was more than just sensual pleasure.

Her eyes closed, those dark lashes drifting slowly shut. Her hands fluttered, unsure of where to go, and then settled against his forearms. The light touch had him gritting his teeth. The feel of her was electric.

Deliberately, he drew two fingers gently down her soaking cleft, rubbing the fabric of her panties against her. Tempting her. The catch of her breath rewarded him, her sexy little whimper shockingly loud in the silent room.

"I want this," he whispered against her ear. "I want you, Nessa. I'm going to convince you to let me do everything you've ever wanted to do. You're going to beg me to."

"I don't beg," she said, but she didn't sound so sure anymore.

His cock was already impossibly hard, and then she moved gently against his hand.

"Hold still," he growled, and he touched her. "Hold still for me now, baby, and I'll make you come." He slid his fingers deeper into that sweet valley because he couldn't deny himself that pleasure. Not under her panties, though. Not yet. This was just a tease, a promise of the pleasure he could give her.

He didn't know if he'd survive.

Her head fell back, baring that smooth throat. "Zer," she said, and he didn't know if it was a plea or a warning. Those impossible eyes of hers searched his face.

"Watch the screen, baby." He paused, moving his hand away from her sweet heat. "Or I stop."

She whimpered but obeyed, and, Christ, that was hot. Wrapping his big hand in her hair, he held her still as he slid his fingers back where he wanted them to be.

On the vidscreen, Nael slid his partner open. Burying his face deep in her pussy. He was going to do that, too. He was going to have all of her, even though he shouldn't. "Next time," Zer promised. "Next time, imagine us doing that together. I'm going to taste every inch of you, Nessa. I'm going to love having you on my tongue."

He gave her the deep, delicious strokes he knew she craved, his fingers moving faster and deeper as her thighs closed around his wrist.

She came so quietly, the delicious flutters against his fingers soaking the silk of her panties. Quietly letting go.

So he held her in his arms, petting her gently. Wrapping her in himself. He was a goddamn selfish bastard, but he wasn't done yet. He'd sleep beside her tonight. He was selfish enough to take that much for himself. That, and the sweet, rich scent of her cream on his fingers.

"Bond with us," he whispered, his words soft against her skin as they lay in his bed. His ragged breathing, the impossible heat of him, and all that strength wrapped around her gave her an unfamiliar sense of belonging.

His offer shouldn't have intrigued her. She'd refused it once, and she had every intention of refusing it now. She wasn't going to do this. She really wasn't. And yet those were her feet beating a path toward him, because something about this Fallen intrigued her. He was a puzzle, a conundrum— and she'd never been able to resist a good puzzle. Maybe, that's all he was. Maybe, if she could figure out what made him tick, she could get back to her life.

"Bond with us, baby," he repeated, his voice a rasping growl of sound.

His words snapped her back to reality. This wasn't about her. This was about what *he* wanted. Her soul. And he didn't even have the decency to pretend that he wanted her soul for himself. "In your dreams, Zer."

She knew *nothing* of his dreams. Or his nightmares.

He had to convince her to do this, and it was killing him that force simply wouldn't do the trick. This relationship business would have been so much simpler if he could simply order her to do something and she did it. His eyes narrowed. "Why won't you do it?" He was genuinely curious, he realized. None of the females downstairs would have considered refusing. They would have begged him for the opportunity. What made her so different? After all, he'd *had* her begging, hadn't he?

He'd seduced her, had his fingers deep in sweet, wet heat, and she'd *still* refused him.

"I don't do shortcuts," she said, as if her words made perfect sense.

She thought he was a shortcut? "Explain," he snapped. Rolling over onto his side, he stared down at her on his bed. He liked that sight.

"I work for what I want, Zer," she said sweetly. "Maybe you should try it."

She believed this was easy? He looked forward to enlightening her. "I work damn hard, baby. This isn't a game. I need your promise." Splaying one large hand over her heart, he let his fingers tease the edges of her collarbone.

Of course, she shook her head. "You're not getting it. I don't want a Goblin bond. You don't have anything I need. Go find someone else."

He had trackers hunting for the three other females on the list, but he simply couldn't afford to waste this opportunity. She was one-fourth of an already too-puny arsenal, and he wasn't giving up any advantage in this war. "We need you."

"You want me," she countered, "and sexual attraction is nothing more than evolution and biology." Her lips parted in an indignant huff that undercut the careful logic of her words. "We don't have an emotional connection, Zer. We have pheromones."

Right. "You can call it what you want, baby, but you wanted me."

She shrugged. "I can want you all I want, but that doesn't mean I have to *take* you."

He wasn't prepared for his visceral reaction to the teasing mental image of her *taking*. Him.

"Let me go, Zer."

"Appealing to my better side? You should know that I don't have one." He'd lost any light and goodness he'd possessed millennia ago, not that the Dominions had been known for their warm-and-fuzzy qualities to begin with. No, they'd been bred to be killers. Protectors. And they'd done a damn fine job of it.

He stroked his hands up her arms because he could, his thumbs pressing pleasurably against the tense muscles of her forearms. Stretching her arms up, over her head. Watching the visible struggle on her face—torn between relaxing into his touch and remembering who he was. Where he had her. Yeah, she thought too much.

"Happily-ever-after." He smiled, and it was a hard, mean smile. "Romance. True love. You females love that shit. You buy it by the truckload. So, what's not to love about this?"

She stared at him as if he had no clue. "Pheromones."

"Bond with us," he repeated. "You were watching us on the vidscreen."

There was a flush of embarrassment—and arousal—on her face. He traced the color with a fingertip, fascinated. He'd never met anyone—human or Fallen—who tried so hard to resist pleasure. What would happen if she let loose? "We're offering fantasies—all your dark fantasies, coming true. You think about it, baby. Dream of it. Because I'm not letting you go."

He levered himself smoothly off the bed, putting distance between them, before she could call him on his bluff. He had blood on his leathers, blood and another female's scent. He'd shower before he slept with her, because he *was* sleeping with her tonight, and he wouldn't lie with her stinking of another's perfume.

"Let me go," she called after him.

"Not a chance. You're staying right here, where I can keep an eye on you."

"Don't trust your jailers?" Her taunt struck closer to home than he liked.

He trusted his brothers with his life, such as it was, but he wasn't going to make the mistake of underestimating her. He had a sinking feeling that, if she tried, she could wrap him around her slender fingers. All she had to do was give him that heat she had stored away inside. If she burned for him, if she let him in, he was going to end up trapped.

And that made her damn dangerous.

"Stay here," he growled, just to watch her eyes widen. With feminine pique.

"I'm not a dog," she began, but he was already pulling his leathers off. Letting the heavy material drop to the floor.

"I'm showering," he said, "and then I'm sleeping. Next to you."

Leaving the door open so he had a full-on view of the suite and its occupant, he hit the shower. The hot jets of water burning his skin were a welcome recall to the present. Reaching for the soap, he watched her. He wasn't stupid. He knew she'd run as soon as his back was turned, so, he wouldn't give her the chance.

Since Zer didn't close the door, Nessa decided privacy didn't rate high on his list of priorities. Even as the hot steam fogged up the room, she had a bird's-eye view of his body. Unconcerned, he'd stripped down right there in front of her, the heavy leathers hitting the floor. His blades, she couldn't help noticing, stayed close at hand. When he'd placed the pair on the edge of the counter, she'd spotted the dark, inky swirl of a tattoo banding both wrists.

The shower was a showcase for luxury living, but its tall, waxy pillar candles and Tuscan-colored tiles were overwhelmed by the male himself.

Impossibly broad shoulders. Powerful thighs. Muscles rippled as he shoved his face into the hot spray, shaking back his wet hair. Water droplets slid down that golden skin, slicking the dark hair back from the strong lines of his face. The steam slowly blurring his outline should have made him seem less dangerous. Instead, the thick cloud made him seem more so.

He was a lethal predator only half-hidden by the clouds of steam.

"Why are you doing this?" she called to him.

He muttered a response and then repeated it, louder.

"Because it's not respectful," he said. "I'm going to lie beside you tonight, baby, but I won't come to you like this."

She'd meant the kidnapping, but his words shut her up fast.

He intended to spend the night in that bed. With her.

He washed with quick, deliberate movements. She didn't think his behavior was meant as an erotic tease, but she couldn't tear her eyes from his body. When he shut the water off and turned around, she frowned. White ridges marred the perfect smoothness of his back—thick, gnarled ridges of scar tissue.

What kind of pain must have accompanied the making of those scars? He had scars on his face and forearms, but nothing like these twisted ropes of whitened skin that looked as if someone had skinned the flesh from his back—or pulled it off in one great sheet.

Spotting her deer-in-the-headlights stare, he swore.

"What happened to your back?"

"Nothing." Clearly nothing he wanted to talk about, and part of her couldn't blame him. Whatever horrific event had caused that pain and suffering was best blocked from memory. Still, she couldn't stop herself from repeating her question.

"What did this to you?" She couldn't imagine anyone getting the best of him like that.

"It happened a long time ago," he growled. Cursing, he wrapped a thick cotton towel around his waist and strode back out into the suite. "Millennia."

She wasn't letting this one go. "Tell me."

He shot her a hard glance. "You really want to know, baby? You promise to kiss it better afterward?"

Standing and walking up to him, she reached out a hand. He didn't move, challenging her. Fine. She wouldn't back down, and he needed to know that.

"You make sure you know what you're doing."

"Tell me," she repeated. "I want to know." She did, and that surprised her. She shrugged when he looked at her. "I do, and I'm persistent. Ask my colleagues."

"Stubborn," he countered, but some of the tension eased from his shoulders. "It happened during the Fall."

"Why did it happen?" He'd handed her one data point, and damned if she was going to let him off the hook now.

"Public education gotten that bad?" He strode over to a wardrobe. Banged open the drawers and rummaged around inside for clean clothes. "You have to know."

"I know the official history. What there is of it. The Dominions, first-line angelic defenders, rose up against the Heavens. There was an attempted coup, and the Dominions—you—lost. As punishment, the Archangel Michael ordered your wings stripped off and sent you here to live with us. I'm not sure I like the idea of my world being considered the heavenly equivalent of a penal colony," she added thoughtfully. "I happen to like it here."

Yanking out a pair of sweats, he dropped the towel, giving her a luscious view of his ass. When he bent over, pulling on the sweats, her breath caught. He was magnificent. All male.

"Yeah, that's the official version." Slamming the drawer shut, he closed the distance between them. He loomed over her, a hard smile on his face. She didn't flinch. "We both know the victor gets to write the history text."

"So." She eyed him measuredly. "Is the official history true?"

There was no simple way to explain what had happened three millennia ago. The memories rushed him before he could respond.

The human female standing in front of him dipped and swayed, the pale golden skin of her bare legs flashing as her skirts moved with the music. Dark eyes watched him with sensual promise. Should have been every male's fantasy, but all Zer saw were corpses.

How fucked up was that?

He could use a week of this R & R, but he couldn't stop the rewind in his head.

Three dead Dominion females in as many weeks. Always, males had outnumbered the females, and, as a result, Dominion women were fiercely protected. Adored. Kept safe no matter what the cost. Now, he had the entire Dominion camp up in arms. Outraged and on a killing edge. Because the recent killings were brutal. The murdering son of a bitch had split his victims open, letting their lifeblood drain away while he sexually brutalized their bodies.

It could have been daemon work. His fingers tightened on the tasseled cushions, and he forced his eyes not to move away as the dancer shimmied lower, her thighs bending, curving as she slipped the first of her veils free. He didn't want the reminder, but there was no escaping the smooth flesh she uncovered for him.

He was a hardened warrior. He'd fought for two hundred years to defend the Celestial throne against the dark daemons that crawled out of other realms. He'd seen death. Witnessed brutality firsthand. Nothing, however, had prepared him for these deaths.

His instincts screamed that, no matter how vicious the killings, these were not daemon work. He'd spent decades learning to track, and the blade marks were wrong. Blades had been stolen before, but the pattern of the strokes was familiar, too, a training pattern taught to all Dominion younglings in the camps. There were no ground signs, either, as if the attacker had dropped down from above, pushing his victim inches deep into the soft ground with his unexpected weight.

Maybe he was wrong. What he wanted to do was get to his feet, palm his weapons, and tear apart the Heavens until he had his answers. Instead, he was stuck here in a Nabatu pleasure camp until the call came for him to fly out. The dancer did the dip-and-sway, and he doubted the sultry heat of the desert would fade any sooner than her impossible interest.

The air was a sensual weight against his bare chest, and, if he flexed his wrist, he had weapons close at hand. A good soldier followed orders. And Zer's Archangel had ordered

Zer down to Earth. So, here he stayed, right? Parked his ass, kept his wings benched.

"Sire." *Gliding her fingers up her stomach, between her breasts, the dancer paused for a long, delicious heartbeat. This close, there was no escaping the sweet, heated scent of her skin or her desire. Desire that filled the air between them with wicked promise as she danced.*

Despite his best intentions, his cock thickened.

A loud commotion outside the pleasure tent broke the mood. Thrusting aside the tent's leather flap, Vkhin strode in. He'd first met the brother a lifetime ago, but no one could claim to know the Dominion cutting across the tent's thick layer of carpets. Wings tightly furled, Vkhin was as controlled, as cold and disciplined, as ever. He should have been the one the Dominions elected as their leader. Not Zer.

Another damn mystery he could puzzle out later.

"Michael has betrayed us," *Vkhin announced.*

Palming his weapons, Zer pushed himself to his feet. "Details."

"Brends has gone back to the Heavens." *Vkhin bit out the explanation, already whirling on one heel to make the return journey out of the tent.*

Moving swiftly to the entrance of the tent, he followed. The girl, abandoned, watched them. Disappointment and something feral painted her face.

Leaving camp was a direct violation of the Archangel's orders, but that was clearly what Vkhin intended. His feet didn't stop pounding, beating out a path toward the camp's perimeter. "Why—" *Zer began, but Vkhin cut him off.*

"Esrene reached out to him." *The other Dominion strode toward the camp's only portal point, clearly intent on following their absconded brother into infamy.*

"Why?" *He laid a restraining hand on Vkhin's arm, but the other shook him off. Brends was not a warrior who disobeyed orders. Ever.*

"*Esrene reached out to him through their pairling bond,*" Vkhin clarified. "*And then she was cut off. She was under attack, Zer.*" Sunset sleepiness wrapped the camp around them. A faint moan of pleasure drifted out of a nearby tent, followed by satisfied male laughter and the soft clink of weapons being removed. Camp was a goddamn fantasy land.

"*If she reached out, she wasn't dead.*" Yet. Running the previous murder sites through his head, he methodically reviewed the evidence. Had to be a pattern there.

"*Brends believes she is in the hands of the killer.*" Slamming a hand against the portal stones, Vkhin snarled a curse as he drew the sigils that would activate the doorway to take them from one plane to another. "*Once we step foot through that portal, we're outlaws. The Archangel, Michael, will hunt us.*"

Zer's brain kept moving even though his feet stopped. The first sigil sprang into glowing life. "*True.*" Michael was not an enemy one would choose to have. "*So, why do you intend to do this? What makes you so certain that Michael has betrayed all we stand for?*"

Vkhin's bleak eyes turned toward him as the second sigil ignited. "*Esrene named him. When she called out to Brends, she gave him Michael's name.*"

"*She could have been mistaken. She could have invoked his name in a plea for help.*" A name was not proof enough. He could not—would not—condemn his commander for a single word.

The last sigil exploded into life. "*And that is why, my sire, I am returning to the Heavens. To see for myself.*"

Sire. Leader. That was his job, wasn't it? To lead the Dominion troops into battle. To be first into the heart of the fight.

And this was a fight.

"*You hesitate,*" Vkhin said. His voice was as cold and flat as ever. "*That is understandable, sire. You should remain*" *here. If I am mistaken in my understanding, you will correct matters."*

And then Zer would be the one to hunt and kill Vkhin. Zer swore. He hadn't asked for this command. Hadn't known how to refuse. And that was another question, wasn't it? Why had he been chosen? At a mere two hundred years, he was still young. Untried. Still, there was no way he'd let Vkhin, his second-in-command, do the job that was his to do.

"I go," he snapped as the portal exploded into life, mazhyk *pulsing through it.*

"We go together," Vkhin countered.

There was no time to argue. Stepping into the portal, Zer let the mazhykical doorway connecting this backward earthly realm with their own Heavens suck him in. On the other side, he hit the ground hard, dropping and rolling, blades in his palms as he came up.

He was younger. Faster. Not waiting for Vkhin, he pushed his wings, muscles tearing as he forced his way through the air, his predator's eyes reading the signs in the fading light. Below him, on the ground, a lighter body had run hard. The footprints were deep and desperate, the bare toes grabbing into the soft earth and pushing away with fierce intent. Behind, though, came the larger pursuer, and Zer's throat closed. He could read the signs of pursuit too clearly. Blood stained bushes he'd passed.

The bastard was playing games with her.

Control slipped away from him, leaving him only sick desperation. No one had wanted to believe him when he'd argued the killer was no daemon. He hadn't wanted to believe the truth himself, but the tracks didn't lie. Couldn't lie. They were the wrong size, the wrong shape, for a daemon. Now, they were all going to pay the price for their disbelief.

The tracks ended abruptly in a small patch of empty space tucked up against the base of a hill.

He'd gotten his ass there before Vkhin or Brends, but he was still too late.

Far too late.

Wings flickered in his peripheral vision.

Refocusing, Zer pulled back, tore his gaze away from the crumpled body lying in the very heart of that small, empty space. Feeling was an unaffordable luxury right now. He couldn't indulge himself in the need to crouch by her fading self, to coax what was left of her to remain. If he went rushing in, he might never know for certain—and he had to see the proof with his own eyes.

Michael, *his heart whispered as the Archangel stalked into the clearing. There was blood on Michael's hands and the Archangel didn't stop his forward prowl until he was looking down at that pale, still form. Bastard didn't so much as blink, and Zer reacted hard, palming his weapons. The sharp edge of the blade cutting into his hand stopped his own forward lunge.*

Esrene's chest stopped its shallow up-and-down.

Behind him, Vkhin cursed, low and vicious. "Now, sire."
Hell if those two words weren't part accusation, part command.

And then Brends burst onto the scene. Zer's brother was all hard-core, ruthless fighter. He didn't hesitate or waste time with eyeballing the scene. No, Brends's blade was free and clear, business end up, as he placed his body between Esrene's and the Archangel's. Zer kept his eyes on Brends's hands. The moment that blade made a move in the Archangel's direction, Brends drew himself a death sentence. Dominions were forbidden to raise a weapon against the Archangels.

"You did this," Brends said hoarsely. That blade didn't waver.

Beside him, Vkhin shifted, readying himself for the fight

they all saw coming. The world stood still for a damn long moment, and then Michael agreed. "Yes."

No regret, no pain. Just the cold, flat tone of a killer, as if the Archangel was ordering the Dominion to take out the trash.

Vkhin was moving, but Zer slammed a hand into Vkhin's chest. "Hold up," he ordered. His own blade hadn't left his hand, and he couldn't deny the protective, possessive urges tearing through him. Anger. Grief. A white-hot wrath. "Michael is mine," he growled.

Vkhin looked like he wanted to argue, but Brends wasn't done suffering out there alone in the clearing. Moving toward the Archangel, he demanded to know how Michael could have done this.

A flicker of hot emotion crossed Michael's face, was quickly locked away. Instead of answering, the Archangel looked at his hands. That bright red stain colored his golden skin as Brends swore to kill the other male.

Vkhin's icy gaze watched Zer. Watched the Dominions' chosen leader hesitate. "Choose," he said implacably. "It's time to choose."

Christ. He wanted things to end differently. He wanted Esrene's chest to move. No chance of that. Instead, Zer either let Brends step up to the plate and take on Michael—or Zer threw the entire weight of the Dominions behind Brends's rebellion. He could make this more than personal.

The minute he stepped into that clearing and didn't put himself between Brends's blade and Michael, he'd drawn the battle lines, and the others would follow. Follow because they'd sworn to and because more than a few of his brothers wanted to hunt this killer who had cut his way through their females.

In the end, it wasn't much of a choice.

He'd loved Esrene. As a sister or something more, he didn't know. So never mind that he'd sworn himself to Michael. He'd take down the male he'd vowed to protect and serve, because life wasn't perfect anymore and he'd hesitated too long.

Esrene wasn't coming back, and Michael's games had to stop now.

He stepped into the clearing and stood beside Brends.

No human had ever asked him about that day.

"Yeah," he said slowly. "It's true." It was—that was the hard part to accept. He'd staged a rebellion against the one he'd sworn to protect with his life. He'd broken his vows, and now he was paying the price. That was the truth.

Before he'd gotten the words out of his mouth, she was shaking her head. "There's more to it than that, Zer, so don't put me off with half-truths. You were a Dominion. There was a rebellion. What I want to know is why."

His reaction to the question startled him. Something unfamiliar and warm uncurled in his chest. He didn't like the off-balance feeling one bit.

"I want the truth, Zer. Why does this matter to you? Why would a bunch of condemned killers want so badly to find a way back into the Heavens? I'm willing to bet that you have a reason. A good reason."

He swallowed. Hard. Nessa didn't take anything on faith. He knew that. She dealt in logic and facts, but now she was reaching out to him. Trusting him.

But he was a damned bastard—literally.

Her fingers stroked lightly over his shoulder. "Tell me what's going on here really, Zer."

Telling her the truth she wanted so badly would win her over. He could taste victory—but, somehow, the taste was bittersweet. She'd believe him, but for all the wrong reasons.

"I'm a killer." He took another step toward her. She made a small, feminine retreat. One more step and he'd have her pinned between his body and the wall. When he inhaled, he could smell her, and her scent was as intriguing as the rest of her.

She gave him the teacher look, the look that said she was running through her facts. Analyzing. "Why did you rebel?" The question wasn't directed at him. "Feel free to corroborate or deny, but I'd hypothesize that there was some sort of betrayal. You had just cause."

Bingo. He had her back against the wall. Reaching out, he braced powerful forearms on either side of her head. "You're good, professor."

Pleasure shone in her eyes as if he'd complimented her eyes or her hair. "You don't seem like the type to just pull a power play."

"Why not?" He leaned in a little, tormenting himself with the delicious heat of her body. He could have stayed like this all night. "You don't know me. Maybe I'm a coldhearted bastard who wanted things his way."

"You want things your way, all right," she agreed.

"You want a bedtime story?" He handed her a pillow, and she wrapped her arms around it. "I guarantee you won't like my stories."

"Try me."

How to explain the deaths no one had been able to explain? "We found a pairling one night," he said finally. "Dead. Her body slit from one end to the other." He left out the details of what had been done to her sexually. This female didn't deserve the nightmares.

"Wait. Back up. What's a pairling?"

He waved a hand. "Think of it as a brother-sister matched set."

"Related." She nodded.

Sort of. The Dominions were bred, not born, but the connection was still there. "Close enough. Which was why her pairling was so upset when he found her." *Upset* didn't begin to cover Brends's rage. The male had been homicidal.

"Was she the first?"

Christ, maybe she did understand where he was going with this. "No. Something had been wrong in the Heavens for months. There were deaths. Disappearances."

"And no one cared? No one noticed?" She sounded as incredulous as he'd been.

He shouldn't be burdening her with this. He knew that. Fighting this battle was his responsibility, not hers, even if she was going to be the weapon he used. "You have to understand how it was, baby. She should have been protected. Cherished. We failed her," he added grimly, "and she died. It was every bit as much our failure as the killer's."

"You told someone," she guessed. "Next in the chain of command."

"No."

"But why not?"

Because he'd suspected that Michael himself was the culprit. "No point," he said curtly. "Better to handle it ourselves."

"You went after the killer."

"We did."

"You knew who the killer was."

"I found my boy Michael at the scene." He smiled coldly. "My gut told me he'd done it, but we didn't have the proof. We weren't going to let the same thing happen to any other females under our protection. We took preemptive action."

"You rebelled."

"Yeah." That was one way of putting it. He'd led the charge in a Fuck You of cosmic proportions. "Insubordination. The Archangel reamed us a new one and tossed us out of the Heavens."

"Christ," he growled through gritted teeth, "don't you see

that it didn't *matter?* We broke the cardinal rule: thou shalt not rebel. Esrene's death was merely an excuse for what we did. We needed a reason to pick a fight with the Archangel who held our leashes, and we found it. We broke every rule in the damn rule book twice and it was all a setup. Cuthah, Michael's lieutenant and second in command, wanted us out and I took his bait. He served Michael right up to me and I fell for it."

"Cuthah played you," she interrupted. "That's what bothers you now."

Christ. It did. "Cuthah was playing a deep game of his own and he set up the Dominions to take us out." Cuthah had been a traitor, but he hadn't been the only guilty one. Zer was guilty of insubordination. Of refusing to play by Heaven's rules. You broke those rules, you accepted the consequences.

"It was a long time ago," he said finally. It felt like yesterday.

"You want me to just let it go?"

"Yes," he said firmly, and he scooped her up, sliding her beneath the covers. "We're just going to sleep," he promised. "No sex."

He sensed feminine trepidation and that damn curiosity of hers. He'd whetted her appetite, for sex and information, and she wouldn't let this go.

She wasn't going to be his. She'd belong to one of his brothers, body and soul, and he wouldn't poach on another male's territory. Still, he didn't mind her outraged reaction to co-sleeping. Turning away from the bed, he reached for the switch to hit the lights.

Too late, he remembered the scars.

Nessa knew instinctively that Zer didn't display his scars. Not to anyone and certainly not to anyone human. She didn't know whether the intimacy seduced her—or pissed her off. So, he wasn't human. And she wasn't an angel. He'd known both those little facts before he'd kidnapped her; if he was experiencing buyer's remorse, he could damn well let her go.

The scars were deceptively simple, thicker, paler twists of tissue that had formed over his injury and that went far deeper than the skin of his back. *Oh, God.* She knew instinctively that those scars cut all the way to the soul. He'd lost what mattered most to him, and those scars were merely the visual proof. Now, she knew what kind of injury a Goblin had to sustain to scar like that. Those twisted ridges of white skin on his back marked where his wings had grown.

She couldn't stop herself from imagining him with wings. She'd never seen a Dominion, but she could easily picture Zer as he must have been. Magnificent. She knew that without a doubt. His wings would be as dark and powerful as he was, making him a fearful predator. Who had her in his sights.

Why hadn't he healed? "I thought you were immortal. That every wound would heal."

"No." The flat look in his eyes warned her she wasn't ready to hear the rest of the story. "Near-immortal, baby. Cut our heads off, and you win. If you were strong enough, you could saw my head off and be clear of me."

The bed dipped and swayed as he got in, settling his weight beside her. Between her and the door. God, how long had it been since she'd slept with someone else? Not been alone in the night?

"Just sleep, baby." His eyes made dark promises, but right now, this was what she needed. Comfort.

He needed it, too, she thought, sleep pulling seductively at her eyelids. His arm pulled the heavy velvet comforter over them. It settled across her. Around them, the candles flickered out. This leader of the Fallen, their sire, was just as alone as she was. She wouldn't make the mistake of thinking that made him weak or any less of a bastard. He wasn't going to back down from his demands, but maybe she could take what he was offering right now, and maybe, just maybe, she could avoid paying the price.

CHAPTER NINE

God, he loved recruiting the Fallen, corrupting the formerly incorruptible Dominions. Loved the almost sensual rush of pleasure as he seduced them—step by step. Leading them right down the path he needed them to take with dark promises of power and pleasure. He'd promised them their wings would be restored so that the entire world would finally know that these Dominions were back on the right track.

Some of them had believed him.

Fools.

Cuthah couldn't stop the cold smile that curved over a face many had called handsome. Handsome or not, it was one more weapon he used. Now, he drank in the bitter rush of air ripping through his powerful wings, the heady rush of flight with each strong beat. *There.* Signaling to his lieutenants, he drove down to meet the ground rushing up toward him. Frankly, he didn't know how the Fallen had survived this long without their wings. He counted his blessings, however, because it made them ridiculously easy to seduce.

Because, God knew, the rogues would do anything to get their wings back. Even sell him what little remained of their souls. Carefully, he scanned the postapocalyptic landscape stretching away below him. The walls of the Preserves glowed balefully upward, their mazhykical wards slipping away beneath him.

He didn't need to pass through the wards when he could simply go over them.

"Land here," he barked, and the others flying with him immediately began their own descent. They knew better than to hesitate, even if the ground soaring up to meet them was rocky and barren and they were hampered by the burdens they carried. The rogues incarcerated here were cheap whores, renting their bodies out to whoever could pay their price. He disliked them, disliked having to use them, but he would put together the army he needed, and then he'd cut off their hope for redemption.

When his feet hit the ground, he folded his wings back. He could have shifted to human form, but he wanted to remind the rogues lurking in the shadows of what they'd lost. Striding forward, he pulled his fyreblades from their sheaths on his back. His lieutenants fell in behind him.

"Everything is prepared." Hesath didn't look at him, just kept on moving forward.

It had better be. Crossing his arms, Cuthah stopped, waiting. The fyreblades were a blazing beacon in the darkness—the rogues couldn't help but come. He was counting on it. The Preserves were a mazhykical wasteland, a prison designed to hold the rogue Fallen who craved just one thing.

Souls.

They would indeed come, like fish to a lure.

His lips curled in disdain. Still, he had no desire to spend more time here than was necessary. He glanced behind him at his lieutenant. "You put out the word?"

"Exactly as you commanded, sire." The lieutenant's eyes were busy dissecting the black shadows around them, the scarred knuckles of his right hand wrapped around the haft of his blade. He was ready to gut the first bastard who sprang at them.

The shadows moved now, thick with life. Of one sort or the other. Soulless bastards were coming to him, exactly as planned. Three millennia without being tossed so much as a bone, and the Fallen were soul-starved. Dying for what they couldn't have. What they'd been denied. The Archangel Michael had cut his own throat when he'd exiled the Dominions to this cold, mazhykless world. The Fallen craved the taste of a soul like the down-on-their-luck addicts they were, and he had just the drug to sell them.

Ten cautious minutes later, the first rogue crept to the outermost edges of the shadows, front-lit by the pool of light from the fyreblade. He was not alone.

Hesath's gaze moved over their new company, counting. "More Fallen coming."

"Good." That was what he needed. The Fallen rogues were going to be the raw fodder for his army.

"They are crazed." His lieutenant didn't shift his gaze from the first male who entered the circle of light. His observation was neither a challenge nor a question, just a careful statement of fact. "I cannot guarantee what they will do."

Truth. These Fallen were lost to the soul thirst. Over time, the transformation had irreversibly etched itself across their bodies. The first male into Cuthah's circle had been tall and broad-shouldered once upon a time. Now, rage twisted his features, bent his back and shoulders into a brutal travesty of the powerful warrior he had once been. Skulking out of the shadows, he was more beast than man as his dark eyes darted toward the source of the light.

"They are what I need."

"It is not my business to question, sire, but how can they be of any help?"

The questions became tiresome. Once, Cuthah would have killed the male for daring to ask. Now, however, he schooled himself to patience. He'd only just replaced Eilor with this male. Striking him down would cause more trouble than it was worth.

"Once," he said coldly. "Once, you may ask. They are malleable. Vulnerable. They want what we can offer them."

His lieutenant considered Cuthah's words, then nodded in comprehension. "They are for sale."

"Even if they do not yet know it, yes." Fortunately, their loyalties were easily purchased—another flaw in Michael's original plan. You could not deprive a male for so long and expect him to embrace his punishment.

"The two females we carried here—" Hesath paused, delicately.

Maybe this new lieutenant was not as stupid as he'd feared. "Yes. The females."

"Bait."

"Precisely. The Fallen here want nothing more than to drain dry as many human souls as they can take. I give them what they want, what they *need*—and they are mine."

Recruiting was so much simpler when the Fallen wanted to Fall. He had the lures, but he'd had to consider carefully the possible candidates. Only a fool would waltz straight into G2's and make his offer to one of those. Those Fallen were hard-core. The loyal. Zer's inner circle wasn't ready yet for what Cuthah had to offer.

"I've brought you a present." He directed his words toward the visible rogue, knowing that he had a larger audience lurking in the shadows.

One of the rogues spoke from the shadows. "What do you want?" Rusty with disuse, the voice hinted at the feral madness that eventually consumed all rogues. Gone, Cuthah judged, mad and endarkened, but still dangerous.

"Service. And, in exchange, I've brought you souls." He paused, waiting.

"No." Thirst had made the male's face savage, burning away any beauty he had once possessed. A long-healed scar cut across his cheek, and the coppery scent of blood hinted at more recent, hidden injuries. Cuthah judged the male should have been starving, but those eyes were shuttered, giving nothing away. The body did, though. The body was tense with hunger and lean, too lean. If soul thirst didn't consume him first, physical hunger would. "I want no souls. None of us here do."

"Speak for yourself," Cuthah replied. There was no leadership in the Preserves, only a brutal game of natural selection. If time had not been so limited, Cuthah might have bothered to destroy the rogue, or try to find out who he had been. But, honestly, why bother? The rogue wouldn't last long in here. None of them did.

"To drink?" Another guttural rasp, this time from Cuthah's left, drowned out the first speaker's pithy curse. This one wasn't so troubled by ethics. Good. This new recruit was dark, like all of them. Undoubtedly, he'd been a handsome bastard before he'd picked the losing end of the Heavens' battle. Now he had hungry eyes and a restless hitch in his gait.

He was perfect.

Zer couldn't keep tabs on them all, and that was an advantage. Better yet, Zer still held to the old code. He wouldn't kill until he was provoked. That was a weakness Cuthah had every intention of exploiting.

"Of course. I've brought two. But if you had your wings back, you could have a steady diet of souls. Access to M City and all the delicious humans still living there."

The growls from the darkness alerted Cuthah to the dark shadows moving closer. He had them now, even as the male who had refused the first offer slipped away.

"What's the catch?"

Most were hardly recognizable as men, too far lost to their rogue side to do more than growl. The Preserves had stood for hundreds of years. Not much of a male remained after that sort of time had passed. Still, he could use these.

"No catch," he assured his unseen listeners. "I offer you a simple business proposition. You threw your lot in with Zer and the other Fallen, and you—Fell. You lost—lost your wings, your rights, and your power. I can give you back all of that. In exchange, you vow loyalty to me. You fight for me, when and how I say."

"We'll be your men."

"Medieval, but, yes. Mine, body and soul."

"And you can truly return our wings?"

Negotiating was a bore, so Cuthah opted for a demonstration. "You," he snapped, gesturing toward the first male.

Pulling mazhyk through his body, Cuthah focused on the male in front of him. He could have been more subtle, but there was no point. These males wanted the flash and drama of a demonstration, so he let the mazhyk spike through the air, rolling across the ground in a lightning-bright rush of light and sound. Power hit the male, pulling a low, animalistic growl of pain from him. As Cuthah pushed more power into the male, his body rose from the ground, bowing. The primitive growls from the surrounding shadows increased. *Now.* Cuthah released the power, and mazhyk was sucked out of the clearing like water down a drain.

Cursing, the male collapsed on the ground. He pushed up onto his hands and knees like a dog. The skin writhed across his back. Red ink covered that skin, blood-red signs and sigils snaking across the heaving surface. Cuthah spoke a final word, and the red ink snapped to life, taking on a recognizable form. A feathered outline. Wings.

"Rise," he said coldly.

The male staggered to his feet, staring blindly into the darkness. The red ink writhed with a life of its own as dark wings uncurled from the male's skin, unfurling into the darkness. With a ripple of sound, the fledgling feathers slid open in a soft hush, testing the air.

"Are you mine? Will you bond with me?"

Raising a hand, Cuthah called in the mazhyk again. The fledgling wings froze in mid-furl, teased by the sudden breeze whipping through the clearing.

The male stared. Groaned once. But there was no hesitation when he spoke. "Yes." The guttural promise sounded as if it had been torn from him. "I am yours, sire, only let me keep *these*." The large hand trembled as he reached behind him to stroke the silky feathers.

All around them, males were stepping out of the shadows, swearing their own promises of loyalty. Cuthah hadn't survived as long as he had by trusting anything so simple as a vow. Words were, in the end, simply words. What he needed— what he *wanted*—was a mazhykical binding. Pulling on the mazhyk, he branded his own red markings on the men. It was a perversion of the bonding mark Michael had given them, but none of them cared.

He had them eating out of the palm of his hand. Crawling to him for what he could offer.

Groans and panting breaths filled the stale air of the clearing as wings tore through skin. Unfurling.

A sharp command to his lieutenants had the two males dragging forward the pair of young women he'd acquired in M City. The aphrodisiac he'd administered almost, but not quite, clouded their senses. Arousal competed with fear, but they'd been paid well—in advance—and so they'd willingly donned the BD/SM-wear Cuthah had provided. Musky ribbons of sensation peeled from their uncertain souls now, unsure whether to revel in the strange pleasures and stranger company or to heed common sense and start screaming.

Too late, darlings.

He'd spent a considerable amount of time considering how best to use these rogues.

"A prize." He lifted a finger, and the Fallen paused. The psychic scent rolling off them lingered deliciously. Lust. Fear and greed. The sweet, sweet residual burn of pain. He licked a drop of blood from his fingers. He'd never promised them that regaining their wings would be *painless*. The Fallen could have swarmed the two women, could have over-whelmed his lieutenants, but they paused. Bitches brought to heel.

Now, they'd hunt on his command. The sky was lighten-ing, the inky blackness paling where it met the edges of the Preserves' walls. Soon, they'd burn to fly. After, of course, he'd given them a target.

"I want you to hunt for me."

The male nearest Cuthah slowly turned his head. Lust streaked his eyes and had the bastard's cock swelling hard and full. Rogue might have been an alpha in his former life, and he sure as hell might want to shout a Fuck You to his re-creator, but he wasn't stupid. He stopped his slow, forward prowl, licking his lips.

"Tell me who you want." Yeah. That one wasn't stupid. He knew who really owned the wings sprouting from his back. And it sure wasn't the Archangel Michael.

"Right now—" He savored the words, because right now he was all-powerful. Those rogues were all *his* now, and he wasn't going to let them forget it. They wanted what he could give them, so they'd roll over for him. "Right now, I want Nessa St. James."

Alpha just glared at him, so clearly he was well out of the G2's loop. That was fine. Cuthah figured that the fewer males who knew what was going down, the easier it would be to control the situation.

"Tell me where to find her," the rogue growled.

Tonight she was at G2's, but surely Zer would move her. If Cuthah had known where, he wouldn't have bothered resur-recting these dregs. These rogues might have been Dominions once upon a time, but that was fairy-tale time—once upon a time and long, long ago. Now, they were less than beasts, trapped in their Goblin forms or worse. Loping on all fours. Hunched. Twisted.

Talk about fucked up. He had to wonder if Michael had known what would happen after three thousand years of hard living—or if it was just a little unexpected bonus.

Fortunately, beasts could be trained. He pulled out the sweater he'd found in the AWOL professor's office. Hell, he hadn't even had to steal the damn thing—the university's dean had been all take-what-you-want as soon as he'd counted the zeroes on Cuthah's latest financial donation. Money talked.

"That's your job." He wasn't going to say it twice. Tossing the sweater to the male, he continued. "You find her. You bring her to me. Alive."

Alpha boy was raising the cotton fabric to his nose. Turned out he was the bitch that Cuthah had guessed. One long, deep inhale and Cuthah could read the satisfaction flooding those eyes.

"She's in M City." No point in wasting time. The sooner his new recruits tracked down the good professor, the sooner Cuthah could take care of his business with her. "Last known location: G2's."

"G2's." The club's name was a low, rasping growl on alpha boy's lips. Yeah, he remembered his former brothers all too well. "You need her all in one piece, sire?"

He didn't have to have all of her. In fact, a little collateral damage might convince his professor that he was deadly serious. "Be careful," he compromised. "No permanent damage."

Alpha boy nodded, his talons shredding the cotton into a dozen lesser scraps. Kibble for his boys, Cuthah figured. "We bring her back here?"

Cuthah shook his head. He preferred to do his business outside the walls of M City. Between the radioactive currents and the burgeoning paranormal population, his tracks wouldn't be as clear.

"Bring her here," he said, and he reeled off a list of coordinates. Alpha boy just nodded as if he had a built-in GPS. "One week," Cuthah warned. "After that, I'm in the market for some new recruits. And, should you think to double-cross me, just keep in mind that those wings of yours are going to need a recharge."

"Got it." Alpha boy's head did the requisite up-and-down. Clearly, he'd gotten the message. The wings were temporary—and, to keep them, alpha boy and his brothers would follow him to the end of the Earth and back. He'd give them this taste, remind them of what they'd lost.

"A token of my good faith." He gestured, and his lieutenants stepped forward, dragging the females with them. One good push and the little darlings stood alone in the circle of fading light. Funny, but the women hadn't considered what could happen to them, alone with a group of rogues. That wasn't Cuthah's problem—it was theirs.

As he and his lieutenants lit out of there, headed back for business in M City, there was no missing the flood of dark rogues swarming the pair. The women's screams were music to his ears.

Behind him, the first of the newly changed took off, dark wings beating slowly up into the sky, breaching the protective wards of the Preserves. His hunters would ensure Nessa St. James did precisely as she'd been told.

Nessa woke up alone. She should have been glad the Fallen had had the good sense to hightail his ass out of the room before she woke up. Part of her, however, was disappointed. She hadn't expected to wake up alone.

From the looks of things, at some point during the night, Zer had vacated the room and left her in sole possession of his large bed. The other pillow was smooth and undented, the only mark hers. The tangle of sheets should have meant sex and morning-after closeness, but, instead, all she had was the soft rub of the satin against the bare skin of her legs where the shirt Zer had given her now rode up.

Yeah. She winced. Not what she'd been hoping for. She'd known Zer was a one-night-stand kind of guy, so this morning's wake-up call shouldn't have been a shocker. For some reason, though, it was, and that made her stomach churn.

A knock sounded on the closed door. A knock that was far too polite to be her jailer.

Sitting up, she pulled the sheets around her and called out her permission to enter. The face revealed by the opening door was flawless, a perfect porcelain oval framed by a long, dark sheet of hair. Almost too perfect. That kind of cool-and-serene belonged on the pages of a fashion spread. And then the visitor smiled impishly, taking in the mussed bed and the man's shirt.

"I'm not intruding, am I? Zer would kill me," she added cheerfully. "I'm Mischka Baran." She paused, as if she expected Nessa to recognize the name.

Since she didn't, she settled for nodding. "Nessa St. James."

"I know." Mischka's fingers tightened on the doorframe, and a low, masculine rumble sounded behind her. "I guess you could say I'm with Brends Duranov."

"The club's owner."

"Yes." She paused, as if she wanted to say more. Then she plowed ahead. "May I come in? Are you in the mood for breakfast?"

Mischka's voice sounded cheerful, but there was uncertainty in her eyes as she poked her head around the door. Whatever she believed had happened, it wasn't what Mischka Baran had expected. This was no routine delivery. Behind Mischka, she spotted the broad shoulders of Vkhin and Nael on other side of door. Yeah. She was still a prisoner—just a prisoner they'd decided to feed.

"Sure." No point in starving just to make a point. Manners couldn't hurt, either. "Thanks."

Nodding, Mischka stepped into the room, followed by another too-large male carrying the tray for her. *Brends,* Mischka mouthed. Feeling stupid, Nessa nodded again. He set the dome-covered tray down on the table in the little sitting area. Turning to his mate, he bent his dark head down toward her, his silky hair closing around them, shutting Nessa out. Nothing new there, but there was nothing to prevent her from catching the end of a soft, private murmur. The large hands that had set the tray down on the table touched the other woman's shoulder briefly. Intimately.

That little caress made Nessa's own heart speed up a little, and that made her mad. Whatever bond these two shared, it was unfamiliar to her.

"I'm going to stay, share a cup of coffee with Nessa," Mischka announced, shooing her reluctant mate out of the room. As she shut the door firmly behind him, her eyes narrowed suspiciously. "You *do* drink coffee, right?"

"Try to keep me away from it." The tray was pure room-service fantasy. Dark, rich Jamaican coffee with thick cream. Fresh oranzh juice. Salted butter and pastries. A nice gesture, she was sure, but it triggered her suspicions instead. Why did they want her cooperation so much? That implied that—somehow—she could withhold it. Was this woman and her tray of goodies merely another well thought out step in Zer's seductive campaign?

Her brain bombarded her with mental images of Zer seducing another woman, and, for God's sake, those thoughts were putting her on edge. She didn't want him. Didn't care if he helped himself to a dozen other women from what was clearly G2's large stable. Did she?

"Nothing happened last night," Nessa said, and immediately she wanted to kick herself. *Way to go, arousing suspicions.* Still, there was no getting around the fact that here she was, planted in Zer's bedroom and wearing only his shirt. Sometime during the night, her clothes had taken a vacation of their own, right down to her panties.

"He wouldn't." Mischka shrugged a shoulder in casual understanding.

Why was Mischka Baran so convinced that Zer wouldn't make a move on her?

Mischka was watching her as she reached for her coffee, and there was that pregnant pause again. Nessa filed it away to consider later. She wasn't falling for that tease right now.

"Bonding can make a lot of sense," Mischka pointed out, and Nessa set the cup back on the tray. Suddenly, this breakfast gave a whole new meaning to the term *dining with the devil*.

"I'm not for sale."

Mischka looked like she agreed, and that surprised Nessa. Maybe the other woman wasn't on her side, but, equally clearly, she hadn't sold out to the Fallen.

Not 100 percent, anyhow.

Getting out of bed, Nessa pulled on the cashmere wrap Mischka tossed her. The wrap still had tags on it. New. When she raised an eyebrow, Mischka smiled helplessly. "Zer asked me to find you something to wear."

"I have clothes," she pointed out. "In my own flat."

That was a mood killer. Mischka muttered something about not being able to take the alpha out of the angel. "They're male." She perched on the edge of the bed. "They provide."

"Pain in the ass," Nessa supplied, and Mischka responded with a wry grin.

"They're that, all right." She raised her arm to take a quick, appreciative sip of her coffee, and her sleeve slid away from her wrist, putting her bonding marks on full display. The thick black swirls of ink were impossible to miss.

She'd grab this bull by the horns. "You're a bond mate."

"I'm bonded, yes." Burying her nose in her coffee cup, Mischka inhaled the rich scent of the brew. The intangible glow of satisfaction surrounding her was as easy to spot as the markings. *Happiness.* She belonged with the male who'd escorted her to Nessa's room. *With,* not *to.* It almost made Nessa believe in the myth of happily-ever-after. Almost.

Cream and sugar, Nessa decided, reaching for the tray. Today was not a dieting kind of a day. "How long have you been a bond mate?"

"I'm not—" she began, then closed her mouth. Nessa filed that strange pause away for future examination, too. "Two months, give or take."

"How long does it last?"

Mischka looked up from the coffee she was stirring. "The bond? It varies. You have to phrase your favor very, very carefully, Nessa. You got that? Think before you ask."

"What's it like?" She had no intention of bonding with anyone, but the question came tumbling out before Nessa could stop it. Hell, she wasn't winning any prizes for tact today, was she?

A pink flush covered Mischka's exquisite cheekbones. "Intense."

"That was too personal," Nessa apologized. Whatever had brought Mischka to bond with one of the Fallen, she clearly had no regrets. Of course, Nessa figured junkies had the same affection for their dealers. Still, Mischka Baran looked like she'd bought every word of the happily-ever-after Zer had been selling.

"So"—Mischka took another long, meditative sip of her coffee, one hand crumbling a scone on the plate she'd balanced on the bed—"I'd ask why you're here, but I've got a good idea." Anger flashed in Mischka's eyes. Good. Maybe there was someone on her side. "Brends didn't tell me in advance what Zer intended to do." She shrugged.

"Should he have?" Nessa got the impression that *feudal* didn't begin to describe the world she'd fallen into.

"Damn right," the woman perched next to her muttered. "I could have told him his plan wouldn't work."

"Kidnapping?" Nessa offered politely.

"Yeah." Mischka slid her cup and plate back onto the tray and threw herself down onto the bed. "Problem is, these guys have some pretty flexible ethics."

That was a fact, not an excuse. "I want to leave."

"I can't help you." Mischka at least had the decency to look apologetic. "Brends closed that loophole. He specifically ordered me not to get involved."

Somehow, the order-giving bit didn't surprise her. "How? I mean—" She paused because, damn, she needed to phrase this right. No point in pissing off the only human she'd met so far. "How come he gets to give the orders and you have to jump?" Maybe that was just Mischka's own personal kink. Somehow, though, Nessa didn't think so.

"You asked about the bond." Mischka lifted her coffee cup and stared across the rim. "Well, that's part of it. We're connected."

"Emotionally, as in you feel really close to him, or some other kind of connection?"

"Other." The small smile spoke volumes. "You really don't care for the supernatural, do you? I didn't, either, which didn't make this whole relationship thing go smoothly at first. Once you bond," she explained, "there's a mental connection between you and your bond mate." She shrugged. "I can always feel Brends in the back of my head."

Lovely. The deal came with a mental stalker as well. "So he's got a 411 on what you're thinking"—she was still highly skeptical, but no point in alienating the first potential ally she'd met since her abduction—"but how does that translate into order giving?"

Mischka set her cup on the bedside table, avoiding Nessa's gaze. Whatever was coming, it wasn't good. "He can do more than watch. If he wants to"—her gaze came up—"he can take charge. Take control."

"Of you." She wanted this out in the open. "He can make you do things."

"My body, yes. I don't believe," she added thoughtfully, "that he can do a damn thing about what I'm thinking. It's part and parcel of being a bond mate. You invite the Fallen in. You give him that access to you." She lifted her cup and sipped again.

"That's slavery. Mind control." No way in hell was Zer getting her bond, even if she hadn't had her own little secret to protect.

"No." Mischka stared at her thoughtfully. "It's trust. Intimacy. Brends is bound to me; I'm bound to him."

No favor was worth that kind of price.

Setting her coffee cup back on the tray, Mischka stood up and brushed stray pastry crumbs off the duvet. "You're the one who's responsible for that pee-on-a-stick genetics test, right?"

That had been either a moment of brilliance or insanity on her part. Part of her was proud of the accomplishment, because it wasn't every day a scientist brought a product to market. Unfortunately, the terms of her contract with the university meant she'd never see a dime of the money the kit had made on the open market. She'd known that going in, and all she'd ever really wanted was her lab and enough money to keep the groceries stocked and the lights on. It wasn't too much to ask. She knew that.

Mischka wasn't handing out accolades, however. If Nessa wasn't mistaken, that was a slightly accusing look in the other woman's eyes. Her run-in with Nessa's genetics test hadn't been the other woman's idea of a good time. "You weren't expecting the test results you got," she hypothesized. Most people didn't. They opened up the box with a full set of preconceived notions—or, worse, daydreams about who they were going to turn out to be related to.

Maybe, no one ever quite gave up on the Cinderella fantasy. God knew, she'd been guilty of it. Some secret part of her had been so very sure that cracking her own genetic code meant she'd find a father and a family. A family that wanted her.

So, Mischka Baran could take her own disappointment and shove it where the sun didn't shine.

"I peed on that damned stick in a gas station bathroom." Mischka glared at her. "I had a pack of Fallen angels standing right outside the door, demanding I fork over the results."

Why had they cared so much?

"Paranormal," Mischka said carefully, but her fingers were curling into the duvet cover, crumpling the expensive velvet. "I was part paranormal. Not human, just like them."

Part paranormal. "There are plenty of paranormals in this world." That was the truth and no getting around it, no matter how much the full humans wanted to believe they could.

"Brends read the results." The idea that the Fallen were using her genetic testing kits made Nessa unexpectedly nervous. "The results said my bloodline came from a small, obscure tribe that moved away from the Jordan River some three thousand years ago."

Mischka's eyes watched Nessa carefully. She didn't seem terribly surprised by the spark of recognition Nessa couldn't quite hide.

"What do you know about the twelve tribes of Israel?" she asked.

Mischka shrugged, picking up a pillow. "That there are twelve?" she offered, going with the change of subject.

"No. There are thirteen. That small, obscure tribe you mentioned? That was the thirteenth tribe."

Mischka blinked. "Since when?"

Nessa waved a hand. "Since forever. The thirteenth tribe doesn't make an appearance in the canonical literature, but that doesn't mean it didn't exist."

"It was a secret?"

"Not precisely. Somehow, though, that tribe disappeared off the historical radar." That disappearance mattered, and it was no longer a purely academic question. That extra chromosome haunting her DNA? All the female descendants of that tribe she'd found so far had had that chromosome. So, the real question was, were there others—and were they alive? Or were they dead?

"You believe my own life has been all smooth and easy?" Nessa went on. The other woman's assumptions annoyed her. "My own genetic test upended my life. Karma's a bitch sometimes, Mischka. Imagine being a junior faculty member in a system that makes that old boys' club you hear about seem like a day at the spa. I worked my ass off to get there, now I've lost it all. I want it back—my lab, my university office, my RAs. I can't afford this little pit stop in a Goblin club, because the clock is ticking for me."

Mischka crossed her arms over her chest. "You can work from here."

With a massive influx of cash and some serious online shopping, she could, but it wasn't the same thing. "I had three days." Why not spell it out? The Fallen already held the upper hand. "One of which is now irretrievably gone."

"Three days to do what?"

Nessa levered herself out of the bed. It was time to stop lying around feeling sorry for herself. "Three days to prove my theories about the thirteenth tribe. That's my deadline. Then, my funding's yanked, and my job's gone. Someone's gone to a hell of a lot of trouble to make sure I'm in a position where I can't say no—so what does Zer really want from me? Because this isn't about sex, and we both know that."

Mischka looked like she wanted to disagree but couldn't. She eyed Nessa. "He wants the women who appeared on Cuthah's list. You're one."

Zer hadn't mentioned that Cuthah was the author of the list. Nessa stared at the other woman, as if Mischka could shed some light on the inscrutable thinking of a Fallen angel. "There could be other women who shared the same name." One by one she ticked off her objections. "A false positive. There could be misdirection. Perhaps this Cuthah added a control group. And *why* were any of those names on the list in the first place?"

The other woman shrugged but answered without hesitation. "I'd like to tell you," she said. "So far, there's not all that much *to* know. The only shared characteristic we've found is gender—we're all female—and that all of the women have a paranormal gene. We're not quite human. You could help us figure that out, Nessa. The Fallen could use some answers, and you're exactly the person to find them. You could break this, be the first to know."

A great big conspiracy theory waiting to be unlocked, sweetened by the bait of what *they* could tell her about the thirteenth tribe. Someone had prepped Mischka Baran well. Someone *knew* her, and that was startlingly seductive. They weren't offering riches or fame or a beach house in Maui. They were offering precisely what she would have chosen— information. The scoop of a lifetime.

"All you have to do," Mischka continued, "is bond with one of them. Get them to trust you."

"And the bond will do that."

"Yeah. And then you do your thing, continue with your research, but this time you have a new sample pool. Plus"— she hesitated—"you'll have their list."

The list on which her name had appeared.

*   *   *

The command room was the heart of G2's, wrapped in a carefully deceptive web of dance floors and club rooms. The high-tech equipment should have been out of place with the Russian antiques. Zer liked old shit, though, so there was no reason to upgrade, was there? Plus, it wasn't as if he wasn't a dinosaur himself. Three thousand years old and counting, so, yeah, maybe he didn't need new furniture. Whenever he ran a hand over the lacquered surface of his desk, he could feel the nicks and gouges in the wood. The desk had come to him from a Russian prince, who had himself undoubtedly purloined the massive piece. That chain of succession was comfortingly familiar.

The strongest won. Simple. Effective. Goddamn brutal.

So it was too damn bad if he couldn't shake last night's memory of Nessa St. James. All that soft skin and those bottomless brown eyes a male could lose himself in. She was a professor and damn smart. Despite that whip-smart brain of hers, however, she was as lost in his world as he would have been in hers. The smile he felt stretching his face wasn't a nice thing. Yeah. As if he'd spend the day caged in a musty office, doing the pen-on-paper thing.

He'd been bred to fight, and that hadn't changed.

The faces looking at him as he kicked back in his chair and landed his feet on the desk's surface, leather duster banging around him, were familiar, too. He wasn't in a mood for subtle, not after last night. *She* was the key to redeeming one of his brothers. Two nights from now, she was bonding with one of them, and he wouldn't stand in the way of that. She was still struggling to come to terms with the way he'd upended her tidy little laboratory of a world, so, if he'd had any shred of decency left, he'd have left her alone last night.

Of course, he'd never been a gentleman.

So, he'd touched her—just a little and just enough to keep her off balance. That was strategic.

"Dog in the manger." Nael rocked back in his chair, kicking his booted feet up onto the desk. Rather than paper and pencil, the desk was loaded with weapons. They were sitting smack in the middle of an arsenal, and that was perfect.

"You think?" He'd never understood Nael's strange sense of humor, but that was fine.

Nael shrugged and slouched lower in his chair. "You don't want this city, but you're not letting go, either."

Of course not. This city was his. His territory. His brain shot him a mental image of Nessa St. James, courtesy of last night. She was his, too. Christ, she'd tasted sweet. Sweetest soul he'd ever had.

She wasn't his, he reminded himself. His job was to keep her safe until she was bonded with one of his brothers. *Just a loaner,* his conscience taunted him.

"Where are tonight's hot spots?" He was done talking about the human female upstairs. He was so not thinking about whether or not she might be waiting for him to come back.

Nael wasn't ready to let go of the subject. "You keeping her or what?"

Zer shot his brother a glare that could have iced over the river flowing through M City. "I told you. She's gonna choose."

"Right." Nael nodded sagely. "The rave. Two nights from now. But, right now, I'm asking what's up between the two of you. Maybe you should consider keeping her."

There was no mistaking the sudden stillness of Brends at the far end of table. The brother's hands stilled on the blade he was sharpening. That one had found his soul mate, and he'd never been the same since. He had feelings for the female, and the one thing Zer had never regretted was losing his feelings.

* * *

Sleek and gleaming, the limousine slid smoothly up to the curb. The driver had his orders.

Cuthah scanned the waiting faces. Bored. Impatient. Greedy. Curious. Glazed-over eyes perked up with the limo's appearance. Humans loved their fairy tales. As long as the car stayed in the bus lane, they'd dream about life-changing events and being picked from the pack. Singled out for some special reason.

Their greed and stupidity made them easy to manipulate.

"A brunette," he snapped to his driver. "You've seen the picture. She has brown hair and the right name to send my message loud and clear."

The car picked up speed, and disappointed faces slid back into their stupor as the fantasy drove away. Two stops later, he found the one he was looking for.

The girl was waiting for the bus, her book bag dropped by her feet. Careless, really. She could have lost both bag and contents to a purse snatcher. One quick grab, a little mad dash down the street, and she'd have been poorer but wiser. That trust would make his job here so much more enjoyable. Because she simply wouldn't see the bad things coming until the nightmare knocked her off her feet.

To his surprise, Zer had kept Nessa St. James locked up safe in G2's, making it impossible for his rogues to get at her. It was time to put Plan B into play. He stroked his fingers along the smooth leather of the armrest and gave her another once-over. Female. Brown hair. Brown eyes. Not a bad approximation on the height. She was insurance. And fun. He'd never liked waiting.

He tapped on the window, and the driver hit the brakes, bringing the car's slow prowl to a dead halt.

When Nessa St. James received his little message, she'd come out of her nice, safe hidey-hole. She'd want to see for herself what had happened to Cuthah's latest pick. Then, she'd run—straight into the arms of his rogues, or right into the arms of the Fallen. Either way, she'd stop straddling the damn fence and make a move. A move that would work for him either way. Life was good.

Whistling, he opened the door, and the girl's head did a 180, peeling away from the empty, bus-less street to try to see inside the car. "Moira St. James?" When she nodded, he added, "It's your lucky day, love." It had been easy to find a girl with the same last name, to learn her habits and schedule.

Sliding back into the darkness of the limousine, he waited. All she'd see was his hand, stroking the empty seat beside him. That hand, and the shadows.

She hesitated, but not for too long. He'd scented the exhaustion and desperation on her. Whatever she believed wasn't going right in her life, she'd also believe he could offer the magic ticket to fix. "You're one of the Fallen, aren't you?" A smile lit up her eyes as excitement replaced the exhaustion. Transformed her face into something approaching pretty. Shape of the eyes wasn't quite right, but he'd known he wouldn't find perfect.

She'd do.

"Get in the car," he ordered.

Sure enough, she did as he asked, even pulling the door shut behind her. The book bag tangled around her feet.

"Do I get to ask you for my favor?" Her voice was breathy with excitement, so eager to whore herself out for the Fallen. Really, he thought dispassionately, he was doing her a favor. Saving her soul for her.

"Not tonight, darling." Pulling out the knife, he made himself wait just a handful of seconds. This close, her pulse beat visibly beneath her skin, and the faint, warm thread of her scent called across the small space to him. Mass-market perfume. Talcum powder. Sweat. He made her nervous, but she'd gotten into the car.

"No one said anything about a knife." Her hand reached

for the door. Lazily, he reached out, his hand crushing those fingers. Her mouth opened uselessly, dragging in air as she tried to scream through the pain. Not that screaming would have done her any good. Limousine was sound-proof, and there were so very few beings in M City who might have been able to stop him, anyhow. No one was riding to her rescue.

He brought the knife up and got busy.

The look on her face, right before the light went out in those brown eyes, told him she understood, loud and clear. Just because he could, he gave her the words, anyhow.

"You see," he whispered against her throat, gathering her up close to him, "right now I need you to do a favor for me. I need you to die for me, love."

The latest body had been dumped on the outer edge of the university campus. Zer's hesitation had already warned Nessa; whatever had happened had transformed a living, breathing woman into a murder victim. Yeah, she understood what to expect.

"You sure you want to see this?" Twice he'd asked, and twice she'd nodded her head. The third time, she'd thrown in a more graphic explanation of where he could stick his concerns. She had to see, and they both knew it.

Still, nothing could have prepared her for the graphic nature of the woman's death. She shifted restlessly. Or for how helpless she would feel. Someone—something—had slashed the woman apart with casual, brutal strength. Blood splattered the street. The killer had made no attempt to conceal the body. Now, she couldn't help watching Zer as he examined the crime scene. She'd known the Fallen were fast and strong, but she'd conveniently overlooked the fact that, sometimes, they were also murderers.

This woman had died fast, and she'd died alone.

Nessa couldn't reconcile last night's lover—the male who

had taken such tender care of her—with the stone-faced, cold-eyed warrior king riding roughshod over MVD. He'd taken charge of the dead woman—and the crime scene— without so much as a please or thank you.

She should run. It was the perfect opportunity. All she had to do was ask one of the MVD techs for a ride. She could be home in minutes. Still, even as the escape plan presented itself, Zer's eyes met hers, those hard lips curving into a slow, male smile. Yeah. Who was she kidding? They both knew that she could take off right now, but he'd be right there on her ass. She wasn't a free woman—she was merely on parole.

She needed to keep her mind on the facts. He was her kidnapper. He was bad, bad news.

"You need to understand," he'd said when the call came in. Then, he'd brought her here.

"Was this random?" Maybe the woman had simply been unlucky.

He shook his head, slowly. "No. This was deliberate. Eyewitness reports place a limousine cruising the bus stops near this edge of campus. That sounds like Cuthah, not just some random rogue. He was looking for her, and when he found her, all hell broke loose.

His eyes examined her and then the dead woman. "She had the same last name as you. Same brown hair and eyes. Not too close, but close enough."

"Are you suggesting she was targeted because she looked like me?"

"No. I'm saying that yesterday's run-in wasn't an accident, and Cuthah hasn't stopped looking for you just because you suddenly dropped out of sight." He shrugged. "You're the scientist, baby. You tell me which way the facts are pointing here. Random rogue kill—or someone who had the misfortune to look too much like Nessa St. James?"

The woman tossed on the ground had the same last name,

the same brown hair, and the same build. Silently, Nael handed her the student ID card. Apparently Moira St. James had been a student on campus.

"She's dead because of me," Nessa said finally.

Zer eyes didn't leave hers. "Yeah," he said. "You could say that."

He was splitting hairs with her. "But is it the truth?"

"You want three kinds of proof?" he snarled. "I can't give you that. What I can tell you is that your name is on a hit list, and Cuthah isn't going to stop until you're dead—or he's dead. Pretend to yourself all you like, but you have to choose sides now."

"That's not much of a choice."

"No." He eyed her for a long moment. "It's not. But it's the choice you get to make."

The familiar campus no longer seemed like a safe haven. Now, the shadows were menacing. She'd walked here a thousand times. Daylight, nighttime—it hadn't mattered. She'd known she was safe. Now, she knew none of that.

MVD had arrived shortly after the Fallen. Their sleek black bodysuits and high-tech gear lent the scene a sleek patina of civilization. Two male techs slid the dead woman into a nylon body bag. The sound of the zipper closing would haunt Nessa for the rest of her life.

The nearest tech paused, then came to her.

"You all right, ma'am?" His eyes methodically dissected her face, the analytical once-over at odds with the sympathy in his voice. "First time at a crime scene?"

"Yeah."

"You know the vic?" He wanted to know why she was here. What role she played in this crime scene of his.

"No."

"Mind if I ask you your name?"

When she told him, she could see him connecting the dots. "There was an incident."

"Yesterday," she filled in wearily. "On campus. Yes. That was my lecture."

"You didn't want to stick around, ma'am, and provide a statement?" His eyes accused her.

"I didn't have much of a choice." Shooting Zer a look, she decided this was his fault, and he could explain. God, she hadn't even considered that campus security would be looking for her. That they would want a statement.

"Eyewitnesses report you were dragged out of the lecture hall by Goblins." To her surprise, he mouthed: *Do you need help?* She couldn't quite conceal her small start at his decency. She should have taken him up on his offer, but Zer was watching her, and she'd seen what a rogue had done to this woman. Whatever was happening between her and Zer, it had gone way past kidnapping. Statistically, her chances were better with the Fallen, rather than alone in her flat or holed up with MVD.

"No," she said finally after a too-long pause. "No, I don't." Disappointment and something else filled the tech's eyes. Great. Now he thought she was a Goblin whore.

When she looked away, her gaze caught Zer's. Something dark flashed in those eyes. When he strode over, the tech took one look and melted away. She didn't blame him. Even she recognized that primitive look of possession on Zer's face.

He knew she'd made her first choice.

Just to make her night complete, the dean popped out of his official car just then, looking harassed. Yeah, she'd just bet he hated when dead bodies appeared on his campus. Now, smoothing his thinning hair with one hand, he flashed his profile at the media camped out on the other side of the yellow tape.

"Nessa," he said, and she stiffened. She wasn't in the mood to discuss her personnel file with him tonight. "You look well."

As if he hadn't been lobbing not-so-veiled threats in her direction yesterday. He sported the same bland suit-and-tie look, and tonight's shirt was just as too-small as yesterday's.

Was she supposed to make polite chitchat with him while the body cooled beside them? Apparently so, because he continued, "Campus security reported a mishap in your classroom yesterday, but, apparently, no ill effects, eh? Had someone at hand to offer assistance?"

He rubbed his hands together, the large stone of his ring catching the light. Sexist bastard. She fought an unfamiliar urge to kick him. Hard. Kicking the dean would be career suicide. Carefully, she pushed down the slow simmer of anger. Facts first. Connect the dots beyond a reasonable doubt. *Then* she'd act. Bastard.

"I did," she replied, her voice tight. Yesterday, he'd been inches from a sexual-harassment lawsuit. Today, he was playing nice. She'd bet the reason for his change of heart was standing right behind her, too.

The dean's gaze slid away from hers, straight to Zer. And stayed there. Bastard was definitely taking his cues from her master manipulator.

Zer leaned in toward her, his breath ruffling her hair. "I'll gut him for you," he growled. "Tell me to do the spineless bastard for you, and I will."

Medieval. Primitive. And highly satisfying, if impractical. "I don't need your help." If she decided to commit murder, she'd do it herself.

He shrugged, stuffing his hands into the pockets of his duster. "If that's what you want."

He didn't sound convinced.

She wanted her life back, but, clearly, that wasn't an option.

The dean watched their exchange covertly. This time his gaze dipped south and stayed there. "Professor Markoff tells me he hasn't heard from you yet."

She'd burned less than twenty-four hours, most of which she'd spent running for her life from a homicidal maniac. What did he think she'd been doing? His self-satisfied little smirk warned her that, campus murder or not, he was going to hang her out to dry, and he was going to enjoy every moment of it.

"Three days, dean. You gave me three days. I've got time left." Her disbelieving glare just had him smiling and rubbing his hands together. Then a reporter yelled a question from behind the police line, and her nemesis wandered over to chat the man up.

"Gratis," Zer rumbled from behind her. "A gift, from me to you." Thoughts of his last *gift* had her squirming with remembered heat. "No more gifts," she muttered.

Zer was playing a deep game—showing her what could be, good and bad. It was just possible that he'd fed this victim to the rogues to illustrate his point. She didn't believe he had, but she couldn't be sure. He was capable of it. They both knew it.

Zer knew he was deliberately fueling her suspicions. He hated like hell that she distrusted him, but he couldn't afford to let her get too close. And, after last night, she'd been softening. It killed him to push her away, but it had to be done. She was going to bond with one of his brothers and live happily ever after, even if she didn't know it yet. Yeah, and maybe if he kept repeating the fairy tale to himself, he'd start believing. It didn't matter. She was the tool he needed, and he wasn't letting her get away. Bringing her here was good. Now, she understood that Cuthah meant business.

Nael and Vkhin peeled away from the small group of Fallen, headed his way. MVD got the hell out of their way. "You got a bead on our killer?" he asked when they'd cleared the path. "Looks like Cuthah's work to me."

He wouldn't have gone far. He hadn't been clean enough or tidy enough to cover his tracks, so all they had to do was follow the signs. Like a neon sign lighting up the M City night sky.

"Yeah." Vkhin stroked a thumb over the blade at his waist. "She get a good look?"

No need to ask who the *she* was. Cold stillness radiated from Vkhin as the brother pulled on his leather gloves. Ready to hunt.

"She did." Zer discovered he didn't like the memory of her paling, but she hadn't puked her guts out. He'd give her that. He'd be willing to bet she'd never seen a dead body outside of a laboratory before. Her face had gone marble-still, those brown eyes of hers widening impossibly in her face. Yeah, she'd gotten a real good look.

"Which way?"

"North. Keros is bringing our satellites online now. If the bastard's on the surface streets, we'll have him."

Vkhin nodded curtly, running the calculations in his head. "Time of death?" Cuthah had played with his catch for a few minutes. That much was clear.

"Last hour." Body was already cool, but between the weather and the tearing, the heat would have gone fast. "Her legs aren't bruising yet." No discoloration meant her killer had finished his work here in less than a two-hour window.

"Good to know." Vkhin strode off, eyes quartering the ground, all his senses on high alert. "I'll lead the hunting party."

"You do that." Vkhin wasn't looking for Zer's blessing, but Zer gave it anyway. Made him feel like he had some purpose out here other than being the figurehead leader watching as the Fallen split off into hunting parties and disappeared into the shadows.

"This is a nightmare," she said hoarsely. "How do you live like this every day?"

He fingered the blade at his side and wondered if she really wanted the truth.

"Do they hunt every day in M City?" She touched her hair, tucking an errant strand back into her chignon. He'd let that delicious, heavy weight sift through his fingers when he'd held her in his arms.

"They do if we let them."

"And do you?" Her eyes stared up at him. "Do you let them hunt here, Zer, in my world? Why would you do that?"

Because he couldn't be everywhere at once, and, sometimes, there was no stopping what amounted to a force of nature. "I do my best," he said quietly. The snow that was starting to fall muted the sound of his booted feet as he urged her back toward their waiting car. It was bone-cold now, in the hours between midnight and sunrise. She should have a scarf. A hat. Something to keep her warm. Cashmere suited her, so he'd get her some more.

"It doesn't always work out, does it?" she said quietly. Her feet crunched over the snow beside him. She made no attempt to muffle her footsteps, to deaden the sound that would alert a predator to her approach. He wanted to protect her from the new world she'd discovered, but that world already knew she was here.

"No," he admitted. "Sometimes, a rogue is just lucky or fast."

"So, what are you going to do about this?"

"Vkhin is the best hunter we have. If anyone can track Cuthah, he can. He'll do what needs to be done, but Cuthah's outmaneuvered us so far. He's got wings, and we don't."

"Is Vkhin in danger?" The genuine concern coloring her voice was strangely warming. Maybe Vkhin could be the one for her.

"No. Vkhin's good. He's hunted for millennia, and he'll hunt for millennia more."

"That's a long time." She shoved her hands deeper into the pockets of her jacket. "You don't think he'll get tired? Or careless? You guys ever slip up, Zer?"

All the time. She just didn't know how badly. "He's a hunter," he repeated carefully. "This is what he does. What we all do. We're not going anywhere—those were the terms of the deal." The punishment.

"Right," she said. "Eternal banishment to this world. No more living in the Heavens for you. There's no way to go back?"

"Not yet." She shot him a glance. He could tell her the truth, but then she'd know what hand she held. Her price would shoot up, and, possibly, she'd refuse. He wouldn't blame her for refusing to bond with one of them for eternity. So, he couldn't tell her the truth: that she was more than just any bond mate. She was going to be a soul mate, the key to returning the wings and soul to one of Zer's males. "You think we wouldn't grab a return ticket with both hands, baby? We're not going anywhere." Not yet. Not without her help and not without their wings.

"So, instead, you live down here, with us." She nodded, as if the pieces of an invisible puzzle were slotting into place. "And you're weekend warriors, taking out your own when you have to."

"Yeah." His voice sounded hoarse, even to his own ears.

"That must be hard." She swallowed. "If you know them from before. Did you know the rogue who came after me yesterday, Zer?"

"No." He gave her that truth. "There were many of us who Fell. I didn't know them all, but, yeah, it's happened before. Sometimes, the thirst is too much to bear, and we lose another of the Fallen." Reaching out, he gave in to the urge to snag her hand, wrapping those delicate fingers in his own leather-gloved ones. "I've hunted my brothers before, known their names when I gave them eternal peace."

Her eyes were distant. "And now you want my help with this."

"I do." Truth again.

"Can I get out of this? Is there any way to convince these rogues to stop coming after me and mine?"

There wasn't. Although, even if he'd known how to stop the attacks, he might not have told her. He needed her to help him. Had to have that help no matter what it cost. He shook his head silently.

"I could leave now," she said quietly. She motioned toward the MVD techs futilely processing the scene for evidence. Their human technology was no match for what Cuthah had loosed on M City. "I could go with them."

He wouldn't let her leave. Still, he didn't want to strip the illusion of choice from her. Not until he had to. Then she shrugged and smiled, a lost little smile. "But that wouldn't make sense, would it? *They* can't protect me from what's coming. *You* can." She rubbed her arms with her hands. "You're the only chance I really have of surviving this, aren't you?"

"I promise that no one will get to you."

"*Can* you promise?"

He couldn't. There were no absolutes. Instead, he dipped his head, pressed a hard, possessive kiss against her lips. "I can promise this," he said gruffly. "Cuthah doesn't get to you—the Archangel himself doesn't get to you—unless they come through all of the Fallen. You belong to us, baby. We're keeping you safe."

"You've fought Michael before?"

"Yeah." And lost.

She looked him up and down. "Two arms. Two legs. Guess it could have gone worse for you."

He wanted to kiss that sassy mouth. Watch her wrap those long legs around his waist. Yeah, and if wishes were dreams, beggars would ride, right? She didn't want any part of him and he—well, he just needed to use her.

"Michael won," he bit out. Admitting his failure burned, but there was no avoiding the truth. Here he was, wingless and cast out. And there Michael was, the bloody Archangel of the Heavens, in charge of defending the Celestial throne. Yeah. Pretty damn clear who had come out on top of that one. Michael was the golden boy.

But that was going to change.

Eyes narrowing, he assessed the female glaring at him. "This time," he said, folding his arms over his chest before he did something he'd regret, "will be different."

"Really." The dry tone of her voice conveyed more clearly than words that she wasn't buying anything he was selling. "You went after this guy before. You lost. What makes you think that picture's changed any?"

You, he thought. *You're my ace in the hole.* Telling her the truth, however, would give her the upper hand in their exchange. "Motivation?" he suggested lightly.

"Right. One supernatural ass-kicking. A little skin-and-bones mutilation resulting in the loss of your wings." She ticked the offending items off on her fingers as if they were a damned shopping list. Having picked up the bread, she moved on to the milk. "Now, you're down here—and he's up *there.* Or whatever metaphysical, invisible-but-you-swear-it-exists plane you're keeping the otherworld corralled in these days. Pardon me if I don't find your logic convincing."

The moon above them spilled silver light down onto the scene, the yellow police tape that hadn't changed color in a hundred years. From the huddle of students held back by that flimsy barrier, he scented fear. Titillation and curiosity.

He stepped up, deliberately crowding her body with his. Face-to-face, he smiled, slow and hard. "This time, I win, baby."

CHAPTER TEN

The damned dress didn't have a single fastening—except for the row of decorative little red satin-covered buttons that marched down her corseted front. Nessa looked like a hooker. A very, very expensive hooker. No way she could blend in to the woodwork in this outfit.

Zer bet she hated that.

Watching her walk down the hallway toward him was pure torture, worse than the three days it had taken for this night to finally arrive. The shimmering red fabric clung to her thighs, and the dress was nothing—nothing—like the business clothes she'd had on when he'd taken her. Thank God. Still, he wasn't looking forward to tonight, to giving her away. Without taking his eyes off her, he punched the button on the panel behind him. The sooner the elevator got here, the better. He'd feel calmer once they were both downstairs and he had her on the club floor.

The elevator arrived, and he placed his body before the doors. Just in case something end-of-the-world had happened downstairs in the club and he hadn't heard of it. Clear. He stepped back, itching for a fight.

She stepped into the elevator cage, angling her body to squeeze past him.

She inhaled—deeply—and that squeezed those breasts of

hers up over the top of the damn corset. He'd spent time choosing his cologne for tonight's rave—for her—but fortunately he didn't have to admit that weakness. He didn't want her to think he was dressing for her. Even if he was.

Two hours—three, tops—and he'd be free and clear, and Nessa St. James would be a soul mate. One of his brothers would be buried deep in all that hot heat, and she'd have her life back on track. Except that she'd be bound for all eternity to one of *them*.

"Ready to go?" Those weren't the words he wanted to give her. No, for some inexplicable reason, he wanted to reassure her. Promise her that whichever male she chose tonight would value her above all others.

If he didn't, Zer would see to it personally.

"I get my life back," she said.

She inhaled again, the pearly smooth skin moving away from the wicked bodice of her dress and then pressing against the stiff fabric as she exhaled sharply. He wanted to follow the motion with his tongue.

"I want my life back. And this is the only way," she acknowledged.

She had no idea.

The doors slid shut, sealing them in.

Zer was too damn big. He filled the elevator's small space, crowding her. She suspected it was deliberate.

"Get out of my way," she said tightly. "I'm doing this, just like you wanted." His too-large body effectively stole any breathing room. This close, she could smell the heat of his body and some spicier, masculine scent. Danger. He smelled dangerous, and she wasn't stupid. She was going to run the other way and not look back. Wasn't she?

"You're dangerous," she said. "You're a killer. I got the message." He didn't deny it, and she wondered if she'd foolishly hoped that he would.

"Yeah," he said hoarsely.

Why was he staring at her like that? It had to be the dress, but since he'd chosen it, fussing like a girlfriend over the fit and the color, she figured it couldn't be such a surprise. He'd gift-wrapped her for his brothers, so he ought to like what he saw.

He must have a closet full of leather himself, because she'd never seen him dressed in anything else. Easy shopping, sure, but it had to be hell on the laundry bill. God, she was babbling. In her head. So, she was nervous.

"But you're not the worst killer out there. I got that, too." He was still staring at her, though, so she babbled on. "I understand Cuthah has to be stopped."

"That's altruistic of you," he growled. "Has nothing to do with your genetic studies, does it?"

"Fuck you," she cursed. "You don't get to question my reasons for doing this."

"So, you'll choose one of my brothers . . . to bond with?"

"What choice do I have, really? I want to help you stop Cuthah." So far Vkhin had had no luck tracking him down.

"Stopping Cuthah. That your only reason?" He'd badgered her into doing this, and now he wanted to argue about her reasons? She didn't think so. Her reasons were her own and none of his damned business.

"Well, it's certainly not because I want some Goblin favor."

"He'll be good to you."

"Who?"

"Whoever you choose," he promised her. "He'll worship the ground you walk on. You'll be his sun, moon, and stars."

Her throat closed up. Panic. That was too much. She wasn't ready to be the center of anyone's universe. He moved closer to her, and she reached out a hand before she could stop herself. There were iron muscles beneath the expensive fabric of his sleeve and a hard, unyielding ridge of metal. He had blades strapped to his forearms. The ink there teased her, dark bands of black escaping the edge of his sleeve.

"I don't know if I *can* do this," she said, giving him honesty because he deserved that much from her. Just because she wanted to do the right thing didn't mean she'd actually be able to follow through. The whole leaping-to-your-death thing only worked if you actually managed to clear the ledge and get into the air. Still, the elevator was purring smoothly downward, and that was a step in the right direction, even if it did seem to be taking Zer's gaze with it. Those dark eyes stopped on the impossibly high heels he'd insisted on. She liked them. They made her feel sexy. Plus, she knew he'd expected her to protest.

So, to keep *him* off balance, she hadn't.

"Why'd you do this?" She touched the dark ink as he stabbed the elevator's stop button.

A confused look crossed his face. Clearly, he'd expected her to protest the elevator's halt. "The ink? No reason."

She drew a finger over the dark swirls. "They look like the bonding mark."

"I don't bond with anyone."

"But no woman's going to ask, is she?" Her eyes narrowed. "You tattooed a keep-away sign right there."

He didn't answer, but she knew she was right. "The others take bond mates. Why don't you?"

"It wouldn't be safe."

"You like my shoes?" Was that her voice that sounded so breathless?

He looked baffled and adorably male at her abrupt topic switch. "Yeah," he said as if she'd asked him a complicated genetics question. "Yeah, I do." He cleared his throat and yanked his gaze up from her ankles.

"You like my dress?" She smoothed a hand over her hip and knew she was teasing the beast, but anything to stop time for another few seconds.

"You look beautiful." The look in his eyes was indecipherable. "He'll love you," he promised.

He sounded gruffly tender. As if he was worried about her, which was impossible. He didn't want her, had made that perfectly clear, but she couldn't stop pushing him. Pushing herself.

"So, are you going to get in line?" She embraced the flicker of anger she felt. That heat felt so much better than the cold ball of terror growing in her stomach.

He shook his head. "You know I'm not. I'm too close to the Change, baby, and you make me want to go right on over that edge."

"What's the Change?"

"You don't want to know," he countered. "But I'm not up for grabs. You choose anyone else you want down there."

"Anyone but you." When he didn't answer, she pushed on. "You don't want me to be your bond mate?"

"There's no redeeming me, baby," he warned. "I'm no makeover project."

She felt an unfamiliar stab of emotion at thought of this male being lost forever. *Stop it.* "Why not?"

His answer was a lazy drawl. "Captain goes down with the ship, baby. You know that. My brothers deserve redemption, and I'm going to make damn sure they get it. That they get *you.*"

"What if I don't want to be the door prize?" She glared up at him.

Zer slammed the button to start the elevator again.

Those too-innocent doe eyes of hers stared at him, dissecting him like an unfamiliar living specimen. Did she like what she saw? It didn't matter. He was way past redemption and even more beyond all that touchy-feely, come-into-the-light-my-son bullshit. When Michael had kicked his ass out of the

Heavens, he'd thrown away the key, and Zer didn't give a damn. He'd stand on his own two feet.

"Don't push me," he growled. "In twelve floors, you're rid of me. Until then, you're all mine, baby." Hell, yeah.

"Oh, no, I'm not," she taunted.

He was going to take this one last opportunity to touch her before he handed her over. Bracing her against the wall, he planted his hands on either side of her face. His stance was dominating. Hard. He had twelve floors, and he was going to use them.

He didn't taste her mouth at first. Instead, he traced a hot, damp path over her skin with his tongue, exploring the curve of her ear like a Tartar lord exploring the virgin expanse of the Russian steppes before he unleashed a flood of ruthless warriors. He gave the trembling flesh a hot lick.

His wicked tongue stroked, penetrated. He knew she'd want to tell him no, that she'd know five good reasons she should, but he also knew she'd been alone a long time, and he'd been created for this. So damned good. He could feel her body softening for him, welcoming his seduction.

His teeth nipping at her earlobe brought a moan to her lips.

"You like that," he said with masculine satisfaction. "The pleasure—or the pain, baby?"

He curled his hands against hers, pinning her in place.

Parted her thighs with a leather-clad thigh, sliding home between them and sheathing himself there in raw simulation of the sex act. The intimate sound of her skirt sliding upward, the whisper of lace and silk as she parted for him, filled the heated silence of the elevator. God. She wanted *him*. He didn't know what he'd done to deserve this, but he had to have her. Just for a few minutes. Then he'd let her go.

She melted into him, and he brought his mouth down on hers, his tongue stroking along the closed seam of her lips.

Sweeping in. Conqueror. Just like a hundred kisses before. Practiced. Nothing could have prepared him for the hot, sweet taste of the female in his arms, the unique scent of her. She was different.

Her mouth opened deeper beneath his. She took a breath. *No.* No protests. Not yet, not when he had to stop in just a minute. Wrapping both her small hands in one of his, he let his other hand trace a slow, deliberate path down her body. She was all liquid heat in his arms. Tenth floor, his brain dimly registered. They were on the tenth floor. He still had time.

"Zer," she whispered into his mouth. No protest. Just sweet, hot welcome.

"Don't think," he urged, lifting his mouth from hers. "Just feel. Just for a minute. Close your eyes, and feel for me, baby."

A minute was all he could afford. The beast in him was already lifting its head, and he knew his eyes were glowing. Her lashes drifted obediently shut.

"That's it," he encouraged. "See if you like this, baby."

Sliding his fingers up her creamy thigh, he dipped into her hot, wet sex. Stroked a wicked path around her straining clit and the heat and damp soaking through her panties.

"You're as wicked as I am," he rumbled.

"Don't stop," she demanded. "Don't you dare stop now." Fifth floor. Armageddon couldn't have stopped him now.

Deliberately, he ripped the panties from her, letting the delicate scrap of fabric slip between his fingers.

Mine.

His mouth swallowed her cry of pleasure, and she rode his fingers hard, arching delicately into his palm. He could feel those sharp flutters of pleasure rippling through her pussy. God, she was coming for him.

He lost himself in her pleasure, opening up all his senses

and drinking her down, down, down. She was vintage Champagne, and, like the worst of alcoholics, he didn't care. He only wanted more of her and wanted that more now.

The man groaned into her mouth, but the rogue growled with satisfaction.

Taking.

Her essence, her soul, flowing from her in deliciously seductive tendrils, and he wasn't stopping, couldn't stop.

With an almost imperceptible jolt, the elevator hit bottom, and he moved his hand, but not the rest of his body. The doors glided apart smoothly, opening up on to the club floor, and then it was all Armageddon. Nael's hands pulled implacably on him, as Vkhin's weapons left their sheaths with a lethal hiss.

I'm a monster, he thought, and he forced himself to move away. To hug the wall on the far side of the elevator's narrow cage. Nael's hands wrapping around the smooth white flesh of Nessa's upper arms made him growl, low and deep in his throat, and then she was pushing those hands away.

"Get. Your. Hands. Off. Me." She bit out the words.

As he fought through the red haze of the soul thirst, her too-pale face wavered in front of him. God. Had she swayed? He'd taken too much. If they'd been in a skyscraper instead of a mere twelve floors up, she'd have been dead.

Nael murmured something, low and hard, into her ear, and she turned all that hot anger on his brother. "No," she said. "Shut up for a minute, and listen to me."

Brother didn't like it, but he paused. Vkhin was falling back to the elevator's perimeter, fingering a throwing star. They both knew that if Zer was truly lost, there wasn't a blade in the club that could stop him in time. Instead, she'd be the bait that held him in place until they could figure out the best way to take off his head.

"I want to talk to him," she said, louder. Nael cursed but

let her go. She took a step toward Zer and stopped. The rogue raged at being deprived of its feast, but the man was relieved. She was scared of him, and that was good.

"You should kill me." He stared at her, unblinking, as he finally gave her the truth. "Ask my brothers. They will do it for you."

"Ask to have you killed?" She looked as if she couldn't believe those words were leaving her mouth, and he knew he'd stood her familiar world on its head. She was never going back to that safe, mundane world. He couldn't give her that, couldn't make that happen for her.

"Yeah." He nodded his head. "You're not strong enough to do it youself."

"Fine," she snapped. "I'll make a note of that little offer, and, if you ever screw with my life again, I'll speed-dial Vkhin."

He eyed her. "You do realize that I almost killed you?"

"No," she said in that smooth, liquid-chocolate voice. "I didn't notice that. What I did notice was the hottest damned orgasm of my life. So, no complaints on my part." She cocked a hand on her hip and glared up at him. "Except for the part where you treat me like a convenience store. I'm damned tired of this touch-me-not thing you've got going on."

Fine. So, she didn't understand what he was capable of. He'd send her the manual later on. *After* she'd selected one of his brothers for her soul mate. Then, she'd understand the danger she'd skirted. He didn't have any soul left to offer her because he was 100 percent cold, hard killer, and even he knew she deserved better.

Scooping up her panties from the elevator floor, he slid it into his pocket. "Souvenir."

Souvenir. From the French, *to remember,* he thought, and he stepped out onto the club floor.

CHAPTER ELEVEN

Cinderella in a ballroom that had taken a darkly erotic turn—that was her. Maybe it should have been enough. God knew, it would have been for most women. Hot sex and an even hotter favor—she should have been all sign-me-up, but instead she was scanning for the exit. An exit that she wasn't spotting because a hot press of male bodies surrounded her. For just a moment, she felt as if the air had been sucked from her lungs by too many bodies crowding into her space, but then Nael's hand, hot and hard and strangely comforting, found the small of her back. When she hesitated, his thumb rubbed a small, soothing circle over the base of her spine. Anchoring her. She needed to leave, needed to get out of here and reclaim her life. Instead, she took another step out onto the dance floor.

"Guard her back," Zer snapped. "Midnight," he warned. "She chooses at midnight," he growled, and he strode off, leaving Nael and Vkhin flanking her like a damned honor guard. Whom did she need protecting from? Him? Or the clubful of males who turned to stare at her with hot, assessing eyes as she stepped away from the brightly lit cage of the elevator.

"This is not a silent auction. He can't make me do this." He couldn't.

Nael didn't say anything. Maybe Zer could. Maybe he had some ace up his sleeve she hadn't considered.

"Come meet them, love. Just take a look. They've come all this way to meet you. See you. You can't send them home now," Nael finally murmured.

This wasn't her fault. The twinge of guilt she felt was irrational.

The first pair of males to greet her were pure fantasy, dark and feral. There was no mistaking the strength of the bodies lurking beneath the leather and blades. The dark tats were warning enough.

"Will you dance with us?" The Fallen standing opposite her extended his hand. She stared at it blindly. *Dance?*

She didn't dance, not that what she was seeing on the club's dance floor resembled any dance she'd ever been taught. Liquid sex. A seething pool of bodies moving sinuously together. Male. Female. Human. Paranormal. All tangled up together in a delicious, hot maelstrom of beat and sound.

"No," she blurted out before stopping to consider her words. "I don't dance." Desperately, she sucked in air like a smoker in need of an overdue fix. For an endless moment, the air refused to go down, her throat closing until she would have sworn she was drowning.

A hard hand pressed against the small of her back, preventing her from stepping back into the elevator and then the doors closed, and the elevator vanished. For a moment, she was temporarily night blind, aware of nothing but scents and sounds, the bone-melting pulse of the music and the primal slide of leather, blades, and booted feet.

"Dance with them. You do this, Nessa," Nael said encouragingly. Too bad he hadn't been the one to introduce her to the Fallen. Maybe then, she'd have wanted to accept their dark offer. She didn't kid herself that Nael was safe—hell, none of them was safe—but she knew instinctively that Nael genuinely liked women. He wouldn't hurt her, no matter what it cost him. Nael was nice—and he was alone, despite the female company surrounding him. She shot him a small smile. Yeah. He was a good man, even if he wouldn't admit it.

"Not too nice," he warned, reading the message in her eyes. "Don't ever make that mistake. I'll take what I can. We both know that."

His hand urged her forward, and she let herself walk. Each step made her acutely aware of the sensual slide of her dress's fabric against her bare, heated skin. Of the sexy saunter those four-inch heels lent her. Music washed over her, through her, the driving, electronic beat almost tangible. The unrelenting sound created a strangely intimate cocoon around her and the males nearest her. All moving to the same beat, she thought. The temptation to give in, to blend in, was overwhelming. They *wanted* her in a way no one else ever had.

So why not dance?

Why not enjoy this one moment before she went back to her everyday life?

Nael urged his sire's female forward, wishing she'd been for sale like the many females he'd seduced in G2's. Nessa St. James was different, and, in this case, different meant trouble.

"Dance with me, baby." He made his request in a low voice that he knew most humans adored.

"This isn't dancing." She eyed the dance floor skeptically, but her feet, he noticed, were moving forward, so he was getting what he needed.

"It isn't?" He eyed two of the nearest Fallen, shaking his head curtly when they moved in too quickly. Nessa was skittish, which meant she was just as smart as he'd suspected.

"No," she said, her brain working overtime. At his subtle signal, her other Fallen watchdog stepped closer. He moved sinuously to the raw beat of the music, his shirt already un-buttoned. "This is spawning, Nael."

He laughed softly, stepping up behind her. Closing off her exit. "You could be right," he admitted. "We're sensual crea-tures, my Nessa. We love females. Love touching."

Twisting her head around, she stared up at him. That cu-riosity in her eyes, the soft, heated flush of her skin was an aphrodisiac for his kind. The beat of the music pulsed through him. Since he couldn't lose himself in the female on the dance floor, he let the raw beat tear through his senses. Felt the rhythm ripping through the floor. The air.

"Why?" she asked

He shrugged and reached for her hips, pulling her loosely back against his body. Damned if he'd play the saint tonight. He whored, and he hated himself for it, but it was necessary. He'd sworn to protect his sire, and that was what he did, body and soul. "When we're with you, we *feel*, Nessa. We can't feel most emotions anymore. It was one of the condi-tions of the Fall." Michael had ripped all the softer, gentler emotions out of them along with their wings.

Another dancer glided closer, hips swaying with the sen-sual beat and a raw masculinity. Not touching Nessa, not yet. But he was in her space, and nothing could conceal the heated power rolling off the male in waves.

Normally, Nael would have shared with the other male. Or would have carried away the prize. It didn't really matter which way things went down. One of them would have the female, or they both would, depending on how she liked it. Tonight, though, either option bothered him. Reminded him that anonymous sex in a nightclub wasn't really a substitute for the emotions he'd lost. Those cold eyes must have warned the other dancer off, because he slipped away into the crowd, and another took his place.

"You have sex to feel," she said thoughtfully. Her gaze slid away from his, but not, he realized, because she was put off.

Or disgusted. No, Nessa St. James was thinking his statements through and coming to logical conclusions. "What happens if you don't?"

"Don't have sex?" He smiled, a lazy, sensual quirk of his mouth. "Why, Nessa, love, you know what happens when a male doesn't have sex."

She stared up at him impatiently, but she didn't stop the sensual glide-and-dip of her hips. "Don't mince words with me, Nael. Neither of us is talking about sexual frustration. What happens to you if you don't find a partner?"

What would happen if he told her? Hell, she was more than halfway to figuring it out already.

Zer had dangled the carrot of a soul mate in front of him, and, even though he'd known he didn't deserve that, he wanted it. Wanted *her*. Christ, yes. He'd *felt* that flicker of hope, even as he'd tamped it down. Every male here had to be reacting to Nessa St. James. She was a beautiful female, inside and out, and he recognized that.

But she wasn't for him. So, he gave her part of the truth. "We go mad, love." He stroked the bare skin of her forearm, drinking in the sensual catch of her breath. "Cut a male off from sensations, from emotions, for too long, and he goes mad."

She licked her lips. "Literally?"

She didn't need to know about the inner rogue they were all hauling around. Not yet. She'd have heard rumors, of course, but he wasn't going to be the one handing her cold, hard facts. So, he confirmed her suspicion rather than give her the truth, let her fill in the blanks in a way she could handle. "Yeah. Literally."

Her hand came up, covered his. He kept up the gentle stroking. Damn, she was soft. Sweet.

"You want me," she guessed, and then she looked embarrassed. As if she truly didn't understand that the entire club was just waiting for her to make her choice and that any one of them would be honored to be so chosen.

"Yes," he growled, and he considered kissing her. Just once. She was waking up, feeling the possibilities. Zer was watching, though, and she could be a match for his sire. Had to be a match for his sire. If his sire found a soul mate, then Nael would be free. There would be no more need to let Zer feed through him.

She was a beautiful female, and he recognized that. Couldn't *not* recognize that. But she wasn't for him. Still, he allowed himself the small pleasure of stroking the bare skin of her forearm again. The sensual catch in her breathing delighted him..

"Chemical reaction," she whispered. This time, her hand gently moved his away.

Right. This was biology and nothing more. He'd fuck her if the opportunity arose and if it was what Zer wanted, but he'd never be more than a third in their pairing. What she had with his brother was more than neurons and pheromones. It was a connection between souls, even if neither of them was ready to accept that truth.

"Yeah," he agreed, but he wondered if she could even hear his hoarse whisper over the driving beat of the music. Something unspoken in her eyes told him, however, that she'd gotten his message loud and clear.

"Just dance with me," she said, her hands reaching behind her to pull him closer.

Stepping up to the plate was activity number one on tonight's agenda.

Unfortunately, what Zer's mind knew and had accepted was not the message his unruly cock had received. No, that poor bastard had decided to stake a claim on Nessa St. James.

As Zer saw it, his cock was doomed to disappointment.

He didn't want a soul mate, and it was damned certain Nessa didn't want him, certainly not for forever. Hell, she still thought she had an out clause on tonight's bond. The one thing he didn't envy her new soul mate was explaining the situation to her. And, eventually, explanations would become necessary. There was only so long they could keep her in the dark; plus, Brends's own soul mate was chafing at the bit. She'd urged complete disclosure from the get-go, but they'd shot her down.

Last he'd heard, Mischka still wasn't talking to the lot of them.

So, he had to step up to the plate. Shoving his hands deep into the pockets of the duster, he wrapped his fingers around a pair of throwing stars and strode back into the club. Well, Nessa wasn't going to pick him, so all he really had to do tonight was throw her to the wolves and stand back to watch the ensuing festivities.

Yeah, and witness her bonding.

Looking up, he spotted her dancing. Nael had his hands wrapped over her hips, and the two of them were locked together in a sensual two-step.

Nael was a good male. He deserved Nessa St. James.

Zer was fucking happy for him.

He really was.

The male dancing with her was sexier than sin, but that was probably the whole point of this exercise. He didn't really want to be here, didn't really want to be touching her. Something about her bothered Nael, and damned if she was going to sweat it. She'd seen him indiscriminately whoring himself out in the club, so whatever was bothering him now was something deeper than she wanted to deal with.

She shouldn't feel sorry for him.

He'd eat her alive without realizing it, and she'd be left

picking up the pieces of her life. Still, he felt good. Warm and solid at her back. A girl could do worse, she supposed, but the situation still made her angry.

She focused on that hot, slow pulse of anger, pushing aside the unwelcome sensuality of the dance floor.

She'd been forced into this predicament. It was all Zer's fault, she decided. He was a sexy alpha dictator—but he was still a dictator. And a consummate seducer. That made her even more mad. He'd aroused her in the elevator, and then he'd left her—making it perfectly clear he didn't want her even if she came gift-wrapped. She flicked a wry glance over her getup. And damn if she hadn't been gift-wrapped for someone in this club.

She wasn't hurt, she decided. She wouldn't let him make her feel that way. Any more than she'd let him force her into this bond of his.

He'd pushed her around, jeopardized her career. And she didn't like the way he made her feel—edgy and aroused and needy. But it was simply a chemical reaction, so she should have been able to pick any one of the other males, right? Wrong. Nael, for all his sexy dance moves, didn't do it for her. Instead, she'd already caught herself scanning the shadows of the club, looking for Zer. He wasn't the kind of male to be dominating a dance floor. No, he'd hang back and watch.

When what she needed to be doing was looking for the club's exit.

She got her bearings, noted a few landmarks on the way out. "Am I the only human here?" Maybe she'd try for a little truth before she left.

Nael clearly hadn't expected her question. He glanced at the female gyrating in front of them and then looked at her. "What do you think?"

"I'm not." She looked around the floor and identified a sprinkling of the non-paranormal. "Why not?" The public was conspicuously absent, but a handful of professionals remained, including the club's bartenders and hired dancers, some of them clearly human.

"Insurance," Nael muttered, his hand pressing into the small of her back.

"Excuse me?"

"Insurance," he repeated patiently. "Thirst starts to get out of control, the dancers volunteer. You're safe."

Hysterical laughter bubbled up. She wasn't safe at all.

"Walk in the park," he murmured into her ear. His hand was a reassuring weight at the small of her back. "You do a little dancing, get to know my brothers. Then, at midnight, you choose."

Except he wasn't suggesting a blind date or even a one-night stand. Nael expected her to choose a bond mate, and she was under no illusions that Zer had gone to this much trouble for a twenty-four hour hookup. He wanted something more, and the real question was: just how much *more* did he expect?

"I'm not choosing," she said. "He can't make me."

Nael considered that for a moment. Nodded. "But it doesn't hurt anyone to think about it, does it? You consider it. Look at them," Nael added softly. "I'll introduce you around. You've got plenty of time to decide if you like what you see or not."

Part of him wished she could have been his. But he knew that wasn't happening. She'd already made her choice, even if she didn't know it yet. Still, he figured she was owed some pleasure, and nobody better to see to that than his brothers. Maybe her body knew that, too, because she melted beneath the gentle pressure of his hand, letting him steer her into the crowded dance floor, where his brothers' hot eyes and the hotter press of bodies swallowed her up.

Just a few minutes. His eyes examined the edge of the dance floor, searching for his sire. There was no sign of Zer, though, so he could let her have these last few minutes of freedom. Maybe she wasn't the same as him, didn't crave the touch of others, but he wanted to give her that pleasure nevertheless.

"Dance with me," he whispered against her ear, drinking in her shiver. "Feel us, Nessa."

The music pulsed through him, a living, breathing techno beat connecting him and her and the other dancers. Here, on the dance floor, you could lose all sense of self in the wash of colors and sensations. "Feel, Nessa."

Male hands stroked along her forearms, her neck, the curve of her shoulder. The stripped-down sound of the music was as raw as the males themselves, and he read all too clearly on Nessa's face her conflict. She felt exposed, naked. Aroused. His brothers were looking at her like she was the sun, moon, and stars of their universe, and she'd never, ever, had anyone—human or not—look at her like that.

The next brother ignored her protests, gently coaxing. Scooping her up and holding her for a brief moment against a hard, masculine chest. Nael knew she was close enough to hear the blades shift, but the male was good. He took his moment, and then, before he could scare her and force Nael to go all Dominion on his ass, he remembered the rules of the game and gently placed her back on her feet in the center of the dance floor. His fingers remained loosely around her wrist for a moment before sliding away. He wasn't forcing her.

"Dance, female. Dance with us."

They were waiting for something she couldn't, wouldn't give them. Since there was no way out but through, she danced.

When she'd finally managed to dance her way across the club, it was almost midnight. Nessa could feel the anticipation building in the room. The problem was, she was the cynosure of all eyes, even the ones discreetly pretending not to stare. The power was seductive but disturbing. She didn't like the desperate hope she felt coming off these males. There was definitely something she hadn't been told.

Who was she kidding? No one had bothered giving her the lowdown on anything happening here, only a deadline of midnight. Well, fine. She'd chosen—and she was so out of here. It was going to have to be the fire door, however, because the main door was clearly out of the question. The door to the alley was no good, either; she had no illusions about how fast they'd be on her. She'd be trapped like a prize heifer in a chute, and that wasn't the way she was planning on ending her evening.

Her only options were leaving—or staying. If she stayed, she put it all on the line, and she chose. She bonded with one of *them,* and then, even if she found out the truth, it would be too late. Her soul wouldn't be her own anymore.

When she took another step, her heel hit carpet rather than the slick tile of the dance floor. Bingo. Damn red dress lit her up better than a neon prey-is-here sign, though. Leave it to Zer to pick out a dress that both pushed her out of her comfort zone and made her wonder if she should rethink her decision. Maybe she'd keep the dress; she didn't need to keep *him.*

Maybe she could find a jacket, something to throw over the betraying color. Problem was, the Fallen didn't seem to leave their possessions lying around. No jackets hanging off the back of chairs or tossed on the sleek leather banquettes dotting the club's perimeter. Plus, she had a nagging feeling that they could scent her. They'd be all over her ass and on her trail in a heartbeat.

Still, she had to try, so she'd do it fast.

Casually, she toed off the killer heels. No way she could run in those. She'd break an ankle—or two—and then Zer would have her right where he wanted her. A barefoot escape was safer, although it was cold as hell outside, and she wasn't looking forward to taking on the pavement.

Wait for it. The music transitioned into another pulse-pounding blend of house and techno, the dancers moving faster in a sensual daze. Sliding quickly between the two nearest banquettes, she plotted her next move. The crowd was turning, looking up toward a second-floor balcony, and that worked in her favor. Fewer eyes for her to evade.

Maybe this could work.

Her hand hit the metal push bar.

And stopped dead. Nael's fingers wrapped around her wrist, and, wouldn't you know it, the damned door didn't budge. He wasn't hurting her, but she wasn't going anywhere without his say-so.

"Let me out." No point in pretending she wasn't leaving. He had eyes in his head.

She didn't like the small smile that touched the corners of his mouth. Regretful. Clearly, he wasn't in an accommodating mood. "Can't do that."

He could; he just didn't want to. She scrambled to think of some way to persuade him. "This isn't right. You can't keep me here." Her voice sounded breathless, weak, even to her own ears.

"We need you, love, and I think you'll find we're not so bad."

"You're Fallen." Hello, Captain Obvious. "How much more bad than that can you get?"

He smiled in acknowledgment and set to work gently prying her fingers off the door. She considered making this easy for him, retaining some shred of dignity, but surrendered to the panic building inside her.

"He told you to convince me, do whatever you needed to." No point in dressing up the accusation. Instead, she focused her attention on the large hand wrapped around her arm. "Hands off."

"Truth," he acknowledged, freeing her hand and tucking it into the crook of his arm. Gentlemanly and deadly. Just her luck. "He needs you. We need you, Nessa St. James." Those large, gentle hands were frog-marching her up the stairs. Toward the damn second-floor balcony, where everyone was staring.

"What is he to you?"

"My sire. The leader of the Fallen." He shrugged but didn't stop his ground-eating stride. "He led us when we were Dominions, and he did it well. When he decided to take up arms against Michael, we followed him then, too."

"Was he . . . ?" Why was she holding her breath?

"Right?" Those leather-covered legs devoured the remaining stairs. Paused. "Who really knows? Maybe he was, maybe he wasn't. You don't need to worry about that."

But she did. He was asking her to trust the Heavens' bad boy.

He eyed her, clearly reading the doubt written across her face. "He's worth fighting for, Nessa St. James. He's a good male."

"You think so?" She kept her words light, but she couldn't stop her eyes from searching the shadows one more time.

"I know so." Something shifted in his eyes. "I swore to protect him. To serve him. I *know* him. He's worthy of much more than this—and you can help him. I can't." He met her gaze. "You can," he repeated. "You ever been thirsty, Nessa?" He didn't wait for her answer, just plowed on with his explanation. "You take that itch in the back of your throat, your body's plea for something wet. Something cool to take the edge off the heat. You magnify that feeling until you're burning and all you can think about is just having one swallow. One swallow—that might be enough. Just enough to wet your throat and get you through the next few seconds. The next minute."

He wasn't talking about water; they both knew that. "It wouldn't be enough," she pointed out.

"No." Some unfamiliar emotion slid over his dark face for

a moment and then vanished behind the playboy mask again. "One swallow, one taste of that sweet wetness isn't enough. We're addicts, and we can't ever get enough. We don't have souls of our own, not anymore. So every waking minute, we're on the hunt for a substitute. For a way to ease that burning thirst."

That wasn't her fault, and she shouldn't accept the heaping helping of guilt Nael was shoveling her way. She couldn't shut out his words, though, the stark images pounding away at her mental barriers.

"He's living with that thirst every day. You could stop it. For good."

"How?"

"How?" Something hot and savage flashed in those dark eyes. "You have to bond with him, Nessa, body and soul. You let him in. You love him."

Zer was right. This wasn't something you could force. Not something you could demand with a blade. Fortunately for them both, Nael was a master seducer. This was what he was good at. So he gave his verbal seduction of Nessa St. James his all—and he told her how lonely and dark and saveable Zer was. He knew human females. She wanted the other male, but she was pissed at him for putting her into this predicament. "He's wrong if he thinks otherwise, and you're the only one who can make him understand that. I need you to go to him." *I need you to bond with him.*

He let her go and stepped forward onto the landing, hand primed to pull the door to the balcony open. His feet were deadly silent on the club's plush carpeting. She hesitated beside him, and he extended her shoes to her, the impossibly feminine red stilettos dangling from his fingers. "You take these. You give him hell." *Heaven.* "He'll listen to you, because you'll make him."

She stared at him. "He'll listen to me?"

"Now," he urged, sinking to his knees beside her, sliding the stilettos onto her bare feet. The delicious warmth of her skin seeped into him as he wrapped his hand around her ankle. *Believe me.* "He needs you. You can save him, Nessa."

She licked suddenly dry lips. What if she didn't want to save Zer? What if she wanted to save herself? Nael must have read her indecision in her eyes, because he reached out a hand toward her. Dropped it when she took a step backward.

"He doesn't want me, and I'm not a party favor he can pass around to his friends."

She was too special for this shit. Briefly, anger flared at his sire, who was this close to the fuck-up of a near-immortal lifetime. Tamping it down, Nael sought words. "Then show him how wrong he is, love. Show him that he's not walking away from *you.*"

Her eyes closed briefly. Snapped open. "At what price?"

He pressed a kiss against the soft skin of her calf, reluctantly sliding his mouth away. "Nothing that you can't afford, love. In exchange, you'll have Zer right where you want him. Eating out of the palm of your hand."

Zer was a powerful predator, one that could never really be tamed. But she could make a difference, and Nael was willing to sacrifice everything on that chance. If Nessa St. James could save his sire, Nael would make damn sure she did.

He stood gracefully, backing away from her. Opened the door.

Even without the silent warning vibration of his vidphone, Zer would have known it was midnight. Stillness and anticipation swept through the club as the dancers pulled back, clearing the way. Above him, Nessa St. James stepped out onto the balcony, wrapping her hands around the glass and chrome railing. Silently, she stared down at his brothers, a living, crimson flame. The wicked scrap of a bodice cupped her breasts like a lover, and Zer itched to be beside her, to stroke his fingers over that agitated expanse of skin. Soothe her. Arouse her.

Midnight. Time for her to choose someone else.

Forcibly, he pulled his gaze away from her, scanning the crowd. One of his brothers was about to be handed salvation. Vkhin's cold, hard face watched them both, arms crossed over his broad chest. The brother blocked access to the stairs Nessa had just ascended. Only male getting up there now was Nessa St. James's new mate. Lucky bastard.

Zer squelched the thought.

If Nael had done his job, she'd be ready. She'd know what the Fallen could offer, would have been seduced by whichever dream called her name. In theory, she could demand to walk out that door. He simply didn't plan on letting her go until she'd given him—them—what they wanted. What they needed. Still, he couldn't stop himself from drinking in the sight of her hair and eyes one last time. She was like the sweetest of chocolates, begging to be unwrapped. God, the unknown brother was a lucky bastard.

The soft curve of her breast rose and fell, a feminine tease framed by the blood-red corset. Nessa St. James wasn't calm, and she wasn't pleased about her circumstances, no matter what that serene face of hers promised. She was liquid heat waiting for the right match. The right male.

He strode out into the empty center of the dance floor. The Fallen nearest him melted away, giving him the respect they owed their sire. He didn't deserve that respect, but he'd make it right for one of them right now.

"Nessa St. James." He came to a halt dead center, crossing his arms over his chest, and stared up at her. He'd picked a fighting stance to make his declaration.

"Choose."

He didn't do fancy words. He figured that about covered it.

She had four hundred Fallen staring at her. One of them had to be the one for her.

Instead of looking his brothers over, however, she was looking down at him. One hand clamped on the railing in front of her, she didn't look nervous. No. What she looked was damn mad. At him. His eyes narrowed. He sought out Nael, but the brother melted back into the shadows.

"You want me to choose?" Her voice was smooth and cool, all professor, but he didn't miss the low, husky note. Yeah, something—someone—had her riled up good. When he'd ordered Nael to make sure she showed, ready to choose, he'd said no-holds-barred. Now, he wondered if he should have been more specific. She was gunning for him, and he didn't know why.

"Yeah, professor," he drawled. A whisper of sound rose from the assembled Fallen, a symphony of leather and steel. "Here's your court, waiting for you. You pick one of my brothers, and he's going to treat you real nice."

Those dark eyes narrowed. He glared back up at her, trying to force her compliance with the sheer strength of his will.

"Let me see if I've got this right," she said, striding back and forth on that narrow slip of a balcony. The lush roll of her hips promised sweet, hot sex. A male could lose himself in that body, but it was the scent of her soul, the delicious tease of her aura, that had the room leaning toward her. Zer bit back a growl. *Focus.*

"You need me to choose one of you," she continued. That lethal gaze of hers raked the room, and he swore the temperature rose. "Just one of you. And you don't care who I pick."

That wasn't strictly true. Hell, he hoped she'd go for Vkhin or Nael, because he knew how hard the soul thirst rode both his brothers. Dead or locked away in the Preserves—either way, they all knew that neither male had time to spare. Still, . . . "You do the choosing," he acknowledged. "Stop talking about it, and get on with the picking."

He didn't like that smile.

"One favor," she said. "In exchange for one soul."

"Right. You need a roll call, or do you see your man?"

He needed to know who she'd chosen, needed to see her in the arms of his brother. Then, his work here was done, unless the brother chose him to witness the bonding. Christ, he hoped he wouldn't be called upon to do that.

"All right." She stepped right up to the railing. Leaned forward, until her arms rested on the chrome. "I've made my choice."

Conflicting emotion pounded through her, obliterating logic. Part of her wanted to slam out the door behind her, tell his high-and-mightiness what he could do with his devil's bargain. There was no way he could force her to do this.

She kept losing her way, though, in the white-hot blaze of desire running through her.

Dancing, all she'd seen was Zer, watching her. And, all she could think about was what happened in the elevator. How good he'd made her feel. Had she ever experienced a thrill like that before in her life? Could she really walk away from that electric current between them?

Hell. No.

Her eyes narrowed. He'd said the Fallen had to find bond mates. So she'd take him. Nael had said she could have Zer eating out of her hand. She was tired of being alone. So she'd choose him and see how he liked having his whole life up-ended. That little move wouldn't be one he'd have anticipated in this sensual battle for dominance they had going on between them.

"You," she said.

The crowd reacted with a deep inhalation, like the ocean sucking out of a bay right before a tsunami hit, exposing the wrecks and rocks and sunken bits that the water had concealed for so long.

Zer froze. Yeah, he didn't like being hunted, either.

"I choose *you*," she said.

His head snapped up, that ice-cold gaze locking on hers. She should have been afraid. After all, she'd just invited the room's biggest predator to make an all-you-can-eat meal out of her. But this didn't feel wrong, damn it. So she said it again. "I choose you, Zer. You want me to take a bond mate—I'll take you."

Stepping back through the door, she slammed it behind her, because the petty gesture was satisfying. Leaning back against the wall, she dug in her pretty new heels to wait. She gave him ten—twenty—seconds, tops.

This wasn't the plan. Hell. The crowd parted around him, moving away. Ceding him the ground because he was the victor in a battle he'd sworn he wouldn't fight.

Disbelief. Anger and shame. Damn her, he'd taken what belonged to one of his brothers. The reaction of the crowd around him only made him feel worse. Loyal to the bone, most of them were. He would have welcomed a blade in his back, though.

It wouldn't be forever. Couldn't be.

"She picked you." Vkhin's voice gave nothing away, the brother himself hidden within the shadows of the stairwell

"Yeah," he answered more sharply than he'd planned to.

"All right." Vkhin stepped aside, leaving the way up the staircase clear.

Christ. He'd never allowed himself to fantasize that he'd be the one climbing these stairs. Not tonight. Not ever. He didn't deserve her, and it was damned sure that she couldn't possibly be his soul mate. He was soulless, and they all knew it. He was the root cause of their Fall, and there was no way he should be the one to pull the first get-out-of-jail-free card.

Before he could start the climb, Mischka reached out and laid a hand on his arm. Brother shouldn't have brought her here, but no one kept Mischka out. Not when she wanted in. "Treat her right."

He looked down at that pale hand. Knew Brends was within an inch of pounding him into the ground for the touch. Did they all know he was an animal? "I will," he growled.

"Right," she insisted. "You take care of her. And"—she paused, sliding her hand away—"you let her *in*. You let her close. Don't shut her out."

"She's not my soul mate."

"Why not?" She stared at him curiously. Brends drew her back against his larger body, and she nestled there, fit into the larger shape of him, his large hand stroking down the length of her dark hair.

"Because she's not."

"You don't know that," she pointed out. "Not until you've bonded with her." Her beautiful face flushed. "And fallen in love with her."

He didn't do love. He wasn't capable of it. All he had to offer Nessa St. James was safety and protection and whatever damn favor she'd set her heart on. He knew he was tricking her into bonding with him, that emotions were riding her hard and she'd have regrets in the morning, but he didn't care. He'd been bred to be ruthless, and he'd accepted that side of himself long ago. He needed her mind, and he needed it now. Her body was just a delicious bonus.

"I don't do love," he said out loud. Mischka just looked at him, and he read the regret on her face loud and clear.

"Too late." Brends's hand dropped to her shoulder, his thumb rubbing a small circle against her bare skin as she spoke. "You made her choose, Zer, and she chose you. She was someone's soul mate, and she chose you. You make this work," she said fiercely. "You have to make this work."

If he didn't do love, he damned certain didn't do happily-ever-after. So how could he tell Mischka what she wanted to hear? He couldn't be anything other than what he was.

"She won't regret," he promised, giving his words to the other male. He hated moments like this. He wasn't a god-damn poet, and they all knew it. He wouldn't let his brothers lose the advantage of this soul mate, either.

He had their backs.

And that was going to have to be enough. Because he couldn't have—didn't want, he told himself—love and happily-ever-after. He'd seen Brends. Whatever that male had with his soul mate, maybe it was worth having, but Brends no longer left the club to fight without looking back. Part of him fought now to go back to Mischka Baran, and that part of him was vulnerable.

And Zer sure as hell couldn't afford vulnerable.

CHAPTER TWELVE

Nessa met Zer at the door, but he wasn't letting her take charge. She'd set the scene, and now he'd damn well finish it, and she'd learn the price of teasing one of the Fallen. "You should have picked someone else, baby." He strode over to her, knowing what she saw coming for her. He was cold to the core, bred to be a warrior and a killer. He wished he could be the gentle lover she deserved, but she'd made this bed for some reason of her own, and now she was going to have to lie in it. Her eyes flickered over his face, searching for something. Whatever it was she wanted, she had him now. He'd either be enough for her or he wouldn't, but there was no going back on this bargain.

Slowly, he settled his hands on her shoulders, mesmerized by the contrast of his large, dark fingers resting on those pale, bare shoulders. That corset was a wicked sin, a walking present he couldn't wait to unwrap. When he'd picked it out, he'd fantasized about slipping open the buttons, one by one, tasting all that white skin it concealed, but he'd known those were fantasies. Not going to happen. Now, she'd handed him the keys to the treasure, and all his good intentions had flown out the window.

Closing his fingers, he pulled her closer. She didn't resist, but she didn't make it easy, either. She swayed slightly on those ridiculously high heels, and he didn't know if it was from desire or fear or some other all-too-human emotion. He'd find out, wouldn't he?

When he had her body flush against his, he stopped. He met her gaze and paused. She was waiting for something— waiting for him.

"You want this?" Taking her hand, he placed it against his chest. "You sure about this, baby?" He wanted them skin to skin. Now. But he figured he'd better give her one more chance.

She didn't look like she appreciated his gentlemanly quali-ties, and damned if he understood where they were coming from, anyhow. "You want me to choose someone else?" She eyed him. "Oh, wait. You made that perfectly clear, didn't you? Anyone. I was to choose anyone else. Anyone but you. News flash—" Her fingers curled into her palm as she shoved him away. Tried to. He wasn't going anywhere. "You're the one I want."

His cock definitely liked the sound of that, springing to life for her. Growing harder. Never mind that he'd been impossi-bly aroused ever since she'd stepped out onto that balcony, fi-nally ready to make her choice.

At the sound of someone else coming through the balcony door, she stepped away, taking the delicious heat of her body with her. He could still taste her soul, though. Anger. Arousal. Heat. She was a delicious cocktail of human emotions.

"You want out of this arrangement you forced on me?" she asked sweetly.

He couldn't read her eyes, got only a swirl of heated, con-fused emotions now from her aura. She was driving him crazy, and she didn't know it. Did she?

"Yeah. I do." And he did, didn't he? He wasn't good enough for her, and that meant she wasn't going to be his soul mate. She couldn't give him back his wings, and that's what he had to have from her. So she needed to pick another male. A decent male. Her eyes narrowed, as if she could read his mind.

"I could pick him." She strolled around Zer, laying a course for Nael, who had just returned through the balcony door. Nael, who looked like a male who saw a train wreck coming but couldn't figure out a way to move his ass off the tracks. "Is that what you really wanted me to do, Zer? Why's he here with us?"

Christ, she really didn't know. Didn't know about the witness required by the bond. Or that, if they were really being honest, Nael was his keeper, his lifeline to sanity. Nael was there to make sure Zer didn't go off the deep end.

Instead, she reached up and captured Nael's mouth with hers, her lips moving gently over his. Her tongue licked along the closed seam of his brother's mouth, and that mouth parted. Opened up and let her in.

His beast growled a warning as her lips explored the other male's. "Nael," he bit out, but Nael threw up a warning hand. Not touching her, except with his mouth.

"You want me, Nael? You going to let your sire here watch us?" she asked, the throaty little murmur doing unspeakable things to Zer's cock. This time, she wrapped a hand around the back of Nael's neck, her fingers gently stroking the exposed skin. Pulling him down to her. Brother went, too, dark lashes drifting shut over those too-old eyes of his.

She kissed Nael deep and hard, until Zer pulled her off him.

He'd spent the minutes since he'd climbed up here with a raging hard-on, imagining what her nipples would look like when he freed them from the sinful fabric cupping them, how they would harden in his hands. Now, the only thing that stood between him and his fantasies was the thin satin fabric of her corset—and Nael.

"Too late for second chances, baby. You're getting no one

else, not tonight." Wrapping a hard arm around her waist, he swung her effortlessly up into his arms.

Kissing Nael had been a revelation. Not bad, not unwelcome—just not Zer.

Wrapped in Zer's arms, she knew he was 100 percent large, hard, domineering alpha. He was making short work of getting her back to his room and the bed she'd imagined the two of them in.

Zer wasn't hurting her, but there was no mistaking his steely determination. She'd intended to push his buttons, push him—and she'd gotten her wish. His desire. For her. The thick outline of his cock strained visibly against the front of his leather pants, and all she could think about was getting her hands on him.

Just sex. That's all it is. Hormones and pheromones and little-used nerve-endings firing. God, she was a liar.

Zer didn't break the kiss once as the elevator shot silently upward. The ride was so smooth, all she could concentrate on was the male who had her backed up against the mirrored panels, devouring her like a starving man.

As if he couldn't possibly get enough of her. His mouth moved like a dream, exploring the sensitive skin of her cheek, her neck, the curve beneath her jaw, before covering her lips. The sweet ache was there between her legs already, and he hadn't even really touched her yet.

The elevator glided to a stop, but Zer didn't. Nael's hand was on his shoulder, as if he'd pour himself into his damn king if he could. Or as if he thought maybe only one of them would be leaving the suite tonight. Could be, he was right. This was reckless and stupid and shortsighted, but she was doing it, and it was too late now. All she could do was hang on and enjoy the ride.

The elevator doors parted silently, and Zer lifted his head, staring down at her with hot, needy eyes. His hands cupped her jaw, his thumbs stroking a sensual pattern along the sensitized flesh. God, she couldn't wait for those strong hands to touch her elsewhere.

Those hands promised a pleasure she wanted. As if he could read her mind—and she knew he couldn't, not yet—he drawled, "I'm going to make you come undone. We're going to figure out everything you like."

"Everything?" She licked dry lips.

His eyes slid over her body, as if he was cataloging that everything. "Yeah," he said, his voice a sexy drawl. "Everything. You can count on that. You're going to enjoy what happens here tonight. That's my promise to you."

He sounded as if there might be some doubt she would enjoy what happened between them. God. He had no idea. She was about to combust on the spot. Any more aroused and she'd be flinging him to the ground. And damned if she didn't actually consider the idea for a moment.

"You think I wouldn't enjoy this?" Wrapping her hands around his, she savored the contrast between his larger, darker fingers and hers. He was so damn big. She wished this was more than a one-night stand, but, just for tonight, she was taking what she could get.

And she wanted this male.

He shot her a look. "Because I'm Fallen, baby. "

"And that makes you some sort of sexual deviant?" Maybe it did, but that didn't explain the new surge of heat between her legs.

"There's nothing I haven't done. Wouldn't do." His hands slid away from her face, and she let him go. "Three thousand years of experience. I've done things you couldn't begin to imagine."

"But you won't hurt me."

"No." He turned toward the open door. "I'd never hurt you." He flashed that dark, masculine smile at her. "Not unless that was what you wanted."

God. His words had her fantasizing about his stretching her out across his lap. His hand taking down her panties and descending on her bare ass.

"Then we're good." Was that throaty whisper her voice? "It's all good, Zer." She didn't know what she was giving him permission to do, but she knew she wanted him. Wanted this night. He was too dangerous, too hard for more than that, but she could have this. One night, and she'd still be able to walk away when it was over, when she'd gotten whatever "favor" he gave her.

She hoped.

Zer merely nodded and strode toward the suite. "Bring her." He tossed the words over his shoulder to Nael.

He was handing her off yet again. Refusing to deal with her. She stiffened as Nael's arms closed around her, guiding her forward. Those familiar dark eyes stared down at her, looking for some answer in her face. "Cut him some slack, Nessa. He's fighting for control."

Was that a good thing? Maybe. She was strangely off balance herself, her heels sinking into the thick carpeting of his room as she followed him inside.

Zer moved toward the bed. He wasn't going to pretend this wasn't going to happen. Behind her, the door clicked softly shut behind Nael, locking the three of them into a room set up for a seduction. Although the lights had been dimmed, she could still see plenty. There were candles everywhere. The sweet, smoky scents of the burning wax had her inhaling deeply, even as her gaze caught and held on the bed.

And the large male sprawled there.

Waiting for her.

He leaned back against the black padded headboard like a military commander at his post, his impossibly large body dominating the room. Like he wanted to dominate her.

God. As if he knew her secret fantasies, the steamy daydreams of being borne off to bed by a male capable of dominating her. Of making sure that she got every pleasure she needed. Her fantasy male had laid her down on his bed and made love to her with no holds barred, hadn't let her keep back a single reaction.

God, the reality was so much better than the fantasy. A blast of pure, liquid heat left her trembling.

Needing.

"Don't," he said, crossing his arms over his chest, watching her with that level gaze of his.

"Don't what?" He'd dropped his booted feet on the velvet counterpane. He looked large, male. Sexy. He was in control. Her body flushed, and she knew it wasn't with embarrassment. She wanted him.

"Don't mistake me for someone else." His eyes examined her face. "I'm no poet," he warned, and she didn't have the faintest idea what he meant. But that was nothing new. "So, strip." His words, however, were a shock. As was the hard rush of wet heat.

"Excuse me?"

"You heard me." He crossed one leg over the other. "Strip for me, baby."

With Nael looking on? Automatically, she opened her mouth to refuse the order. And closed it. She was going to do every damn thing she'd ever fantasized about. She flicked open the first button.

The hunger was a freight train roaring through his head, the beast demanding out. Which was just too bad. He didn't particularly like letting his rogue out to play, and he sure as hell wasn't inviting that kind of kink into bed with him when he finally had Nessa St. James in his arms.

She was the sexiest damn sight he'd ever laid eyes on.

Now that she'd started, she didn't hesitate. She unbuttoned the corset one wicked button at a time until the satin slipped open, framing the soft, rounded mound of her stomach and those breasts. The hard pink nipples begging for his touch.

"Show me what you like, baby." He'd make this fantasy good. It was the least he could do for her.

She was so damn gorgeous, and those breasts of hers were going to kill him. He dragged the sweet scent of her deep inside him as her hands stroked slowly down the soft curves of skin. Not tentatively, as if she was shy, but as if she were considering his question. Exploring possible answers. Christ, that was sexy.

"This," she decided. "I like this."

She cupped the weight of her breasts in her own hands, her fingertips caressing. Rubbing those hard little nipples. Lust ripped through him, stronger, harder than anything he'd ever felt before. His cock pulsed, demanding he get inside her. Now.

"What do you like?" she asked.

Her straight-on gaze unmanned him, shocked him down to his core. This was her night. Tonight was about her fantasies, not his.

"You," he growled, wrapping a hand around her wrist and tugging her down onto the bed as he swept back the covers with one arm. She let him guide, settling onto the sheets beside him. "Hot. Wet. Coming on my fingers for me. Against my mouth. The taste of you is candy-sweet, baby, and we've got all night. Lie down for me." The smoky rasp of his voice lit new fires inside her. "Do it."

She lay back, but her face broadcast her disappointment when he didn't follow her down. Instead, he was bending over her, and he knew he was too large. Too male. All her feminine instincts were rioting in protest, screaming for her to run. "Relax, baby," he whispered, his voice a silky promise as he stripped off the red satin, tossing it away to land on the floor behind them in soft whisper of sound. The dress fell away from her like a cocoon, leaving her only the wicked garter belt and shoes.

"Take them off, too," she whispered.

"You sure?" He was asking about more than just her heels. When she nodded, he slid his fingers down her calf, pulling off the stilettos and discarding them but leaving her the garter belt he'd secured for her.

"Yes." Tonight, she was taking what she wanted. Tomorrow, she could go back to her old life. Do the responsible thing. Tonight was her one chance. "Yes, Zer." Leaning up into his hard chest, she reached for the buttons of his shirt. Wanting to undo him the way he'd undone her.

She undid buttons, fascinated by the thickly muscled male chest framed by the sides of the shirt. Pulling off the shirt, she wanted to lick him all over. The deep golden color of his skin, the earthy scent of him, were an open invitation to touch. To taste.

When she gave in to the temptation and ran a hand over that dusky skin, he groaned. "Be sure, baby." He inhaled deeply, as if he wanted her inside and out. "Be very sure. Last chance."

"Bond with me."

His primitive growl of satisfaction was all the warning he gave, and then his large hand was gently pressing her forward. She went. Wrapping her legs around him, rocking her garter-belt-framed pussy against that delicious strength.

The candles flickered dimly; Nael was just a shadow beside them.

A thousand wicked fantasies boiled through her mind. Zer would do what he wanted; she knew that. And she would enjoy it. Would enjoy every dark taste. His touch. After tonight, he'd know her better than anyone. She was okay with that, she decided.

He helped her settle back against his sheets until the decadent fabric slid against her stocking-clad legs. "We're doing this my way," he warned. "You're going to give it up to me, Nessa. Every bit of pleasure. I'm going to be watching *you*. You're not hiding from me tonight. You're going to come for me."

Nessa St. James was not an easy woman, and Zer knew she didn't open up for just anyone. But now she was spread deliciously wide beneath him and not just in the sexual sense. Her cream teased him, but not half as much as her soul. The sweet, hot heat of her essence was flooding him.

Unable to resist, he allowed himself the smallest sip of her soul. Her aura reflected heated shock, feminine curiosity and—God—arousal. Pure, sweet arousal.

She wasn't afraid of him—or this.

She *wanted* this.

Deliberately, he wrapped her hands around the frame of the headboard, bending his head toward hers. "I need to tie you there, baby, or will you stay put?" Those sweet brown eyes of hers widened. Hesitated. Then she nodded, and a dark lick of pleasure shot through him. She'd play this game with him, would give every bit as good as she got.

When he slid his fingers from hers, sure enough, she stayed put. "Now we're going to get you wet for me, baby."

Moving down her body, he stripped away her garter belt and hose, uncovering those last few inches of soft flesh.

Damned if he couldn't stop staring at her. She was beautiful. Not an airbrushed, lingerie-catalog kind of beauty, but something else. Her body was blatantly feminine, the soft lines drawing him downward. In. The dimpled curve of her belly was an invitation he couldn't resist, so he ran an exploring finger over that soft skin, watching as she stilled. The lush heat of her warmed some part of him he hadn't realized was cold.

He ran his knuckles down her jaw, along the line of her

throat. "You're so beautiful," he whispered hoarsely. "Let me show you."

Losing this battle wasn't an option, so he planned his attack as he moved down. Pressing hot kisses down the length of her.

Her hands flexed on the headboard.

"Don't let go," he warned, and he turned his attention to her breasts. He had to touch her. As he drew his knuckles along the smooth curve of skin, her nipples pebbled before he'd even touched her with his mouth. He couldn't hold back the rumble of pleasure welling up inside him. The sweet scent of her skin, the slide of the satin sheets beneath them threatened his control.

"Hell," he muttered. She was coming apart in his arms, coming without his really touching her, and he was coming undone right alongside her.

"Open up for me." He deliberately put a hand on her thigh. She'd do this for him. He wouldn't force her. "Let me taste you."

She hesitated, her gaze sliding to Nael. Maybe she *was* shy, after all. "He won't watch you, baby. Not unless you want him to."

"Who's he watching, then?" Her voice was a husky whisper of sound in the room. He wasn't sure Nael was still breathing. Christ, he was holding his own damn breath. Who would have believed that one small female could be so damn powerful?

"Me." He shrugged his shoulders. "No one. Whatever pleases *you*." Pausing a beat, he slid a finger down her side, loving the way her wary gaze followed. "Decision time, baby. What do you want?"

His hard mouth bent toward her, blazing a heated trail over the sensitive skin behind her ear, his hands sweeping the loose hair away from the vulnerable nape of her neck. A shiver she would feel straight down to her pussy.

She'd watched Nael, after all. She'd seen Zer's brother take the woman in the club. Slipping out of the shadows, Nael pressed a small kiss against her fingers. "I'll be right over there, love, unless you want me." His dark eyes promised only sweet, sinful pleasure.

Her hands tightened deliberately on the headboard, her thighs parting as she whispered, "He can watch us."

Zer's control snapped.

God. She'd never known that a ménage à trois—even this bare hint of a threesome—would make her so needy and aching for his touch. It was strangely, intensely seductive, this pleasure of being watched rather than watching.

He pulled her up and over him, smoothly reversing their positions, so that she straddled him, her legs parting around the delicious ridges of his belly. His cock was thick and hard, a delicious heat that pressed against the sensitive flesh of her pussy.

His fingers wrapped hers around the headboard once again; then he was sliding down her body, promising un-speakable pleasures. Pleasures she'd only dreamed about. She wanted to touch him, but instead her fingers flexed against the smooth wood. The gardenia-and-jasmine scent of the candles swirled around them, fragrant evocations of long nights and lovers.

Behind them, half-hidden once again in the shadows, Nael shifted. Stilled.

Beneath his gaze, she felt every inch of her nakedness. She'd never felt so intensely desirable, so feminine.

The knowledge of his watching, of that dark gaze explor-ing her, *enjoying* her, added a new dimension to her pleasure. Nael thought she was beautiful. He hungered for her. Sud-denly, she felt beautiful, swept away in the heat of the mo-ment.

Anticipation had her pussy tightening as Zer raised her higher, sliding his head lower. His hands stroked softly along her thighs. Opening her farther. The contrast of his dark face, his head between her thighs, was shockingly explicit. Pleasure. Wet heat. She was going up in flames.

"Wait," she breathed, fighting for control. Losing the battle.

"No." The gruff command warned her, the rough words an erotic shock reinforced by the short, hard tap his hand delivered on her ass.

Pulling her over him, he buried his face in her sex and dragged his tongue briefly over her clit. A muffled squeak of surprise escaped her before she could choke back the shocked protest. Another sharp tap landed on her rear, and the blazing pleasure jolted her forward onto his wicked tongue. God, she could feel the orgasm coiling tighter and tighter. She couldn't hold back. Not when he touched her like this.

"I'm going to really kiss you now, baby." His voice warned her that he was telling, not asking. He was taking what he wanted tonight. Sure enough, his next kiss was not delicate. But sure. Bold. Parting her first with his fingers and then the thick, luscious glide of his tongue. Oh, God. She knew her eyes were drifting shut, but the pleasure—she'd never imagined pleasure like this.

He drew back. Waited.

They were locked in an elemental battle she'd never imagined. She was fighting to keep from coming against his mouth so quickly. Letting him know just how badly he'd undermined her defenses.

Wet and tight, the pleasure coiled fast and hard inside her.

"More." She gave him the words he demanded, ripping her hands from the headboard to wrap them around his wrists as sensation rocketed through her. "Give me more."

"No." Dark eyes watched her from that devilishly cold

face, but there was nothing cold about his eyes, not anymore. Those black eyes were pure, liquid heat as they moved over her face.

The sensual smack on the curve of her ass shocked her, the sharp sting fading to a heated burn that shot straight from her pinkened flesh to her weeping pussy. God. All she wanted was to beg for more. For him to touch her harder, deeper. She'd never felt such total pleasure before, the liquid jolts of sensation tearing her apart.

Wordlessly, she stared at him.

"I told you to do something." She heard the sensual threat in his voice, the promise of heated punishment. His fingers moved, stroking lazy circles so near where she wept to be touched. Her fingers slid away from his wrists as she scrambled to make sense of his words.

Another sensual tap followed, and she moaned helplessly.

"I told you not to let go."

Would she? Wouldn't she? She weighed the savage challenge of his eyes with her desperate need to come. God, he was hot. Deliberately, she wrapped her hands around the headboard again.

"Good girl," he purred. Resentment flickered through her, but too late. Her nerves were on fire.

He dipped his head, and his fingers stroked through the thick folds of her sex as he parted her. Licked at her again, dragging his tongue through her sensitive flesh. The sensual rasp was her undoing.

"God, Zer."

Her fingers clamped on the headboard with a death grip as she arched her back, giving in to the incredible pleasure.

His husky groan filled her ears as his hands cupped her ass, separating the cheeks as he devoured her. Her entire world narrowed to him and his wicked touch. She knew she was lifting herself to meet each stroke, and she sure as hell didn't recognize the throaty moan filling the room. God, what had he done to her? She didn't care, didn't care, only wanted more. She wanted to touch him, but he wouldn't allow that, so all she could do was hang on.

It was going to be so very, very good.

"One finger." His wicked promise made her sex tighten in unfamiliar anticipation. "Let's see if you can take that much of me, baby."

A small cry tore from her throat as he followed up on his promise, sliding a thick finger inside her. She could feel herself opening. Parting before his gentle invasion. God, she was so wet.

His penetration was so damn good. "Zer!" She cried his name, sliding her thighs wider, arching into his touch. His mouth. The wicked press of that talented finger, seeking a hidden spot, rubbing gently.

"One more." His heated promise was all the warning she got before he slid a second finger inside her, sheathing himself in her. "You can take this." She could hardly hear the intimate growl of his voice over the blinding pleasure consuming her. "You can take me."

His groan told her he wanted her, too. He wanted this. She wasn't alone here.

Sensation exploded, a bright burst of pleasure beating behind her closed eyes. She came long and hard, riding his fingers. Drawing him deeper into her until she didn't know where she ended and he began.

The erotic stillness of her body as she tried to make sense of an overload of sensations rocked his world, teasing all his senses with sensual promise, and then she melted into his embrace.

Good. "First time, baby," he promised. He moved up her body, bit lightly at the smooth skin of her throat, marking her beneath her ear. Next time she wore that damn chignon of hers, the whole world would see his mark of possession. Would know that she belonged to him.

He shouldn't be doing this, but the pleasure was a torment now. So long since he'd felt this sense of welcome. Homecoming. As if, in all the universe, this was the one place he belonged. A male could drown in this pleasure.

Christ, he wanted this to be right for her. For him to be her fantasy the way she was his.

Ruthlessly, he stripped off his boots and pants. Shot a look at the shadows. Solid as a rock, there was his boy. Nael hadn't moved from his position in the darkness. Safe. So, he slid his weapon under the pillow but didn't remove the pair of blades strapped to his upper arm. Nael had his back, but no way would Zer risk Nessa now. She was worth too damn much. Losing her wasn't an option, and for reasons he didn't want to explore. Not now.

Covering her, he deliberately bore down with his weight, pinning her to the bed. Her husky feminine moan went straight to his head.

"Bond with me," he growled.

Her answer, when it came, rocked his world.

"Yes," she groaned, licking at his ear. "You bond with me."

Chapter Thirteen

Ignoring the unexpectedly primitive pang of possession he felt, he decided he would mark her. She'd never forget the Dominion who'd held her in his arms first. Zer was going to make damn sure of that.

Her hands exploring him weren't passive. He wanted to throw back his head and howl with the pleasure of it all. Gripping her hips, he pulled her closer, his cock nudging her opening. She was soft and wet. Delicious. He knew exactly how she tasted now.

When he slid deep inside her, her hot, slick passage clung to him even as she struggled to open up to him. Her breath caught.

"Open up," he growled, his voice rough with arousal. "Let me in, baby."

The heat building between them was a delicious surprise, her legs wrapping around his waist, her hips rising up to meet him. Her fingers curled around his shoulders. He'd known her touch would be unforgettable, but he hadn't expected the burning heat that was consuming them both.

Sliding his hands beneath her to cup her ass and pull her harder against him, he pressed deeper. Closer. His entire body was consumed by the building pleasure. He'd never wanted anyone the way he wanted this woman in his arms.

She whimpered, a throaty promise of pleasure as he stretched her, moving deep and hard inside her. Branding her. Shaking with his own need, he took her hard and deep, driving in and out. Her soul was wide open, and the delicious taste seduced him even more thoroughly than the woman had. He had to claim her now. Before he went over the edge. "Bond with me," he groaned again.

His. She was all his.

"Yes!" Her hips arching up to meet his. He'd meant to make this night unforgettable for her, but now he was lost in the maelstrom of heat and dark pleasure and Nessa. There was no forgetting who he held. "Is that it?" She breathed the words against his skin. Then demanded, "Don't stop."

"No, baby," he growled. "I'm not done with you yet. The favor," he bit out. "Tell me what you want." His body was driving into hers as he buried himself deeper with each hard thrust. Pleasure consuming him, eating him alive. Ecstasy and pleasure. Almost pain. She felt so good. So *right*. He never wanted to stop moving in her. And that almost scared him. Then his cock was throbbing, sinking back into her, and he couldn't, wouldn't stop to think about the sensations flooding him. Just held on to this woman and every moment.

"Good. I'm not done with you, either." Her body twined around his, her teeth sinking into his shoulder. His body clenched in erotic pleasure. His fierce little human. She gave as good as she got. "I want *you*," she growled. "All of you. That's my *favor*."

Shock boiled through him, with anger close on its heels. Hell. She had no idea what she was asking. Hadn't someone warned her? Didn't she understand how the favor worked? He stared down at her, but it was too late.

Behind them, Nael cursed foully and murmured, "Witnessed."

The guilt and anger wasn't enough to stop the orgasm from pounding through him. The incredible, impossible sensations tearing out of him as he poured himself out for her. To her.

"Granted," he growled through gritted teeth, because he couldn't refuse, wasn't allowed to refuse. Michael's mocking laughter played through his head as he poured himself into her, unable to stop.

The dark ink of the bonding marks blossomed on their skin, wrapping the visible sign of their pairing around their wrists. Tying them together for the whole world to know. The ink didn't bother him. No, he had the feeling that the real problem was the invisible tendrils of *something,* some unfamiliar and entirely unwelcome emotion, connecting his soul to hers. With every stroke of his body, every new, dark layer of ink, he felt that connection growing. Binding *him* every bit as much as it bound her.

Her flesh clenched greedily around his, her hips arching up one last time as her body melted into his. Through their fledgling bond, he felt every soft, sweet clench and throb. He felt her unspeakable pleasure even as her orgasm forced a cry from her lips, and savage satisfaction filled him. She'd come for him. With him. She'd screamed, and he knew nothing, no one, had ever made Nessa St. James lose her careful composure like he had.

She wanted all of him. All. Of. Him.

No way that was a quick fuck and a favor. No way at all.

Resting his forehead against hers, he sucked air into his starving lungs. He didn't know where to start with her request. Didn't know how to open up and let her in. Which meant she'd tied them together for a damn long time.

He wasn't handing her off to one of his brothers anytime soon.

CHAPTER FOURTEEN

Nessa woke up alone. And, after a night like last night, waking up alone pissed her off. Her body felt pleasantly sore, every inch of her exquisitely aware of the man who had rocked her world.

Unfortunately, that man was nowhere in sight.

Stalking out of the bed, wrapped in his velvet comforter, she managed to make it into his over-the-top-luxurious bathroom. Maybe hot water and soap would improve her mood. Dropping the fabric wrapper, she examined her body in the mirror. He'd been dominant but strangely gentle. Her body was almost unmarked—except for the bonding marks.

Shit.

Pulling a thick cotton towel from a nearby bar, she wrapped the towel around herself, sinking down onto a padded bench in front of the vanity. Bonding marks that were still there.

Keep it together. Genecore's president had been very, very explicit when he "strongly suggested" that she avoid bonding with any of them. She hadn't worried about his little "suggestion" because she'd had no intention of doing something so stupid. God. Obviously, she needed to learn how to control her emotions.

And her mouth.

Carefully, she turned her wrists over, examining the marks.

Yeah. Everything was *so* not right here. "What have you gotten yourself into, Nessa?"

This was supposed to be a one-night stand and a favor. She'd deliberately picked an easy favor. A simple favor. Except, clearly, it wasn't that simple. Her gut was shrieking that she'd be lucky if this turned out to be a one-week stand. Because the damned bonding marks were still there. The marks that were supposed to be gone this morning. *Be careful what you ask for.*

God. What had she asked for? Reviewing the previous night's events in her head produced only a deliciously sensual fog and some scattered snapshot memories. Dancing in the club. Pushing Zer's buttons because she was tired of being pushed around. Succumbing to the heat he raised in her. Demanding that he bond with her—in exchange for what?

Think. How, exactly, had she worded her demand?

The bonding marks were thick, broad swirls of ink around both wrists, a gorgeous pattern of curves and lines extending from the top of her hands, around her wrists, and up her forearms.

She'd never seen this much ink before.

She was in so much trouble.

His new bond mate blew through the doors of his study as if she had hellhounds riding her ass. He considered warning her that the muttered curses preceding her had given him all the heads-up he needed if his goal had been to avoid her. Somehow, though, looking at her face as she strode across his priceless Karabagh rug and slammed her hands onto his desk, he didn't think she was in the market for strategy tips.

Behind her, Nael looked like a male who was dying by slow inches. He jerked his head up, clearly trying to communicate something of the wordless variety. Too bad the subtlety jerk was lost on Zer. Story of his life, though.

"Leave," she ordered, not bothering to confirm that Nael

was still behind her. No, she took his bodyguards in stride, even if they were flanking her like she was the queen of Sheba.

In her next breath, his new mate fired the opening salvo in her campaign. "We need to talk," she announced.

"Right," he agreed, even though he probably should have made her wait. He needed to establish who was in charge here.

Still, he couldn't stop himself from giving her a quick once-over. She wasn't carrying concealed, that was for damn certain. He was bastard enough to appreciate the view. His mate was wearing a sexy little cashmere tank top and soft lounge pants that clung to her slim thighs and remarkable ass. Mischka hadn't bothered finding his bond mate a bra, and the breasts he'd enjoyed so much last night were threatening to spill out of their skimpy confines with each indignant breath she took.

"You left," she snapped.

Right. He didn't have much experience with this morning-after stuff. Probably, he should have consulted with Brends, but that male had just shot him a knowing look earlier. When he could have given Zer a heads-up that this shit storm was en route.

Zer made a mental note to return that favor at a later date.

"We had sex. And. You. Walked. Out." Her eyes drilled holes through his head.

Agreement seemed like the right move. "You wanted me to stay." It wasn't a question.

They were bound to each other now, whether they liked it or not. Bond mates, even if they were not meant to be soul mates. Somehow, he needed to work with her.

"Damn right. Or leave sooner. Like—three days ago. But, no." She leaned forward. The tank top slid down, baring the soft upper curves of her breasts. There was a smug smile on her face. His eyes narrowed. Was she deliberately teasing him? "You waited until you'd pulled this bonding crap, and *then* you disappeared." She tugged the top back in place.

"Is this about our bonding?" He propped his feet up on his desk because, Christ knew, he wasn't interested in using it for paperwork at the moment. No, what he wanted to do was toss his uptight, indignant bond mate onto the antique surface and remind her—intimately—that she hadn't done a whole lot of complaining last night. He didn't think she was really in the mood, unfortunately. "Or is this about my leaving?"

She stared at him wordlessly for a moment. Yeah, score one for him. Then she inhaled and, damn, he was a dead man. "I'm pissed about all of it." She thought for a moment, tapping a finger against the lacquered surface of his desk. "So much for bonds and connections and all that sentimental bullshit you've been shoveling. It's just the same old, same old. You saw something you wanted, and you took it."

"You had a choice last night," he pointed out. Behind her, the door closed quietly. Nael getting the hell out of Dodge. "And you made it."

"I was not fully informed." Her eyes narrowed. "And you did that on purpose. Undo it. Now," she snapped. Mmm, she tasted delicious. All that feminine anger, the sweet edge of arousal. He drank in her soul like she was a particularly fine Veuve Clicquot.

"Can't," he drawled. "We're bonded, sweetheart."

Hell. He'd known from the start that he should have steered clear of her, but she was just too great a temptation. Those long legs and the sweet soap-and-water scent of her, innocence mixed with just a bite of some more exotic scent. He liked his women with a hint of surprise. Maybe it shouldn't surprise him, then, that all he'd been able to think about when he was around Nessa was burying his cock in her sweet depths and letting the pleasure burn them both.

If she'd known what he really was, she would not have

picked him. Unfortunately, as his little professor was learning, desire wasn't logical, and it sure as hell didn't care about
would-could-should. Even now, the faint, smoky spice of her
arousal was driving him crazy. Had him jamming his fingers
into his pockets before he reached out and touched her.

"This was supposed to be a one-night stand and a simple
favor," she snapped, and something stabbed him. He didn't
care what she thought about him, did he? He *couldn't* feel.
Good thing, too, because she was barreling on with her accu-
sations. A lesser man would have been heading for the hills
by now. "But this is not looking like a short gig. How long
before we're done?"

"I don't know," he gritted through his teeth. "I don't
know, okay, Nessa? What you asked for isn't something I can
pick up in a store, now, is it? You were supposed to ask for
your lab. For grant funding."

"My apologies that my shopping list didn't match yours. I
have a tattoo," she swore, rubbing at her wrists. "You have
any idea how a tenure committee feels about female academ-
ics with tattoos, Zer?"

He could guess.

Righteous indignation colored her voice, and he thought
she'd come straight over the desk at him. This was not going
well. Well, he wasn't happy, either, was he? She was supposed
to be a soul mate. But her choosing him meant that one of his
brothers wasn't getting a soul mate and therefore wasn't getting his wings back.

"You," he said deliberately, "were supposed to be a little
bit more than you turned out to be. You, darling, were supposed to be a soul mate."

"And here I thought you were shopping for a simple bond
for a favor," she mocked.

"Maybe I was in the market for an upgrade. You know
what a soul mate is? Happily-ever-after." He smiled, and he

knew he was handling this all wrong, but damned if he could stop the train wreck. The words just kept coming out. "Romance. True love. You females love that shit. You buy it by the truckload. So, what's not to love about this? When Michael kicked our asses out of the Heavens, he gave us one out clause. Find our soul mates, and we could go back, wings and all." She stared at him, and he had no clue what was going through her mind. "There was supposed to be one soul mate for each Fallen. One perfect female."

She stared pointedly toward his back, looking for the damned wings he didn't have.

"Obviously you're not *my* soul mate," he continued wearily. The bitch of it was, that had to be the truth. He'd bonded with Nessa St. James, had laid it all on the line, but here he was, the morning after, and he still didn't have his wings back. Worse, unless he figured out an end run around her favor, he was *hers* for a damned long time, and so it didn't matter that she should have been a soul mate to one of his brothers. She was stuck with him. And he'd screwed one of his brothers out of his chance of redemption.

Now, she finally looked shocked. "You didn't really think I was a soul mate, did you?"

He shouldn't have unloaded the happy news on her like this, but in for a penny, in for a pound, right? "We did. Your name was on Cuthah's hit list." He shrugged nonchalantly. "He's gotten it right before. What did you think there was between us?"

"Pheromones." She dismissed the strange shock of attraction between the two of them with a casual wave of her hand.

A treasure hunt across her world. For *women.* She was fairly certain she'd never heard of a more misogynistic plan, and she told him so. In no uncertain terms.

"Yeah. A wild goose chase." He closed his eyes, leaning his head back against the ancient leather of the chair. "Or so we thought, until Brends bonded with Mischka."

How would you each find one person, one perfect match? She could calculate the odds of finding one person in all the billions living on Earth—and those odds were infinitesimal. "How?" She found herself stepping closer to the man sitting in the shadows. "How did they find each other?" The words slipped out before she could stop them. He was drawing her in, despite her best intentions.

"Mischka Baran was an accident." He shrugged, not opening his eyes. He looked decadently sexy. And cold. "Brends Duranov wanted her, so he pursued her."

"Harem, much?" She had no intention of endorsing the Fallen's sybaritic lifestyle. They'd made choices—just like everyone else in this world—and she figured they could live with the consequences of those choices.

His eyes opened slowly. "It is what we are. We are hunters, fighters, seducers, love. He wanted her. He convinced her. After they were bonded, however, something else happened. Something"—he shrugged—"unexpected."

When he tossed her the slim vidpod, she caught it automatically. It couldn't hurt to look, right? Data points were good—and the black-and-white images were shockingly clear. Male. Tall. Six-foot-plus. Good-looking bastard, but the bare skin of his back had been marked with some sort of intricate tattoo of a pair of wings stretching from his left shoulder to his right. The thick swirls of darkly inked feathers curled down his spine and were, she decided, stunningly realistic. When she punched the play button, however, she did a mental 360. Now, the tattoo writhed with life. Skin split, and bone reformed as wings tore out of the man's back.

She replayed the vid. Impossible.

"Brends Duranov regrew his wings." Zer stretched out his hand, and, reluctantly, she handed over the vidpod.

"The Fallen don't have wings." She'd have known if there were legions of winged seducers flying around M City. She'd spent enough time staring off into space when she was supposed to be working. Pigeons, yes. Clouds and the usual assortment of weather-related phenomena, absolutely. Winged angels? No.

"We didn't," he agreed. "Most of us still don't. Still, Brends's metamorphosis changes things." He tilted the glass he held loosely in his hand, the ice cubes clinking musically as the neat squares shifted. She'd have bet that one drink cost more than her last grocery bill.

"And yet Brends Duranov suddenly sprouted wings. Does he still have them?"

"Yes, and yes." He eyed her over the rim of his glass. She ignored the frisson of sexual awareness zinging southward as his lips parted to take a sip. "Although I'm not convinced that there was any 'suddenly' about it," he volunteered. "He didn't regain his wings until he bonded with Mischka Baran."

"True love?" She had her own opinions on that. Her mother had spent a lifetime chasing after Mr. Right. Determined, time after time, that *this time*, she'd gotten the right man. It was always the right one—until the next time. When she'd last talked to Mommy dearest, her mother had been preparing for nuptials number seven.

Zer just shot her an inscrutable glance. "You're a scientist," he suggested. "Do you believe in true love?"

"You want me to be this soul mate of yours?"

"No." He sighed. "I don't have any emotions left in me. That's part of Michael's curse, Nessa. I don't feel anymore. I can't."

Had she been hoping he might feel something for her? She was damned if she'd let him see that his words hurt. So she took refuge in hot anger. "You know what I think, Zer?" She crossed her arms over her chest and leaned forward to stare at him. She'd bet he suddenly had a good idea how a lab specimen felt. "I think that's your excuse. It's not that you can't feel. It's that you don't want to." She shrugged. "Fine by me."

He glared right back. "I'm way past redemption. I think most of the Fallen are."

"You don't believe Mischka Baran had something special that brought out hidden depths in your friend?"

He shook his head. "Not that way. Mischka Baran was— is," he corrected himself, "special. But not, I think, unique."

"You don't subscribe, I take it, to the theory that every human is unique and special?" She didn't even bother to hide the mocking lilt to her voice. "Science would disagree with you. We're all genetically unique."

"Evolution." The dark purr of his voice did unspeakable things to her insides. "You're programmed to be different, no two alike. But that still doesn't explain why there were fireworks when Mischka and Brends hooked up."

"Why don't the rest of you have soul mates?" She dared him to answer her. There had to be a scientific reason.

"Because we haven't found them."

"Explain."

"You want the short version or the longer version? When the Archangel Michael booted us from the Heavens three millennia ago, he exiled us here." She knew that. There were books on the subject. "He took back our wings."

Zer smiled, and there was no mistaking the cool menace of that grimace. "Forcibly.

"Of course, none of us was eager to take this deal. But the alternative was even less pleasant." He didn't elaborate, but Nessa could fill in the blanks just fine.

"Michael claimed there was an out clause. All we had to do was find our soul mates." Zer looked away from her.

Nessa had a sickening idea where this conversation was headed.

"*Soul mate* being another euphemism for a *needle in a haystack,*" she murmured.

Zer nodded, and she figured the *Titanic's* captain hadn't looked more bleak when he'd gotten his first eyeful of the iceberg headed his way. "Might as well have been. Michael promised there would be such females out there, one for each of us. All we had to do was find them."

"You were supposed to single-handedly canvas every female human on this planet? Over multiple generations? No wonder you never found any matches." It was a Sisyphean task. Rolling boulders endlessly uphill would have been a walk in the park in comparison.

Zer shot her a wink. "Searching hasn't been *all* hardship, love."

"Sex? You searched for soul mates by having sex with every woman you met?"

He shrugged. "You have a better idea?"

"There has to be one," she scoffed, the wheels in her head already turning. "How many have you found? Honestly?"

Zer looked over at her. "Two. Mischka and her cousin, Pell Arden."

Two. That certainly redefined *needle in a haystack.* "You thought I was one."

"Yeah. Cuthah's hit list"—he rolled his shoulders—"should have been a list of soul mates."

Should have been. Because he sure as hell didn't have his wings back.

"You've found these women?"

He shrugged. "Not yet."

Mischka Baran had read as paranormal on her DNA testing kit. If Nessa knew her genetic codes, that meant Mischka's cousin, Pell Arden, also had. Now, here *she* was. What if there was a genetic marker? She didn't buy that one-man-for-one-woman, happily-ever-after line, as nice as it would have been to believe. What she would believe, however, was that these males were biologically programmed to be attracted to women carrying a certain DNA strand.

After all, she'd been sent here to find DNA evidence.

"I'm not a soul mate," she said again, because it had to be said. "You need to hear me out on this one."

"You were on the list."

She wanted to smack the patronizing smile off his face. So she dropped her little conversational bombshell and prepared to stand the hell back. "I'm a ringer."

He leaned back in his chair, crossing his arms over his chest. "Right. Nice try, baby. I appreciate the effort you're making here."

"Check it out." She slapped her hands down on his desk. "Do your mental voodoo. My name was added to your list. Deliberately."

He shifted, coming to attention. "Explain."

Fine by her. Maybe if he'd insisted on a little more conversation and a little less sex, they wouldn't be stuck in this boat together. Genecore had played the lot of them, but she was the one who was going to be paying the price. All the pieces were falling into place. A day too late.

Which sucked.

"Look," she said, "what you don't know is that I'd gotten put on probation that day you came to my lecture hall."

"I know about that." Zer's level gaze didn't waver. "Who do you think put the pressure on your dean?"

"Right. You decided to upend my life—so you could get what you wanted."

"I offered you something in exchange. This wasn't a freebie," he growled.

"You took away my choice. Or you thought you did. I had that meeting with the dean, and you know how that ended up for me? He gave me an ultimatum, Zer. Three days to se-cure the funding I needed to finish my research on the thirteenth tribe of Israel, or he pulled the plug on the whole thing. My life circling the drain."

"You're more than just your research."

Was she? "I am my research."

"No. You're not," he bit out. "Let me be the first to assure you that you are way more than that."

"Right," she mocked. "Because I'm this soul mate you've been searching for. News flash. Ringer, remember? When the dean pulled the plug on my career—at your instigation—I called in my backup plan. Genecore Foundation had been after me to do some independent work for them. They had DNA samples, Zer. Samples that could prove my theory of a thirteenth tribe. I said yes. What else was I going to do? I had absolutely no idea then that they were anything other than research scientists. That my name was on some list they'd leaked."

"You agreed to work for Cuthah," he said flatly.

"I'm a researcher. I research. Genecore offered me that opportunity—and I took it."

The room was deadly silent. Then, "Fuck." He scrubbed his forehead with his hand. "You made a deal with the devil, darling. Your buyer's remorse is understandable, but pardon me if I don't give a damn. It's not my problem. It's yours."

She stared at him, stunned. "This is not my fault. Genecore came to me—before all this shit hit the fan, I might add—and put a genuine research proposal on the table. I took it."

"And then you found out your new boss was a wee bit psychotic. Right."

"I didn't know he'd added my name to that list you found," she argued.

"Yeah. Finding that out must have been a bitch." Anger churned through his gut. He couldn't lose this advantage. Wouldn't lose it.

Her research had to be the key, after all. If Cuthah wanted

those answers, Zer wanted them, too. And Cuthah would be back for them, he was certain. This could work to his advantage, after all. Thanks to their bond, she was all his. She couldn't refuse him. Not now.

"Way I see it," he drawled, "you get to work for me now, baby."

CHAPTER FIFTEEN

"Close your eyes." The gruff rasp of Zer's voice sent shivers zinging down Nessa's spine and lower. Definitely lower. Nessa had never been playful. Ever. Still, she closed her hands over his and let him lead her forward, one tentative step at a time. "There aren't any walls to bump into," he rebuked her, and she could only hope he wouldn't find it necessary to read her mind. Ever. "Now. Open."

God. His command had her remembering last night. The sweet, hot pleasure and the male who wouldn't allow her to hide from those unfamiliar, overwhelming feelings.

Instead, she opened her eyes and discovered heaven. He'd led her into the heart of a small but state-of-the-art lab. All gleaming stainless steel and glass, the room was crammed full of enough equipment to keep an entire team of scientists out of mischief. "Yours," he said.

Mentally, she compared the new space to her laboratory on the university campus. She'd ruled there. Now, he'd handed her the keys to a new kingdom. It was no little blue box from Tiffany's—it was much better.

"You like it."

God. She loved it. Wordlessly, she nodded.

"Good." He leaned against a wall, folding his arms over that broad chest she'd explored last night. "I've brought your files. Your hard drive." He indicated her aging hardware with a wave. "So, you have everything you need."

To do what? "Why?"

He looked at her. "Why what?"

"Why this? Why give me a lab?" Her eyes narrowed. "Especially since I already *have* a lab, Zer." Did Zer want *her*— or did he want a world-class scientist?

"Across town."

"It's my lab."

"You work here now." There was no mistaking that uncompromising tone. The lab wasn't a personal gift. It was an edict. "You'll be happy here." He shrugged. "Have something to do. You want to study the twelve tribes of Israel. I want you to do it here."

"Thirteen," she said, unable to let his inaccuracy stand. If he was going to upend her entire life, he could at least get the details of her research correct.

He stopped, arrested. "You know that for certain?"

"I've been tracing that diaspora through history."

"Yes, but why, exactly?"

"That's obvious, isn't it?" She blinked at him and stretched her arms over her head, the lithe yoga move full of sleek, feminine strength. "I'm one of them. The real question is: Where do *you* fit in?" She'd like to have the Fallen under her microscope, but she'd always found the Bengal tiger at the M City zoo interesting, as well. No way, though, had she waltzed into its cage to collect a specimen. Did the Fallen deserve the same measure of respect? No. They were the ones who'd forced her into their lair.

She pulled on a pristine white lab coat and added a pair of latex gloves with a decisive snap.

Reaching forward, she plucked several hairs from his head and dropped them into a test tube. "I know I'm part paranormal. You, however—you're a mystery. No one's gotten a good look at your DNA yet."

* * *

Hell. He was jealous of the covetous tone in her voice. His dick hardened, demanding he find a way to make her pay attention to the rest of him with that kind of thoroughness. He wanted her lips curved around him, wrapping her mouth around him with the same kind of pleasure she'd reserved for his DNA.

While he was standing there, staring at her like the worst kind of fool, she was already moving around the lab, her movements precise and economical. Yeah, she was in her element here. He was the one who didn't belong. This was what she did day in and day out, picking apart genetic puzzles the rest of the world had no idea existed.

"Basic biochemistry. We're going to purify you." Her hands moved confidently, adding unfamiliar liquids to the tube from the bottles lined up on the workbench. Discarding pipette tips between liquids. Precise. Pristine. He shouldn't have found watching her work so damn sexy. "You can't be all that complex, Zer."

"You don't think so?" He couldn't keep the amused smile from his face. Maybe they weren't soul mates, but there was something between the two of them. And he was fairly certain she didn't hate him. Even, he frowned, if she apparently had decided he'd make the perfect lab rat.

Capping the tube, she held it up. "Here you go. Your DNA sample. Reaction buffer. A little primer. Purified water." She made it sound like a witch's brew. He sure as hell wasn't drinking her Kool-Aid.

"That's it?"

She smiled, the unexpectedly mischievous grin lighting up her face. "A few other ingredients. Don't get me started, or I'll bore you to tears."

He gave in to the urge and grinned himself, leaning his hip against the wall and crossing his arms over his chest. "You do that often?"

"See? You *can* smile. And boring others to tears is an occupational hazard," she admitted cheerfully. "You came to my lecture. Didn't you notice the meager audience? Plenty of open seats."

He'd had eyes for no one but her, hadn't been able to take his eyes off her, but he figured she didn't need to know that. Instead, he watched her handle the test tube with cool confidence, as if that narrow piece of glass was the focus of her entire universe. When she finally slid the damned thing into a centrifuge and shut the lid, the soft whir of the tube spinning rapidly filled the air.

"Crap falls to the bottom. The good stuff rises to the top. Plus, this cools things down."

Just like life.

Using a pipette, she swiftly transferred his sample from the first tube to a smaller, second tube. She could have been deliberately damaging the sample for all he knew about the scientific process, except he didn't think she had it in her. She had her own code of honor, true. But it was a code, and it wasn't worth any less than his.

Moving confidently, she extracted liquid and dropped colored dye onto slide plates. "Stops the reaction," she explained, sliding the newly christened plates into an oven.

The temperature she punched in made his eyebrows rise. "You want to boil them?"

"Incubate them." She shrugged, sliding off the used gloves and disposing of them in the trash can.

"Now what?"

"Now we wait. You've got five minutes to kill."

And he knew precisely how he was spending each and every one of those minutes. Winning her over was the smart thing to do, and kisses were part of any man's arsenal. Hell, maybe he was winning himself over. To her.

Stepping forward, he pinned her between the lab table and his body. Gently slapped his hands down on either side of her so he could wrap her in the heat of his body. Her shiver wasn't born of fear. Opening his senses, he let himself have just the smallest taste of her soul. Sweet arousal. A delicious uncertainty. Her body tuning itself to his, melting just a fraction.

Dropping his head, he rested his cheek against the soft skin of her throat where the pulse beat hard. God, she loved their games as much as he did, and that knowledge sent arousal pounding through his body. As if he needed the assist. He'd been hard since he stepped into her lab—her territory—and now all he wanted was her. The raw intimacy of losing himself in her body and mind.

She didn't move, but that meant she wasn't moving away, either.

Maybe, she was tired of all the fighting. Maybe, like him, she wanted this moment of quiet.

He pressed his lips to her skin, and she jumped. Inhaled sharply and then just stepped into him. Gave him her weight, her head tipping back so she could search his face for something he didn't know he had to say.

"Do it some more," she said, and he carefully wrapped his arms around her waist. Just holding her and losing himself in the sweet heat of her body and the even sweeter taste of her. One hand tangled gently in her hair, erasing the knot of tension in back of her neck while his thumb drew small circles on her smooth stomach through the thin lab coat and soft cashmere of her top.

"Whatever you want, baby," he whispered hoarsely, the sweet catch of her breath turning him inside out. She smelled so right. Felt so right.

The *ding* of the timer broke the dreamy stillness. He let her go before she could respond. Sliding him a look he couldn't interpret, she stepped away, retrieving her slide and pulling the microscope toward her.

When she bent to look into the narrow eyepiece of the microscope, she frowned, and he wanted to kiss away the sexy little furrow in her brow. If she was allowed to age normally, she'd have a delightful little crease there by the time she was ready to be a grandmother. She wouldn't age while they were bonded, however, and he didn't know if she'd welcome the perpetual youth. Or curse him for it.

She straightened. "Look."

When he looked down the microscope's eyepiece, he liked the idea that he was touching what she'd touched. Unfortunately, that sexy little transfer didn't include any useful knowledge. Whatever she saw on the slide, it was still Greek to him.

"DNA tells us what eye color, hair color, height a person will have—all the physical characteristics." She gestured toward her face. "You look at my DNA, and you don't have to look at me to know that I have brown hair, brown eyes. That DNA is packaged into the twenty-three chromosome pairs we get when we're conceived. Every human has his or her very own recipe."

"It's like a cookbook." He looked at her.

"Yeah. An enormous one. DNA testing can determine your race and your ancestry. We're all walking, talking family trees."

Walking over to the printer, she picked up the printout. She knew that the printout looked dry and dull to the untrained eye, a simple string of letters. But none of it was meaningless, not to her. The patterns sang to her, called her. She was hunting for a very special snippet of DNA, and today could be the day she hit pay dirt.

"I get it. You want to tell me who my parents are."

"Not really." She flicked through the long ribbon of paper, her eyes scanning the dense text. "The direct paternal line isn't what I'm after. I want the mother's. Mitochondrial DNA tracks the maternal line, traces our ancestry back to a mitochondrial Eve. I'm looking for distant matrilinear relatives. Women who share a common ancestor would also share certain mtDNA sequences. I type them, and the same sequences should be highlighted."

"Just the women?"

She smiled slowly. "Yeah. Just the women. Mitochondrial DNA is a female thing, Zer. It passes down through the matrilineal lines only. It turns out we're all related. There are approximately thirty known maternal lineages." Deftly, she plucked the tube from the centrifuge. "So some of us are just more closely related than others, but I believe I've found a new haplogroup."

"What does that mean?" Her eyes watched him, that wrinkle between them deepening. So he kissed her, hard and fast, kissing away the doubt, the little pucker of a frown.

"Many of those maternal lineages and haplotypes are continent-specific. It means," she said with a satisfied smile, the pieces of the puzzle finally falling into place, "that your soul mates share a common maternal ancestor. They're related, and I can spot the markers in their DNA and find them that way. I can identify your soul mates by their DNA."

She would run her own bloodwork and DNA again. This time, she wouldn't be distracted by the red herring of the paranormal gene. She had Genecore's mystery samples, and should could get fresh samples from Mischka Baran. The paranormal gene was a great big blinking neon sign if you knew what to look for. And she did. It would take someone else months and months of study to find the marker. But she'd been researching the genomes for years and would make progress much more quickly.

She wasn't kidding herself. This wasn't the fairy-tale happily-ever-after she'd been hoping for. She'd been looking for aunties and uncles, a grandparent or two. Instead, she'd found the bogeyman. In researching her own bloodline, her own genetic inheritance, she'd found a startling surprise. "We're connected."

"I know."

"Not like that—not this bond of yours. We're connected on a genetic level." It pained her to admit it, but there was no getting around the facts. "You knew this," she accused.

"No, I did not." Those large hands of his examined a tray of glass tubes. "I did not expect you to examine my bloodline."

She shrugged. "It's what I do. Get me more samples, so I can confirm. I need samples from all of you."

"We are not guinea pigs, but I will see what I can do." This was an outcome he sure as hell hadn't foreseen.

"You can identify the soul mates."

"No. Maybe." She hunched her shoulders beneath the white lab coat. "It's not that simple. I can give you the gene pool. I can tell you if someone is a likely match or not. Somehow," she argued, "your DNA got spread around down here. Hypothesize," she ordered. "How could that have happened?"

He wanted to give her a fairy tale. Make it sound romantic. But it wasn't. "Dominions occasionally came down to Earth." For fucking and fighting. Yeah. There wasn't a whole lot of romance going on there. More like shore leave for a bunch of heavenly berserkers.

From the look on her face, she'd drawn the appropriate conclusions. "Reproductive activity." She made it sound like a disease, but, hey, she'd just found out she was the love child of a Dominion slumming with a human woman. He could understand her distaste. "Was that expected?"

"No. Most times, there was no offspring."

Tapping a finger against her teeth, she nodded slowly. "Infertile unions. Typically. But not always. That's just lovely, Zer." She paused, thinking. "But there had to have been more than a few isolated incidents. This kind of genetic change—you find it in a community. People who lived together, in close proximity, for centuries. Long enough for their DNA to reflect that proximity."

He grimaced. "Clearly, not impossible." The ethics of those couplings were strangely disturbing. How could the salvation of his brothers' souls be tied up with the shore leave R & R of their forebears?

"You can tell who the soul mates are by looking at their DNA," Zer repeated.

"I could. I think." She paused, then threw down the gauntlet. "But I won't. I won't give you my research, Zer."

"Why not?" His voice was hard and implacable, all leader now. "I need that information, Nessa. When I gave you the lab, I thought you would work for me. Now, you want to hold out on me?"

"I can't do it." Her voice got real quiet, real fast.

"You won't." He wondered what was going through her head. He supposed he could have pushed his way in, found out for himself. It was what he should do. Instead, he slapped a hand down on the table beside her, rattling all the damn glassware with a shimmy-and-shake of epic proportions. He didn't want to threaten her.

But he would.

This was too damn important. He couldn't afford emotions.

"All right. I won't." She lifted her head and glared at him. "I don't know what you think you're going to do with this information, Zer, but I can hazard a pretty good guess. Tell me you're not going to go haring off after these women. Tell me you're not intending to drag them back here and pair them off with your brothers."

"You don't know these women," he pointed out. "You don't owe them anything."

"No," she agreed. "I don't. But I still think they should have a choice. You may be a barbarian, Zer, but I'd like to think I have a few manners. And some ethics."

"It's not a question of choosing." Hell. He ran a hand over his head. "At least, not yet. Those women aren't safe, Nessa. Don't you think they deserve a chance to live? Because, I can assure you, Cuthah isn't going to play nice. He knew you were looking for this information. If he doesn't get it from you, he'll find someone else to put two and two together."

"Good luck to him," she said confidently. "I'm the best. He can try, but I can assure you, it will be a cold day in hell before he finds himself another researcher who can do this for him."

"Can you guarantee that there were no leaks in your lab?" He drove his point home ruthlessly. "That no one planted a bug in your software? Never looked over your shoulder while you were working? Hell, you had an office full of notes on the thirteenth tribe before I met you. You were that close, Nessa, and he's going to know that, sooner or later. Why the hell do you think he came after you?"

"I know why he came after me," she snapped. "The real question is: Why did you?"

Zer was no poet. No, he was large and bold, all warrior and very, very male. Maybe, just maybe, he could see her for both the researcher and the woman. Clearly, he wasn't threatened by either. He didn't need to prove he was as smart as she. And he sure as hell didn't have anything to prove in bed. He prowled toward her with hungry eyes.

"Let's examine this question of yours." His large, hot hands wrapped around her waist, lifting her effortlessly onto the lab table. "Why did I come after you?" He grinned wolfishly. "Your name was on that list, of course, but the minute I saw you . . . all prim and proper and buttoned-up. You were obviously brilliant, but so much more, too."

Distantly, she realized she was melting into him, her fingers curling into the heavy leather of his coat. His mouth covered hers, one hand sliding up to cup her neck, tracing an erotic pattern on the sensitive skin of her throat. His other hand deliberately flicked open the buttons of the lab coat and pushed down her top.

"This pleases me," he whispered hoarsely. "Very much."

"Good," she moaned, leaning deeper into his touch.

"Sooner or later, you're going to give me what I want," he growled. "Don't underestimate me, Nessie."

Lowering his head, he resumed his hot, heady exploration of her neck. Talented fingers stroking delicately down the exposed curves of her breasts. The soft kiss of his knuckles gliding across her sensitive skin teased her with wicked promise.

When he tongued her nipples, pleasure exploded through her.

Her hands clutched his shoulders. To hell with keeping still. He'd promised to deliver on all her fantasies, so, closing her eyes, she let her hands explore. Slid them down that powerful back, ignoring the obvious bulge of weaponry. His ass was a work of art.

"You're beautiful," he growled as he pushed down her lounge pants. "I like you better in a skirt. You were wearing one when I found you. You challenged me," he growled. "Then, when you picked me at the club, you really threw down the gauntlet, baby. You know what happens when you push a predator?"

She was too busy sliding her hands around to the front of him, sliding open the buttons on his leather pants and wrapping her hands around the thick, hot length of him. "Right. Predators. It's just simple anthropology, isn't it?"

God, it was hard to think with the delicious haze of lust rolling over her. Screw thinking. She could do that later.

Much later. Instead, she slid a hand down him. Smooth. Hard. His husky groan was music to her ears.

Challenge a predator, and he needed to dominate. His teeth closing gently over her earlobe sent a bright thrill of sensation shooting through her, so, wrapping her arms around him, she urged him down onto the table.

CHAPTER SIXTEEN

Snapping on the latex gloves, Nessa pulled material for a dish card. The glassware was still hot from the sterilizer, so she was good to go.

For the past week, she'd worked her ass off in the lab. And when she hadn't been working, she'd settled for staring out the wall of plate glass looking down onto a small courtyard. Right now, the pink glow of the early morning came through the glass, lighting up the rows of tables and workstations. Computer fans beat out a steady hum as the processors did their thing.

Two weeks ago, she'd have named the place paradise. Now? Well, she'd acquired a partner, a heartache, and the equivalent of a biological time bomb. Since she really couldn't stare out the window all day, she settled for rolling her chair over to a lab table loaded with glass beakers.

Zer hadn't stinted on the equipment. Somewhere, somehow, he'd ordered an entire lab picked up and delivered right to her doorstep. She had enough glassware to equip a small country and high-tech equipment that was so cutting-edge, there were probably entire governments who'd never heard of it. And would likely kill to obtain it.

And all the effort had paid off, hadn't it? She could identify the genetic marker in her DNA that identified the soul mates. Yeah. Confetti and champagne all 'round. Of course, she hadn't shared that little tidbit with Zer yet.

Right on cue, the door to her state-of-the-art laboratory opened quietly, and damned if it wasn't her nemesis. Zer had brought coffee and some sort of Danish to sweeten her up. She'd known he was smart. She took the paper cup he offered because she was smart, too, and there was no point in turning down good coffee.

"You got built-in radar?" she asked. Right now, she'd believe anything was possible.

"You find something for me today?" He set his cup down on the table and looked her over. Yeah. This wasn't an accidental visit. None of them were.

"Maybe," she admitted, because she could tell him that much. He needed to know that much. He just didn't have to have the deets. "I've been going through the microbial DNA sequences." Again. Because she couldn't afford to be wrong about this. There was way too much at stake. "I can identify the start and end of the gene sequence. Alpha and omega." She shrugged and waited for him to make the connection.

"The software routines." He ran a hand over his head, and damned if he didn't look interested. "Your computer analysis of our DNA strands."

"Code," she agreed, and she sighed. "I've spent this week processing millions of records and sequences, searching for a particular pattern." A pattern she'd predicted. If there were anomalies in the gene model, she'd intended to find them. One by one, she'd coaxed the fragile DNA strands onto glass slides, scanned them with a microscope, and uploaded the results into a database. The freezers lining the lab wall came with a backup power gen and bank-worthy alarm systems. Locked inside those stainless-steel doors was raw material for decades of research. Genetic gold. So, she'd had no illusions. She'd known he'd be watching.

What had surprised her, though, was tracking the shift in the genome from the purely human to the paranormal.

You wanted to build a human body, the instructions were out there on the Internet. She was piggybacking on generations of scientists who'd picked apart the human genome and cataloged its idiosyncrasies.

Human genomes made humans who they were.

Twenty-three pairs of chromosomes, with the last pair dictating boy or a girl; the others had always fascinated her more. Some things were more fundamental—more *unique*—than gender could ever be. The genomes were a living record of everything her species had done and accomplished in the evolutionary picture of things. Genes that had been there since the first human breathed and stood upright. Genes that reflected all the turns humans had taken on the evolutionary path.

If she was right, one of those turns had happened three thousand years ago, when the Dominions had Fallen from the Heavens. Some of her kind had acquired a new gene. A gene marking them as potential mates for the Fallen.

"What did you find?" His dark eyes examined her face, but he stayed out of her head, which she appreciated.

"We've tracked the migration of the human race from one continent to another. We can tell you how different races of people evolved, by examining their genes. I can trace the soul mates the same way."

There was a long pause, and then he swore colorfully. "You're sure of this?"

"Yes." She took a sip of her coffee, not surprised that it was perfect. He knew precisely what she liked. "I've been looking at mitochondrial DNA as it passes from mother to daughter. I can trace a maternal lineage from one woman to the next. What might have been a harmless genetic mutation once upon a time"—if they were talking fairy tales—"is now a neon soul-mate-here sign. A daughter inherits the genetic marker from her mother and then passes it along to her own daughters."

"Does that make your mother a soul mate?"

He was quick. "It makes her a likely candidate. If I'd had a sister, she would have been another likely candidate. It's not a guarantee, though. Just like not all brown-haired mothers have brown-haired daughters, not all women with the soul-mate marker pass that gene down to their own daughters."

Except the mutation seemed to be regional. The change would have originated with a small group of women—her thirteenth tribe. The lost tribe of Israel.

"So, what's the connection?" He raked a hand through his hair. "You and Mischka are not closely related, if at all."

"We can both trace our ancestry to the lost tribe. As the tribe dispersed and the women moved, the genetic marker moved with them, disappearing into the general population. Have that particular marker in your DNA, that X-chromosome mutation, and you're related to the women who were originally born near the Jordan River and lived there in the same community. Mischka and I share a common ancestor; people who lived in the same geographic region often share certain genetic patterns. Not all of them will have the same genetic patterns, but enough will. We can trace the outward migration of that group, look for that common allele."

From the look on Zer's face, he was connecting the dots fast. "So your research on the thirteenth tribe of Israel wasn't a crock of shit after all."

"No." She shot him a bitter look. "It isn't. It's the academic breakthrough of the century. There's not a journal in the world that wouldn't rush to publish the paper I could write."

"Can you find the other women?" No missing the fierce interest in his voice. Yeah, he'd want to know that, wouldn't he?

"Not all of the women may have had the allele, but

enough of them did. They likely lived in that area for several generations and then migrated from there. They share the same genetic variant. Test a woman, and I can tell you whether or not she's got the marker Mischka and I share."

"You weren't a ringer, after all," he said, savage satisfaction filling his voice.

"No." She couldn't keep the sadness out of her voice. "No, I wasn't." He'd been right. She was a match. Just not for him, it seemed.

"Tell me how I find them."

She understood now that she needed to help Zer find the women. Keeping their identities to herself would not keep the potential soul mates safe.

"You can give me the list and bring me biological samples from each woman on that list. If I type their DNA, I'll know whether or not they're the ones you're looking for. Or—"

"Or?"

"Or, you can approach this from another angle. Go through a larger sample set, typing for hits." When he didn't answer, she continued. "Blood banks, Zer. Hospital records." God, she was suggesting felonies as if they were flavors of ice cream. "Anywhere you can get me the biological matter I need. Hell, you can go scraping the Metro if that's what you want. I can't tell you where those women will be, but I can tell you if they're carrying the mutation you're looking for."

"I don't want you involved in all this anymore. Just tell me how to identify the DNA, and we'll set up a team of scientists to do the actual work."

"Don't ask me to do that, Zer."

What would happen if the whole world knew exactly what the genetic marker was? Her mind supplied a mental picture far too easily of the media feeding frenzy that would result. Worse, what if it turned out that her kit, her little pee-on-a-stick genetic test-in-a-box could identify potential soul mates? She'd upend all their lives. And paint a great big fat red bull's-eye on their foreheads. She hadn't made anyone's life better. No, what she'd done was plunge them all straight into a living hell. Worse, the kit was already out there. It identified those traits—it just didn't say one line for nice, normal human life and two lines for a destiny as the eternal soul mate of a soul-sucking Goblin.

"I'm not asking," he growled. "I'm telling."

CHAPTER SEVENTEEN

A spectacular fuck and a hot favor. Most women would have been pleased with the bargain. It was just too damned bad that she wasn't one of them, Nessa thought as she fled the lab and Zer's demand. She refused to give him all her research yet, and she was afraid he wouldn't take no for an answer. Which explained why she was out here, on the sidewalk, racing toward the university.

He was Fallen. He didn't *have* emotions—she'd had that explained to her, up front, and she'd still refused to believe. He wouldn't hesitate to go looking for the research he needed, even if it meant raiding her former lab. When he wanted something, he took it. She should know.

She'd laid a course for the nearest Metro station. Logically, she knew she couldn't have gotten away unless he allowed it. She knew he could beat her to the lab if he chose to. But she was running, anyway.

All she got now was the tinny voice of a train operator and the soft *shush* of the train sliding into the station, doors opening. She'd hopped on before she could think it over. Part of her couldn't believe he'd just allowed her to walk out. That was the hopeful, naïve part. Logically, she knew he could call her back any damn time he pleased. The bond made sure of that.

By the time she got off the train, he'd made it pretty damn clear that he didn't care where she went.

Some long-dead Soviet architect had decorated the Metro exit with reliefs of entire families of happy Soviet workers. Sadly, their utopia hadn't worked out any better than hers had. She'd known better than to believe in the happily-ever-after Zer had been pushing. Sure, he'd held out the promise of a favor. That was the one funny spot in a pretty damn bleak landscape. He'd expected her to demand a building or a salary. A useful leg up on the university ladder. What she'd actually requested had really thrown him for a loop.

Because she'd asked for something impossible. She'd not only asked him to feel something—for *her*—but she'd demanded it. Yeah, and how was that working out for her? Straightening the cuffs of her no-nonsense cotton blouse, she carefully picked her way up the stairs to the street level, her heels clicking a steady beat. Just to be on the safe side, she wrapped her hand around the railing, despite the germs, because slipping and falling now would be too damn ironic.

Walking across campus this time of year, it was impossible not to observe the student hookups going on around her. It was spawning season, her colleagues liked to joke.

Shoving the sleeves of her shirt up, she examined the dark markings that circled both wrists. Yeah, it was spawning season, all right, and she'd made a mistake of epic proportions. The black markings curled around her forearms, tracing an uncompromising pattern over veins and bone. No hiding these for long.

Still, here she was, right back where she'd started. Heading into her lab. Her time was past up, but she had bigger problems on her hands right now. What she had to do was get in and destroy her notes. She couldn't risk the possibility that either Zer or Cuthah might find them. She needed to destroy her samples. It sickened her to think of deliberately flushing away years of work, but the alternative was unacceptable. Don't think about it, she warned herself. Just go in there and do it.

Sliding her key card over the sensor pad, she pushed open the door when the light blinked green.

She was back where she belonged.

Because she couldn't shake a feeling of restlessness, she took the stairs, not the elevator. In all truth, she wasn't sure she could face an elevator anytime soon. Not until she'd somehow manage to bury the hot memories of Zer's large body pinning hers in one. Pleasuring her. He'd feared he'd hurt her, and maybe he had, but not in the way he'd worried. He'd been concerned about her body. Instead, she'd handed him her heart.

No, she'd take the stairs, thank you very much, until the bitter sting of those memories faded somewhat. Exercise had to be good for what ailed her.

At this hour of the day, the building was still mostly empty; 8:00 A.M. was the crack of dawn for her students, and she knew it. A few lights were on down the hall in her laboratory, though, so some of her RAs had made it in already. Her second clue was the rich, burned smell of coffee and artificial sweeteners. Maybe coffee would be the pick-me-up she needed. Or not.

Pouring herself a cup, she headed for her office. She had to decide what she was going to do next. Looking down at those damn tattoos again, she knew he'd *let* her walk away from him this morning. That burned, but facts were facts. She'd made a deal with a Fallen angel, and there was no going back. Maybe she should have done some begging and pleading, but to whom? Zer was the damn leader of the pack, and he'd already admitted that there was nothing he could do to change the nature of the bond.

Not until he granted her the favor she had requested.

Damn. She should have settled for the lab upgrade.

Setting the coffee cup down on the first book-free surface she spotted, she slid into the banker's chair behind her desk and shoved a hand through her hair. Yeah, and that was another problem. What the hell had she been thinking? She'd demanded all of him, all of that sensual, infuriatingly alpha male. He blamed her for that, and he was right. She'd been so mad that she'd forgotten Mischka Baran's warning: be careful, be specific. Instead, she'd demanded—and gotten—a colossal, open-ended, impossible-to-fulfill favor. Chances were good she and Zer were bonded for life.

And he didn't want that.

Which made her feel like hell.

Not, she mentally added, even as that little inner voice she couldn't quite quash mocked her, that she wanted forever, either.

Shoving aside a stack of professional journals, she pulled the coffee cup closer. Stuff was thicker than tar, despite the handful of powdered creamers she'd dumped into it. Worse, whenever she relaxed, she could *feel* him. Zer. A dark, solid presence in the back of her mind and a constant reminder that that mind wasn't her own anymore. Mentally, she tried shoving him out, but he went nowhere.

Just how powerful was he?

If she could feel him, could he feel her?

The next moment, all she was feeling was a massive explosion from down the hall, knocking her off her chair and onto the floor.

Hot coffee splattered everywhere. Defying all known laws of physics, the cup seemed to contain at least a gallon of the scalding brew. The dark brown liquid pooled, soaking into the books and papers piled everywhere.

"Damn it!" Automatically, she leapt into action, shoveling still-dry books away from the minilake she'd just created, reaching for the roll of paper towels she kept stashed in a desk drawer for these sorts of emergencies.

Wait. Explosions weren't Monday-morning routine here. Only lab on this floor was her genetics laboratory, and explosions were foreign currency there. They didn't traffic in volatile chemicals. Ever. So what the hell had just happened?

Reaching for the landline, she lifted the receiver. Nada. The line was dead, and that was not a good sign.

Grabbing her cell, she flipped it open as she headed for the door. She didn't know who to call, but having a plan felt good.

The plan ran out at the door, however. She should have insisted on a window office. The small, windowless space made her feel trapped, and, given the commotion down the hall, trapped wasn't going to be good. She had only two ways out: the door or the air duct in the ceiling. Since she was no ninja, it was going to have to be the door.

Okay. Next step.

After testing the doorknob for betraying heat, she cracked the door a half inch and listened. All she got was a dull roar—flames?—and a whole lot of screaming and yelling.

Rogues?

Sliding the door open another inch, she peered out. The wall to her laboratory was gone, blown out. This was no natural accident. As the flames licked hungrily at a piece of loose-hanging drywall, the sprinklers finally engaged, dumping water. Worse, looking through the weak flicker of the flames, she had a dead-on view of the large hole blown through the exterior wall. Even from her end-of-the-hallway perspective, she could catch glimpses of sky over the campus quad through the billowing smoke.

So, okay. No way campus security had missed that blast. Calling them was going to be a moot point.

No one was looking her way, which was good.

What was bad, however, were the four very large, very un-familiar males filling up her lab space. She didn't need intro-ductions to recognize them for the predators they clearly were. Equally clearly, they weren't human.

As the fourth male shoved a woman toward a pair of hu-mans, a fifth male came through the hole. His wings rippled as he landed on the floor, sending out a shock wave of raw power.

Yeah, she definitely had trouble on her hands.

Weighing her options, she tried to estimate just how many of her RAs or students might be in the lab.

Worse, she was playing sitting duck where she was. The minute she stepped out of the office, she'd be right in their line of sight. Maybe she'd get lucky and catch them off guard, but she wasn't going to bank on it. It was growing smokier in her office, too, despite the valiant efforts of the building's antiquated sprinkler system to dampen the flames. Nothing lethal—yet—but she couldn't stay where she was, not forever.

Voices echoed, bouncing off the walls of the lab, and booted feet crunched over broken glass. Outside her office, someone sobbed, and a male yelled. She recognized that voice. It was Brad.

The rogues were rounding up her students.

The carnage was delicious. Opening his senses, Cuthah drank down the delicious cocktail. He didn't need the emo-tional drug the way the Fallen did, but that was like saying he was a recreational drug-user and not a hard-core addict. He could walk away, but why should he? This was pleasure, pure and simple. Here he was, stronger than ever and front and center at M City University. The university where the Fallen's newest soul mate had her lab. He hadn't missed the protective streak in her—any more than he'd misjudged her stubbornness. She'd left G2's an hour ago, running as if someone had lit a fire under that lovely ass of hers.

Since she hadn't gone back to her flat, and since she had nowhere else to run, Cuthah figured she'd do the predictable thing. She'd go to the university lab.

All he'd had to do was wait for her, and then part two of his plan could kick in. He was betting that Nessa St. James was still 100 percent human, even after her close encounter with the Fallen. She wouldn't like hearing that Cuthah had gotten his hands on her students. In fact, Cuthah was betting she'd go after him just on principle.

She'd want to stage a little search-and-rescue, and he had just the welcoming party for her. She wasn't going to know what hit her any more than the students at her university would. There was no better way, he figured, to lure her away from her Goblin's protective embrace.

Sympathy. It got humans every time.

The new doorway he'd opened up in her lab wall was going to be useful in more ways than one. No point bothering with the stairs, he figured, when an explosion made his point so much better. Snapping his wings closed, he ran his gaze over the room. The mazhyk tingled over his skin as his wings shifted back into the tattoo on his back.

The laboratory was standard-issue and nothing much to look at. Of course, his boys had created a hell of a mess here. The broken glass, collapsed shelving, and burn marks made quite a calling card. Indeed, the chaos was downright delicious, but even better were the hostages. Early as it was, three of Professor St. James's research assistants had already made it into the building. He'd bet they were regretting that. Two girls, one boy. More or less intact, although the boy was nursing a snapped wrist and a bruised jaw. Shouldn't have tried to take on his rogues, but humans seemed to give in to the adrenaline rush first and use logic later.

Much later.

"Ladies and gentleman," he said, and heads snapped up. "Now that I have your attention, I have a question for you."

The girl nearest him merely sniveled, but the boy snapped to indignant attention. "A question?"

"Yes. Have you seen your charming professor this morning?"

"No." Boy human shook his head vehemently. Of course, even if he had, Cuthah knew he wouldn't have shared that information. Not willingly.

Not yet.

"Really?" He said the words lightly, stepping forward. The crying girl only cried harder, but the other two students were watching him. They knew things were headed south, and they were right. When he pulled out his fyreblade, its bright light lit up the room. All eyes tracked the sharp edge, so he was certain he had their full attention now. "Are you quite sure?"

"Yes." The boy sounded desperately glad, so Cuthah figured he was telling the truth. Pity.

"Well, then," he said, and he stopped talking. Drew just the tip along the edge of the boy's throat until he could see the crimson trickle of blood against the soot-streaked white lab coat. The boy swallowed hard and tried to take a step backward—the adrenaline must have been wearing off finally—but a quick jerk of Cuthah's head had two rogues stepping up behind him, forming an impenetrable wall. So all the boy met was an immovable surface.

"We could wait for her," Cuthah suggested. "Or, perhaps—" He stopped, and the blade stroked down the exposed throat a second time.

Nessa's graduate student stared at the winged creature holding him, a lamb in the teeth of a wolf, and there was nothing—nothing—Nessa could do to head off the disaster she saw coming. Did Brad have any clue what was headed his way? Of course, the lab's new entrance should have been all the heads-up he'd needed.

"Perhaps what?" Brad swallowed again, the blade nicking his Adam's apple. The move might not have been intentional on Cuthah's part, but he clearly didn't have any issues with bloodshed.

She'd seen the dead woman on the quad. She should have had a plan. After all, she never went into a situation without one. And yet, here she was, facing public enemy number one, and she didn't have the faintest idea where to start.

Cuthah's face twisted, the snap of his wings folding and closing on his back too loud in the tense room. Somehow, she'd expected angels to be terrifyingly beautiful, all golden skin and hair. Cuthah had the terrifying part down, all right.

Her fingers flipped open the cell. She was way out of her league here, and she knew it. *Call Zer.*

"Perhaps Professor St. James hasn't made an appearance yet," Cuthah said softly.

Her grad student didn't blink, caught in that cold gaze.

"Or perhaps she has. Perhaps"—Cuthah moved the blade to the other side of her student's neck—"you know that." The girl on the floor had stopped crying. Marlene. She'd started last week. Professor Markoff's lab was going to look damn good after this episode.

Cuthah looked over the boy's head at one of the rogues. "What do you think?"

"Sire?"

"Do you think this human knows where our professor has gone?"

The rogue's eyes flicked down to the student's face. Paused. Moved back to Cuthah's face. "Unlikely, sire."

Cuthah sighed. "Undoubtedly, you're quite right."

God, maybe, this could end well. "Then," Cuthah continued, "I suppose there's really no point in my keeping him, is
there?"

A single, casual flick of the ethereal blade sliced Brad's
throat open. When Cuthah released his grip, blood foun-
tained, and Nessa hit send on the phone. God, let Zer be
there. Bond or no bond, she needed the sound of his voice.

She needed his help.

His low, hard greeting made her pause. Would he still help
her even though she'd refused to help him? He'd want to protect his investment, right? Even if he didn't think she was his
soul mate, he still believed she was a match for one of his
brothers. Suddenly, watching one of her students dying on
the floor of her lab, she didn't feel like splitting those hairs
with him anymore.

"Zer—" How did she start? Where did she start? She
knew he had to hear the noise coming from her lab. The
screams as the two women realized what had happened. She
didn't want to think about what the other noises meant.

He didn't hesitate, didn't waste time rehashing their early-
morning argument. "Tell me what's happening."

Her throat froze up, but she still had her eye pressed to the
crack of the door like a damn coward. She should make herself go out there, but she couldn't.

"Nessa." His low growl was all the warning she had before she felt him pushing at her mind through their mental
bond, tasting the fear paralyzing her. He snapped an order to
someone in the background.

"Tell me where you are, baby."

"The lab," she managed. "I came back to the university
lab."

"And then what?"

Her mind blanked, and she had to force herself to focus.
To examine the evidence. It was just another experiment. Not

real. "There was an explosion." She whispered the sequence of events rapidly.

"How many of them are there? Tell me who did this, baby." She could hear the sounds of Zer's males in the background, a low rumble of sound that was strangely comforting. She wasn't alone. "This is my job, Nessa, not yours, so you let me do it." His voice was firm. "I'm moving now, so you keep your head down and stay put. We'll be there in ten. How many of them are there? Give me a heads-up here, and it will be taken care of sooner."

She pressed her eye to the crack again, counting once. Twice. "Four rogues. And one other."

Snapping a vid, she punched the send button on the cell. Her efforts didn't seem like much.

She felt rather than heard the short, pithy curse from the other end of the line. "You know him," she guessed.

There was a telling pause. "Yeah, I do. That's Cuthah. He's not going to bother you for long, though. Are you doing what I asked? You got a place there to lie low?"

She looked around the small office wildly. Not as if she had an abundance of choices. Hiding under the desk seemed like a desperate measure. She looked out the door again. Cuthah and his rogues had secured her two female graduate students. One sharp gesture, and two of the rogues peeled off. The hallway suddenly seemed way too short to hold the rogues strong-arming office doors open.

Think. She had to think. "They're coming," she whispered.

Zer's curse blistered her ears. "Eight minutes, baby. Buy me eight minutes. Tell me where you are inside the building."

"My office."

"Exits?"

"There's just the door." A door that led straight in a direction she didn't want to go. "And the air vent." Although she suspected that nothing human would fit up there.

She registered a momentary pause on the other end of the line, followed by the slam of a door and the roar of an engine. No way he would get here in time. "Can you fit up there?"

She eyed the narrow space, the distance between the ceiling and the floor. Impossible. Still, she hurried to flip the lock on the door. No way that would keep the rogues out for long, but since she had a feeling she was counting her life in minutes now, she'd take every second she could get.

CHAPTER EIGHTEEN

Crashing the SUV through the glass doors of the lobby was remarkably satisfying. Fortunately, the university provosts were cheap-ass bastards who hadn't upgraded the facility in years. The glass was old and the doorframes even older. When he hit, the frames pulled away from the building's Sheetrock with a dull roar and the high-pitched shriek of twisting metal.

Showtime.

Rolling out of the SUV, Zer came up firing, Vkhin covering his back. The first rogue out of the chute went down hard and fast, temporarily disabled by the full clip in his lower intestines. Zer ignored the snarl of pain coming from the endarkened face glaring up at him and settled for taking full advantage of the bastard's temporary incapacity. One clean slash of the blade, and the bastard's head rolled from his shoulders. Zer was pissed enough to have done it barehanded, but the knife was quicker, so he used that.

Moving fast, Vkhin took out the second male while Nael pulled gear from the SUV's trunk. Plenty of incendiary party favors for this little shindig.

"We're in," he snapped into the mouthpiece of his headset. "Get me rolling."

He toed the body with his boot, but he'd done his job, and

the rogue was still dead. He didn't know where the dead Fallen went, and he wasn't in the mood for philosophy, anyhow.

Keros's familiar voice in his earpiece barked quadrants, and Zer flipped into full soldier mode. Right now, he knew precisely what to do. Whom he was going to kill to get to his bond mate. Right now, that was the plan. What he did afterward, when the mission was accomplished, he had no idea.

He'd figure it out later.

"Got it," he acknowledged into the mouthpiece before relaying their new set of directions to Vkhin and Nael.

Reaching into the totaled SUV, he pulled out his duffel bag and slung it over one shoulder. The familiar weight made his back a walking arms depot.

He was getting his female out, even if he had to shoot the whole place to pieces.

Inhaling, he scented trouble right away. Another rogue was holed up, waiting for him to come sauntering down the hallway. As if this was some sort of gentlemanly hand-to-hand combat like the Archangels used to have. Well, the Heavens were a long way off, and none of them were the warriors they'd once been.

"I want a clear path," he snapped. Dropping down behind the wrecked SUV, he took aim and fired, taking savage satisfaction in the dull thud of the bullet hitting flesh. One more down. A single shot like that wouldn't be fatal, but the bullet would buy Zer time. Take the bastard a while to regenerate a spinal column.

In his ear, Keros barked a heads-up, the click of his fingers working the keypad audible even over the static-filled connection as he pinpointed incoming.

Sure enough, a trio of rogues edged out into the hallway. More, then, than Nessa had thought. Some tactical Einstein had dragged all the classroom furniture out into the hallway, and piled everything up to block off easy access. As if the tangle of ancient desks, portable whiteboards, and metal storage cabinets would stop Zer. Well-armed, one rogue was palming a sweet Glock while the second lay down covering fire. Ducking down behind the SUV, Zer sent up a quick prayer the rogues didn't score a lucky shot and hit the gas tank. Baby was armor-plated, but that would only get him so far.

Beside him, Vkhin methodically squeezed off rounds. Up, aim, and fire—the brother's weapon never stopped. The bark of each bullet was followed by the hollow, wet sound of lead punching through flesh.

"Move it," Vkhin said, dropping down behind the SUV and holding out a hand for the reload Nael slapped into his open palm. Yeah. He'd noticed that the rogues' bullets were punching a Lite-Brite pattern in the SUV's black paint job, trying to connect the dots with the gas tank.

"You know where we'll find your mate. We'll clear a way in." Nael palmed his own weapon, laying down a thick hail of bullets when one of the rogues decided to take a chance during the brief pause. Bastard hit the ground hard and didn't move.

"I need a route," Zer hissed into the mouthpiece. Keros wouldn't let him wait out this shit, and Nessa didn't have time to burn anyhow. "Hook me up now, damn it."

"Park your ass, and take a number." Zer could hear Keros exchanging information with another brother in a low, hard commentary. Since bullets were kicking up the linoleum under the other end of the SUV, peeling back the faded checkerboard in short, hard bites of sound, Zer figured he needed some hurry-the-hell-up. They were in serious danger of being pinned down if they stayed here too long.

"Logical north," Keros relayed. "You got one corridor clear of debris straight ahead. Take that. I'm uploading building schematics now."

Zer checked his handheld. Shit. Of course, that laid a course straight through the welcoming posse. Couldn't be helped. "We go through there," he said, jerking his head toward the too-full hallway. "Nessa is that way. Upstairs."

"Got it." Jamming down the safety lever of a concussion grenade with one hand, Nael grabbed the pull ring with his teeth and lobbed the bugger nice and easy at the posse of rogues while Zer and Vkhin laid down a little covering fire of their own. Dropped flat as the grenade hit the rogues' barricade and bounced. Three, two, one. The blast rocked the kill zone, generating five meters of hell as the TNT exploded out of its iron casing. The resulting shock wave rocked the lobby.

The grenade didn't have the pincushion effect of a frag grenade, but Zer was more than happy to hit cleanup. Hell, yeah.

Vaulting over what was left of the SUV, he took out two remaining rogues: the first had been well within the ten-foot burst radius. Another bastard was staggering like a day-old drunk, hit hard by the shock wave.

Stepping forward, Zer raised his blade up and over his head, bringing the sharp edge straight down in front of him. Drew the blade through flesh and out as he stepped back.

The path was clear enough now. Silently, he examined the dead rogues at his feet.

The males were unfamiliar. Soul thirst had worked its usual carnage, twisting their faces to mirror the endarkening of their souls. Rolling the bodies, Zer sliced open the military-issue flak jackets to uncover the crimson tats on their backs. Sure enough, the bastards had cut a deal.

"Sending pics," he bit into the mouthpiece, whipping out his cell to snap shots of the wing-shaped markings. "I'm going in," he snapped, nodding toward the hallway Keros had called out. "The two of you are going to find yourselves a nice little spot for a diversion. I want every rogue left in this building headed your way—we clear?"

Vkhin's hand tightened on the Glock he hadn't bothered

holstering. He would buy Zer some time, some space. But there was going to be plenty of fire to go around.

"Christ, Zer." Nael didn't look happy, but Vkhin's eyes locked on Zer's, cold and knowing.

"I need time," Zer repeated. "You buy me that time, and everything's good. Split off, and go around the other side. Blow some shit up. Do what you need to do. But. Get. Me. That. Time."

Vkhin's hard nod was all the acknowledgment he needed. He didn't like sending Zer in alone, but the brother had never gone back on his word. Not once in three millennia.

"You go after her, but we're going to be hard on your heels once we've given you this diversion," he warned.

"Go," Zer ordered, and Vkhin and Nael peeled off, headed down the opposite corridor at a quick jog.

The grenade had opened up the hallway nicely, blasting a new entrance. Fine. He'd take what he could get. His rogue was in full-on hunting mode, demanding out. It wanted to rend. Tear. He could feel his control slipping, but right now he needed to keep a cool head. In his ear, Keros spat more directions as Zer ran up the now-clear corridor.

"Upstairs," Keros finished. "Two more rogues. And Cuth-ah." Savage satisfaction filled his brother's voice. This hunt was going well.

"Any civvies?" The information was good to know, but nothing was going to stop Zer from cutting his way to his mate and hauling her ass out of here. Today, he was listening to the instincts screaming for him to go in, guns blazing. The civvies could drop and cover—or not. Mentally, he added them to his checklist as he took to the stairs. He'd avoid it if possible, but he'd take the collateral damage, too.

"You got two closing," Keros warned, and Zer inhaled, confirming the targets as he cleared the stairwell. "Nessa's halfway down the corridor. Five doors. On the right."

Moving down the hallway on silent feet, Zer counted off offices and lab space. Glass blown out of the doors littered the floor, and someone had stamped a bloody handprint on one wall. His rogue growled at the scent of blood and fear in the air, because everything screamed that humans had bitten it hard here. One body, but that was all he saw. He didn't stop to check the stats. Maybe, the human was dead. Or not.

"Got one up ahead," he acknowledged into the mouthpiece.

Showtime.

The rogue charged out of the blown-out laboratory door on Zer's right, going straight for Zer's throat. Sidestepping, Zer let his opponent's momentum drive him into the opposite wall. The crunch of the rogue's face hitting Sheetrock was satisfying.

The second bastard was already charging out the door. A quick look-see over his attacker's shoulder revealed a windowless office, a soulless cubbyhole of space with no way out. Zer spared a thought for the poor bastard condemned to work there day in, day out. Should have taken today off, that was for certain.

The rogue came flying at him, pulling a fyreblade. Shit. He hadn't seen that coming. Backpedaling, he swung his weight to the side, blocking the blow with his own blade. Space was too close for grenades—and he sure as hell wouldn't be able to get off any shots with the Glock tucked into his waistband.

"Dance with me," he growled.

Hand-to-hand it was. Baring his teeth, he grabbed his opponent's wrist and twisted. The rogue backed up two steps, but not far enough. Bastard still had space enough to bring the blade back up. And down again.

A ribbon of liquid fire streaked along his side. "Hit," he cursed into the mouthpiece. The angelfyre wound burned like a motherfucker. Only advantage to being Fallen was, he no longer had a soul. Sure, the injury hurt like a bitch, but it wouldn't take him out. Not yet.

"Zer, my sire, you okay?" Keros's voice came over the earpiece, hard and loud. "You want me to send in reinforcements?"

"I'm good," he gritted out and then waited through the pregnant pause.

"You tell me if you're not," Keros said finally. "The rest of us will come. We've got your back, my sire."

Yeah. That was the problem. They'd had his back when he'd taken on the Archangel Michael, and look where he'd led them. One-way ticket to hell, so he wasn't making matters worse now.

"I bite it, you come in after Nessa," he ordered. He could justify that much. She was too valuable to lose, and not just because he wanted her so bad, he ached with it. She had some powerful knowledge locked up in that brain of hers, not to mention her potential to be a soul mate. None of them could afford to lose her.

"Will do." Keros paused, and Zer knew his brother was still considering making an end run around his sire. Hell, it was what he would have done.

"You stay there," he ordered. "I need my gatekeeper. I need to know that this isn't a distraction, that Cuthah isn't unleashing his own personal hell on the rest of M City. I'm out, Keros." Battle lust had his rogue struggling for freedom. "You hold the fort down for me, and I'll be back."

The rogue with the fyreblade was already making the return trip, swinging with everything he had, but the narrow space was hampering his blow. A hard kick to the chest sent him plowing through a specimens cabinet, the metal doors banging open and spilling a shitload of glass beakers and vials onto the floor.

"Sure as hell looks like our new sire can give us our wings back, now, doesn't it?" The bastard facing him taunted. He had wings, all right, and his eyes tracked Zer's quick up-and-down flick over his back. Hadn't shifted, though, which made sense. Wings in this small a space could be a death sentence. "Yeah," the rogue went on, "I figured, if there was a way to get my wings back, you could count me in. I spent three thousand years in fucking exile, and it seemed pretty clear that you weren't going to get the job done. Every brother for himself, man, and I don't plan on getting screwed. Again. This time, I'm aligning with the winner." The rogue paused a beat, clearly enjoying what he believed was the upper hand. Since the intel was handy, Zer didn't disillusion him. Yet.

"You come looking for someone?" The rogue smiled, a mean, hard smile. "She walked right into it, didn't she?"

Cursing, Zer pushed back, wielding his sword in short, hard strokes. Pushing the rogue toward the wall until he'd wiped the smile from the bastard's face and backed him into a corner where he couldn't get that blade of his up. Only one of them would walk away today, and they both knew it.

"You shouldn't have brought her into this." He raised the blade overhead. "She's mine." The truth of that reverberated through him.

"She's bait," the rogue argued, but Zer was done conversing.

One clean cut through the spinal cord, and he was wiping his blade on the rogue.

"She's mine. And you lose."

Now, all he had to do was get in, get Nessa, and get out.

The image of her in his head was his only anchor, the only thing keeping him from drowning in the soul thirst. Violence rode him hard, his inner rogue clawing for release in mindless depravity.

Moving carefully, he slipped through the building. In his earpiece, his brothers barked directions. Instructions. Hell, he didn't like drawing them into this. Any other time, he'd have hunted on his own. Today, though, he didn't have the time to spare. He needed to get to Nessa. Fast. She'd turned off her cell, but he didn't miss the fear spilling through their bond. She was keeping it together, but she was no match for Cuthah, and they all knew it.

He should have been sending her waves of reassurance through their bond, but he was fairly certain that all she was reading from him was 100 percent, pure, lethal killer.

"Blast in three from our boys." Keros's soft warning sounded in the earpiece, warning him to stop his forward momentum and brace. Vkhin and Nael were in place and had a little incendiary what-the-fuck for Cuthah. Still, even knowing it was coming, Zer was shaken. The blast rattled the building; shelving collapsed all around him with the musical crash of breaking glass.

When the power died on cue, he counted out the long seconds in the dark, moving swiftly on memory of what he'd seen. When he hit the ten-second mark, the emergency gen kicked in, and the lights sputtered back on at half power. Perfect.

"Hard right. Five paces." Keros's voice lasered in. "You've got access paneling above you."

Sure enough, moving aside the paneling in the ceiling, he pulled himself up into an air duct. The piping took a hard right, and Zer followed it.

Sitting in her office, Nessa ran through her options. Thank God, the explosions seemed to have distracted Cuthah and his rogues. No one had come knocking on her locked door. But it couldn't be much longer before someone discovered her.

The air vent sliding open overhead just about gave her heart failure.

Zer dropped down lightly, landing smack in the middle of

her desk. Now, she decided, probably wasn't the time to quibble about her paperwork.

No greeting, no explanation, no soothing words—just the hand he extended to her, which she took before she could overthink it. His sharp tug pulled her to her feet. "You evac, now."

CHAPTER NINETEEN

"I'd love to get out of here," she snapped back. "But how? Last time I looked, the hall was full of rogues."

"I'm going to battle my way out of here, with you right behind me."

"Then you're just going to go on out there and die," she said, and she could hear the desperation in her own voice. "Why?"

"Why not?" Was he not speaking the same language as she? "Fighting's what I do, baby. I'm not a politician. That's not what I was bred to be."

"You weren't bred to be anything, Zer," she said, and he recognized her stubbornness. This was where she'd start the whole you-chose-your-destiny schtick, and he'd have to disappoint her. Again.

"I defend," he repeated gently, because part of him wanted to be who she believed he was. "I kill. It's who I am."

"But Cuthah and his rogues are on the other side of that door," she pointed out. "You're outmanned and outgunned."

He stopped loading up on weapons for a minute and stared at her. He was packing an arsenal, and they both knew it.

"We need a plan," she said. "Some kind of an edge. If only you could get your wings back, like Brends did."

He looked at her as if he was half expecting her to take

notes. "He found his soul mate," he pointed out. "That's the key."

"All right." She stared at him expectantly, as if somehow he came with a mazhyk wand he could wave and—presto— she'd be his long-lost soul mate. "That's your hypothesis."

"It's not a hypothesis. It's the truth." He glared at her and started sliding weapons out of the bag.

"It's what you believe," she said unflappably. "Tell me exactly what happened when he regrew his wings."

He shook his head. "You want a play-by-play of his love life, baby? I can do that, but I don't know if we have enough time here for either of us to enjoy the story."

She shot him that look that made him want to undo all her buttons. See if he could shake that unflappable calm of hers. "He was having sex?"

Best damned sex of their lives, if Brends's account was to be believed. "You want to give it a shot, baby?"

She stared off into space for a second, clearly thinking. "But he and Mischka had had sex before?"

"Yeah. They had."

"Were they"—she blushed—"trying anything unusual?"

He hadn't demanded too many details, but he'd witnessed the bonding ceremony for Brends. "It was just sex, baby."

"Right. So no unusual positions, no—"

"No," he growled. "But I can promise you, they both enjoyed it."

"So, what made it different?" She looked up at him. "Or was it the number of times?"

He hadn't asked for those kinds of details, but maybe she was on to something here. Maybe there was a pattern they weren't seeing.

"What makes the wings happen? If it's not kinky positions and not a certain threshold of events, then what causes the wings to appear? Why didn't it happen the very first time?"

"What difference does it make? I'm not getting my wings back, because we're not soul mates." He wasn't letting her go there.

"Are you sure?" She eyed him. "I'm not saying I *want* to be soul mates with you—"

Hell, she made it sound like taking out the trash or paying a particularly unpleasant trip to the dentist.

"But how do we really know, Zer? What did they do that we haven't done?"

He shrugged dismissively. "We know you're a soul mate because you were on Cuthah's list, and he's been dead-on right so far." Emphasis on *dead*, given what had happened to most of the females on that list.

"But obviously you're not *my* soul mate."

"Prove it." The professor voice was back.

"No wings. There's your proof."

Her eyes narrowed. "You're holding out on me, Zer."

She wanted facts? He'd give her facts. Before he could re-think it, he described exactly what Brends had told him about the night his wings had regrown.

"Brends said he gave Mischka everything that night. No holds barred." He hesitated. "He gave in to every dark urge he had, came close to going rogue."

Leaning forward on the desk, he braced his forearms on either side of her. Caging her in his heat. "We all run that risk. All those emotions, those feelings you humans have, we drink them and then, sometimes, we don't stop. We keep on drinking, keep on drawing on your emotions through the bond—you end up dead. That was Michael's little price tag when he exiled us from the Heavens, took our souls and our wings from us. You want to tempt my control?" He smiled against the skin of her throat, feeling the pulse jump and throb as she processed what he was saying. "Brends didn't hold back, love. And I won't either."

"Show-and-tell—or something more, Zer?" She rose and turned in his arms until she was trapped between the desk and his body. The pure, sweet heat of her jolted through him.

"You think that's sexy, love?" Deliberately, he slipped his mental chain just a little. He knew his eyes glowed silver in the dimness of her office. "You think you can handle what I've got?" He shrugged casually. "I'll do you, if that's what you want. If that's your fantasy."

"I'll be unstoppable," he growled, and the damn scent of her skin, the shell-pink flush of her arousal, made him want to say to hell with this battle. To hell with Cuthah. He wanted to wrap her in his arms and carry her away somewhere safe and love her. That was the fantasy, though, and not the reality.

"I won't be gentle, and you're not going to be able to stop me."

He ran his hand down her forearm. A shudder rippled through her, leaving a trail of gooseflesh "You want an edge of violence to your sex, that's fine." He could dig that kind of fantasy. "That's what Brends gave Mischka. He had her on that bed of his so fast and hard, she didn't have a chance to scream. Just him and her and the bed. You want that kind of hard, rough sex? That make you wet? You want a warrior riding you, dominating you in bed?"

"Maybe." Her voice was a husky whisper in his ear.

"You want to do this, or not?"

She glared at him, and damned if he didn't get a raging hard-on. He was a sick bastard, no doubt about it. He knew *he* wanted it, and that scared hell out of him. But he wasn't in any mood to man up and discuss how he felt with her. That was his business, not hers.

So why was his hand stroking a soft little path down her arm?

His eyes narrowed. And she wasn't saying no, thank you,

now, was she? Color flushed her face, and her fingers were curling around his forearm.

"You want to try that with me?" Was that his voice, making that request? "I should warn you, though, that I don't have a good track record, not when it comes to the females. Last female under my protection, she died, and it was my fault. I didn't keep Esrene safe, so maybe you should think that one over first."

She froze. "Esrene?"

"I didn't love her," he said quickly. "But she mattered, yes. She was Brends's pairling. I was his leader. I'd sworn to protect both of them."

"And you did." She was sure of this.

He eyed her grimly. "I did. I went after the Archangel, vowed to cut him down him on sight."

"The Archangel Michael."

"Yes." He rolled his shoulders, training his gaze to the weaponry spread out on her desk. His large hands assembled the small arsenal with lethal familiarity. When his gaze met hers again, his hands stilled. "Yes," he said again. "But it was all a setup. I still don't know why Michael took responsibility for Esrene's death. Hell, maybe he *felt* responsible. I did. I let Cuthah lead me around by the nose. Worse, when I attacked Michael, I broke the cardinal law of our kind. I defied an Archangel's orders. I refused to accept his authority. The penalty for that should have been death." He fit the barrel onto a gun with a soft *snick*. "Instead, I started a war. Too many of the males who fought under me decided to fight for me, instead."

She moved to stand behind him. Trouble was, her hand was on his neck, rubbing at the tension there. She wanted to comfort him—and he didn't want that comfort. "You did what you thought was right, Zer. How can that be wrong?

The other Fallen chose to follow you. That was their choice to make."

"No." No point in candy-coating what had happened. Loading the clip into the gun, he sighted down the barrel. "I was their leader. Hell, I *am* their leader. That makes it my responsibility." Setting the gun down, he looked around at her. "I started this war, and now I have to finish it."

He was warning her off. She got that. So she shouldn't have savored the hot, hard heat of his body for even a moment before stepping away from him. "How? What's your plan, Zer?" Striding around to the front of the desk, she slapped her palms down on either side of his. "And what's my part in it, really? Is there a part for me—or have I already played it? I may be mostly human, but that doesn't make me any less than the rest of you."

He sighed. "Believe me, I'm aware of that."

"Are you?"

"Yes." He shoved away from the desk, and she watched him come, filling the too-small space with his heat and size.

"I'm not this soul mate you were searching for." Even though part of her traitorously wished she could be that woman.

He made an impatient gesture. "I never thought I had one."

Why not? "Then, what—?"

He cut her off, gently turning her around. Sliding her up onto the desk. Weapons shifted with a metallic chime as he slid them to one side. Making room for her. She couldn't even protest the soft rain of paper—her paper—onto the floor. She didn't care, she realized. Time had stopped.

Placing one finger against her lips, he cupped his other hand gently against the back of her neck. "I wanted you for one of my brothers. I wanted to save at least one of them."

"You can't make those kinds of choices for them."

Something dark flashed through his eyes. "I know that."

"Now."

His slow, masculine smile had her melting. "Yeah, now. So maybe you chose the wrong male, or maybe, Cuthah's list was wrong, or maybe, he got the wrong woman. Even if you're not a soul mate for one of the Fallen, you're helping us defeat Cuthah's army. You've brought us one step closer, and I won't forget that, Nessa St. James." He said her name like it was a promise. A vow. "I owe you for that help, and I swore I'd keep you safe, no matter what the cost."

The sounds from outside—from what had been her lab—grew uglier. More violent.

"You don't need to do this for me."

Looking her deep in the eyes, he hesitated. "I need to do it for me." He paused, then plowed ahead. "For us. Whatever you are or aren't, Nessa, you mean everything to me."

She had never thought to hear those words from him. And now that he'd said them, he meant to go out there against impossible odds and lay down his life for his brothers. For her.

Zer filled the too-small space of her office. His large hands spread out on the cluttered surface of the desk. Large, strong hands that drew her eyes and held them. Hands that had brought her exquisite pleasure, hands that would protect her, no matter what the cost. She was mesmerized by the way his dark T-shirt clung to his chest; he was wearing his usual black leathers and those damned boots. He'd shed the duster, but only because, she was sure, dragging the damned thing through the air ducts would have been impossible. When he moved, she couldn't tear her gaze from those strong, muscled forearms and that devilish swirl of black ink. Ink that screamed he belonged to her every bit as much as she belonged to him.

"We go up." He jerked a thumb toward the air duct in the ceiling. "That's the plan. I take you out through the ducts before I take on Cuthah."

"I'm not leaving you. And what about my students?"

"Your students are collateral damage, Nessa." He spoiled his tough-guy image by adding, "I can't get them out. Cuthah has them pinned down in your lab." He could have forced her acquiescence. They both knew it. Between the bond and sheer brute strength, he didn't have to ask her permission for anything. But he didn't.

"No," she repeated. He folded those arms over his chest, then settled into in her poor banker's chair, kicking his booted feet up onto the desk as he smiled that slow, devilish smile of his, accepting the impossible odds she'd just handed him. "You got a new plan for me, then, baby? You want to take me up on my offer?"

Scrambling to straddle him, she threw one leg over him, letting the sides of her white lab coat slide open around them. He grabbed her shoulders, halting her downward slide. Beneath her spread thighs, he was hot and tense. Nowhere near as relaxed as he pretended.

Brushing her thumbs over his jaw, she mimicked his earlier actions.

The strong, hard line of his jaw was as uncompromising as the man himself. Sprawled on his lap, she had a front-row seat when his eyes swept up and met hers in a cool, mocking challenge. "Sex, right now? You surprise me, baby." There was something else there, though, lurking under the surface. He wanted this. Wanted her.

What if she could be what he needed, after all? According to her genes, she *could* be his soul mate. Okay. Someone's soul mate. She had the genetic marker—all she needed was the man.

She eyed the male lounging below her with a purr of satisfaction. And she'd found him. Now it was up to her to convince him to stay.

With her.

It was up to her to make him lose control. So he could find his wings. And keep his life.

Lowering her head, she took his mouth in a hot, slow kiss. God, she loved his lips. Hard and firm. Just the brush of her mouth against his had now-familiar desire uncurling through her. He felt so good. Sliding her tongue deeply into his mouth, she feasted on him. Beneath her, he groaned, a husky, masculine sound that had her creaming.

Lifting her head, she stared into his dazed eyes and smiled slowly. "Take me, Zer."

"You sure you want to do this?"

She leaned forward, cradling his cock in the sweet vee of her spread thighs. He could see the pink flush of excitement on her face as she nodded her head. Her hands went to the hem of her skirt, sliding the fabric upward. The gentle brush of the fabric shot straight to his cock. "I'm sure," she whispered. "One hundred percent."

"You told me nothing can have a hundred percent success rate."

Her tongue licked delicately at the corner of his mouth, and he shivered. "This can. *We* can."

She wasn't holding anything back anymore—and that was sexier than hell. She was giving him everything she had. No holds barred.

He leaned back in the chair, giving her more room to work her magic. Her fingers teased open her clothing with deliberate, sensual provocation. The tempting curves of her breasts had him tunneling his fingers through her hair to hold her still for his kiss.

She melted into him, and he never wanted the moment to end.

When he finally broke off their kiss, he realized what he wanted to say to her. What he needed to say to her. "I love you." His eyes sought hers. "I love you, baby."

She pulled back, her gaze suddenly uneasy. "Why?"

Stroking the tumbled hair away from her face, he said,

"It's not science, Nessa. It just is. Can you tell me why you love me?"

"I never said that I do."

"But you do." If she didn't, the phrase *an eternity of hell* took on a whole new meaning. So, he'd just have to coax the truth out of her.

Smiling wickedly, he reached for her.

CHAPTER TWENTY

His smile should have warned her. Sensual. Male. Arrogant. His cock stirred beneath her, the only thing separating them her panties and his leathers. Her arousal was a thick, liquid swirl of sensation between her legs. Shifting, she spread her thighs wider, rocking against the thick, delicious ridge. He was so damn beautiful.

"I'm going to make you say it, baby." His sensual warning made her wetter. He leaned back in the chair, the powerful muscles in his arms flexing as he settled her more firmly into place, wrapping one arm around her waist.

"Maybe," she teased, sliding her hand between them. Unbuttoning his pants was the work of a moment, and then she was wrapping her hand around the impossible girth of him. Long and hard, his cock was a delicious weight in her hand. Fascinated, she slid her hand up and down the satiny, heated length, rubbing her thumb over the engorged head.

"Tease me, baby," he growled, "and I'll make sure you keep every promise you make." His hand on her waist tightened, his face twisting with pleasure. So she leaned forward, deliberately fisting him.

"I want you." He was impossibly hot and large, his flesh straining against the hand she'd wrapped around him. All that golden, heated skin so near was a tease she couldn't resist, so she settled against his chest, using her tongue to trace a sensual pattern down his chest. When she tongued a nipple still covered by the soft cotton of his shirt, a harsh growl tore from his throat.

"Be sure," he warned. "I've tried to keep you safe, baby. You didn't know what you were getting into when you entered my world. I've held back, before." His free hand stroked a path up her arm. "I don't know how this will end. You need to tell me you're good with that."

His fingers flicked at her nipples. Her eyes watching those diabolical fingers, she stared at him. "I want you." Resting her hands on his chest, she looked him in the eye. He wanted truth, so she'd give him truth. "I want this. Whatever happens, Zer, I want this for us. I want us to try. You'd never hurt me. I know that."

"Be very, very sure. Sure enough for both of us." That wicked hand now rested over her heart. "Because I can't be, baby. I want to keep you safe. I want to hold you here, forever."

But he couldn't. No one could. Outside this room, there was a storm waiting to break. Somehow, together, they had to find a way to stop what was happening. And, if they couldn't stop it, she wanted these memories, for however long they lasted.

The expression on his face was fierce, protective. "I would do anything to keep you safe," he vowed.

"Then let me do the same for you," she whispered. "Let me keep you safe, Zer. Let me help, if I can."

An expression of near pain crossed his beautiful, dark face, and then that hand was moving again, exposing all of her to his gaze. "You win, baby. You want to give me what I want to take, I'll take it. I'll take you."

All primitive, hard warrior, he filled her office, filled her world, until there was room for nothing and no one but him. He was the answer to every secret fantasy she'd had at night, alone. His words plucked a raw chord hidden deep inside her. His gaze on her bared breasts burned through her, and she reveled in the exposure.

"You're beautiful," he promised, his voice reverent. She *felt* beautiful. His eyes glowed with heat. But his hands. Those big, rough hands were strangely gentle. Petting the soft skin he'd exposed as if she was something—someone—rare and precious. As if she was the very center of his world, too.

His hands cupped her breasts, the calloused fingers stroking the bare skin softly.

"Undress for me." She wanted to see as well as touch him. Wanted as much of him as she could have. She was shaking with the pleasure he was giving her.

"No," he said, and she whimpered. "Not here, baby. It's not safe. I need to be able to protect you."

"Then take this off at least." Her hands tugged at his T-shirt, and he let her pull the material over his head. The feeling of being naked while he was dressed, her bare skin brushing his, filled her with incredible pleasure, but she wanted to be closer still. Skin to skin. "Please undress for me," she begged, but he shook his head. "Why not?"

"Because," he said gruffly, "when I need to fight, I'm not doing it bare-ass naked."

She'd have to make do. Get a little creative. She could do that, couldn't she? Pushing him farther back in the chair, she slid down his body. His powerful arms tensed, sliding away from her waist to grip the chair.

She smiled slowly. He was so hers. All hers. "You want me to do this, don't you? Want me to taste you?"

"Yeah, baby," he growled hoarsely. His hands came up to fist gently in her hair, guiding her down. "I want to watch you, too."

Teasingly, she lowered her head, letting her hair brush against his straining erection. Her reward was another husky groan, his sensitive flesh jerking toward her. Arousal pounded through her body, thick, heated jolts of pleasure. She'd never been so hungry for him. Knowing that this might be the last time she held him. Had him.

"You're killing me," he murmured, his eyes half-closed. "This is not a good idea." Unmistakable tension filled his large body, had him riveted to the edge of the chair. He wasn't in charge here—not anymore. She was, and, God, it was every erotic fantasy come to life.

Bending down, she took the thick, hard jut of his cock into her hand. Delicately scraping her nails down the smooth shaft, she licked a decadent path up his straining flesh, tasting the musky salt of him on her tongue. "I want you," she whispered against his flesh. "I'm going to have you just like this. I don't care who or what comes through that door— right now, you're all mine." Just mine.

His answer was a husky groan that shot straight to her core.

"I'm going to kiss you," she promised, looking up into his eyes. "And I'm going to watch you, every step of the way. Every touch." She paused, sliding her hands around to cup his balls. "I want to feel close to you."

She wasn't closing her eyes. Not this time. She was desperate for every inch of him. She wanted—needed—to see what the raw intimacy of this kiss did to him. For him. There was every chance that they were all out of tomorrows. If this was the last chance she had to touch him, she wasn't going to miss a single second.

Gently, she sucked on the firm head, tracing the damp slit with her tongue. If she turned her head, she could rest her cheek on well-worn leather and the hot, smooth flesh of his thigh. Cupping his balls with one palm, she slid her other hand around the base of his shaft, guiding him into her mouth.

The large head of his cock filled her mouth. She fisted him

as she pulled him in deeper. Palming what wouldn't fit. The raw intimacy of the soft, sucking sounds and the glide of her palm over his wet flesh wrapped the two of them in an intimate world of their own. His hands tangled in her hair, guiding her into an intensely personal rhythm even as his ragged groan of pleasure drove her crazy, the wet ache building deep inside her.

His big hands closed gently in her hair as he slid slowly in and out of her mouth, her gaze watching the thick, wet shaft.

Let go, she whispered through their bond. She opened up, letting down all the mental barriers, letting him feel her arousal, her feelings through their bond. She could feel his pleasure, the hot sensations tearing through him, and she sucked harder, pulling him deeply into her.

His mate's wicked mouth was killing him with the hot, wet pleasure of her touch. Arching his back, he drove himself deep into that willing mouth, losing himself in the emotions sweeping through their bond. As she tasted him, drew him deep into a sensual maelstrom, he could hear the sexy little sounds of her pleasure. The fiery burst of sensation made him grit his teeth, as she raked his aching cock with her tongue.

He'd done this before, but never had the act felt so intimate. He'd never felt so connected. The sensations tearing through him were white-hot in their intensity, a liquid burn that threatened his control. God, he had to touch her. Know her.

Before he could come, he pulled away from the wicked heat of her mouth. He wanted to be buried deep inside her when he came. Ignoring her whimper of protest, he tugged her upward. "Your turn, baby," he whispered hoarsely. "Now, I'm seeing to you. Time for you to come and come hard."

Flipping her onto her back, he was on fire for her. She

arched into him, her hands sliding over his shoulders, down his back. Pleasure for pleasure as he parted her legs and crashed against her.

"Zer," she moaned, as he nipped at the sexy curve of her ear.

She was his, and she was killing him. He couldn't think about the battle. Couldn't look beyond this moment, this woman in his arms. This wasn't a weapon—*she* wasn't a weapon. There was only her and him and this pleasure growing between them.

Dipping his head, he kissed her. The brush of his cock against her sweet opening almost had him coming on the spot.

Fuck. He had to keep it together. Had to make this good for her.

"I'm going to take you, baby." Had to. He couldn't, wouldn't, stop. Not now.

Sheltering her with his body—just in case, his rogue side whispered—he slid into her, hard and fast. Filling her. Beneath him, she cried out in pleasure, arching her body up into his.

"You feel so good." He lowered his head, burying his face against her neck. "So damn good, Nessa."

"More," she pleaded, arching up against him. "I need more."

She wanted more; he gave her more. It was that simple. He set a hard, fast pace, moving in and out of her with smooth strokes. Lifting his head to watch her. Watch the pleasure overwhelm her as he moved deep inside her. God, this was something *more*.

You couldn't ever *know* a person, not completely. But you could love someone with every fiber of your being.

Hell, he didn't know himself.

Still, he knew one thing. "I love you," he growled against

the damp skin of her neck. Wrapping his arms around her, he pulled her closer. Driving in and out. The sweet, tight friction of her flesh wrapping around his, holding him close, was sending him right over the edge. And she gave, her sweet flesh parting, taking him in completely. He couldn't control it anymore; the room filled with the raw, intimate sound of flesh on flesh and her breathy moans.

He'd have crawled right inside her if he could have. Curled up inside her soul.

"Oh, my God, Zer," she panted, her hands flexing, her nails driving into the flesh of his shoulders. He reveled in each small, possessive prick. He belonged to her. He was *hers*.

"Nessa . . ." he whispered.

His hands were pulling her closer, closer. No him. No her. He'd lost both himself and her in the impossible pleasure. When he came, his roar of pleasure almost—but not quite—drowned out her own long, low moan of ecstasy as she went to pieces around him, her pussy sucking on his cock in short, hard quivers.

Panting, breathless, he buried his face in her neck, inhaling her scent, as he poured himself into her.

Her hand came up, stroking over the nape of his neck. "I love you." Damned if her words didn't rock him right to the bottom of his lost soul. Before he could figure out what to say, she pulled him closer, wrapping her arms around him. "I love you, Zer."

Opening his eyes, he stared down into her wide-open eyes and her wide-open soul. Christ, she was giving it all to him. Everything she was—right there on display for him.

And then the indescribable pain hit him.

The skin of his back split wide open, as if someone was peeling the muscles from his bones one by one. His mind blacked out for a blissful moment, and then the pain hit him like a semitruck barreling down the highway his body had become.

Beneath him, Nessa tensed. "You okay?"

He rolled off her, onto his side, onto the floor, with a groan. He figured *okay* was the overstatement of the year.

He wasn't. Something impossible was happening here, and he was helpless to stop it.

His lips peeled back with the pain and rage of it all. He didn't do helpless. Ever. And yet here he was, laid out on the floor, completely incapacitated.

Another liquid bolt of agony jolted through his body, and he panted his way through it. When he fought free of the fog slowly squeezing him, Nessa's hand was stroking his shoulder.

Wrapping a hand around her wrist, he pulled her back down to him. Sudden knowledge roared through him. *The Change. The* real *Change.*

God, he was Changing. For the first time in millennia, his words were pure prayer.

She hesitated, clearly worried. "You okay, Zer?" She didn't have to add that he looked bad.

"Yeah," he groaned, breathing through another gut-wrenching contraction that had his spine bowing. "We're just getting what we wished for."

"No!" Her gaze shot to his back, horrified, and he knew it looked bad. "You didn't tell me it was going to hurt."

With one last, agonizing push, the wings tore through the skin of his back, slowly unfurling. He hadn't realized how empty he'd felt until now, when he was overflowing.

He wanted her to stay.

Unfamiliar joy hummed through her veins. He really did love her. After all, he'd said the words—and she'd said them back, hadn't she? And she'd meant them. Telling Zer exactly how she felt—well, that had felt right. They were no poets; she figured that theirs had to have been one of the briefest declarations of love in M City's history. Still, warmth flooded through her.

He was spectacular. His new wings were flexible, pure muscle where the base of them connected to his body—and a fifteen-foot wingspan to lift his two-hundred-plus-pound frame from the ground. He shuddered and stretched, expanding the dark wings as he sat up, running a hand along her arm.

"You okay?" he asked.

She nodded. She wasn't the one who'd just, for all intents and purposes, birthed a pair of enormous wings. She had a pretty good idea, too, of just how painful that process had been.

"May I touch them? Your wings?" She had to know what they felt like.

He eyed her cautiously. "You go right ahead."

Before he could change his mind, she stretched out a hand. The tip of the wing closest to her was firm and light. Birds, she knew, had strong, light bones, hollowed out by millennia of evolution to give their owners every advantage in the air. Like a bird of prey, he'd be a powerful flyer. Those wings would push him through the air with hard, brutal strokes. Not intended for a lazy, slow glide, she thought, but for the short, hard bursts of speed necessary for taking down prey.

And for the sheer brute power required for flight.

Running her hands over the soft surface, she cataloged what her senses reported. The central section had three bones, with two in the lower section to fuel the powerful downward thrust of those wings when he lifted his body upward into the sky. Evolution or divine planning had designed his wings for maneuvering quickly and taking off rapidly. They were, she realized, exactly like the wings of a raptor.

That description fit. Zer had the wings—and the heart—of

a predator. Even now, as he shoved himself off the floor and came toward her, his every move was fast and sure. He didn't hesitate, just laid in his course and stuck to it. Behind him, his wings gleamed blackly, the midnight inkiness of the feathers on the outer edges blending with the gathering shadows in the room. No, those wings weren't built for lazy, graceful flight but for speed.

"What did we do?" she murmured. Because this had taken both of them. Together.

And something had been different this time.

He extended a hand to her, but she couldn't take her eyes off those wings covered with deceptively soft feathers. Stroking her fingers over them, she savored the softness that was such a stark contrast to the male himself. The wings were all satiny weightlessness where he was hard, heavy, dark. Savage.

He didn't hesitate, the words he gave her as brutally direct as the man. "I love you," he repeated. "Those words changed things. Changed *me*."

She wanted something, but she wasn't sure what that something was. He wasn't the only one who had changed. She wanted to pull him back into her arms, savor the unexpected closeness.

"You think that's all it takes?" Because she'd loved him before he'd stepped into her office today, and there had been no wings.

He shook his head. "We have to talk about this now?"

She wasn't naïve. She understood what Cuthah was capable of. But *now* might be the only time they had left. "I want to understand," she said.

"Christ, Nessa." His big hand cupped her jaw, turning her face toward his as he drank in the sight of her. Resting his forehead against hers. Impossibly close. "It's about not holding anything back, okay? You *know* me. You've seen parts of

me, parts that shouldn't see the light of day, let alone someone like you."

"Someone like me? I *love* you, Zer." She wasn't ashamed
to admit she loved him. He might be dark, but he was still a
male of worth. A fighter. Her warrior. He'd made hard
choices, and he'd kept on fighting. He wasn't a consolation
prize, wasn't a dirty little secret she needed to hide away
from the rest of the world.

"I love you, too," he said roughly. "You're part of me,
body and soul, Nessa. And I wish—" He hesitated, then kept
right on going. "I wish all my brothers had found their soul
mates. Because, what we have . . . it's more than the wings.
What we have, it's me and you and . . ." His voice trailed off.
"I'm no poet. You're the heart of it all. The heart of me. And
that," he said forcefully, "is why I have my wings back and
we're even having this goddamn conversation."

CHAPTER TWENTY-ONE

Keros was on the headset again, barking out a 411 Zer didn't want to hear. Diversion time was over, and Cuthah was headed back. He'd chased Nael and Vkhin halfway around the building, but there were only so many things his brothers could blow up before they brought the entire goddamn building down. They'd bought him the time he needed, though. That was all that mattered.

Zer ran a quick mental check of the new arsenal he was packing: wings. Holy shit and then some. He didn't know if regaining his wings would give him the tactical advantage he needed against Cuthah, but he'd take any weapon fate handed him. Except they were more than just a weapon, weren't they? He couldn't shake the memory of Nessa sliding her fingers through his wings. And the sensation was more than purely sensual recall. Sweet and intimate, it was the kind of feeling that made a male forget he was about to head into battle.

Pull it together. That's what he had to do. Focus on the fight. Afterward, maybe he could take in the incredible possibility of happily-ever-after. But to get there, he had to take care of Cuthah first. A quick look around the too-small office made it clear wings were a liability and not an asset in the confined space, so he needed to take the fight elsewhere. No problem.

"He's going to be here soon." He pulled a blade from his belt. Nice and light, the edge was still killing sharp. "We're clear on the plan, right? You stay here, nice and tight. Just in case, though, you're taking this."

She didn't hesitate, reaching out a hand to wrap her fingers gingerly around the handle of the blade.

"You ever use one of these before?"

When she shook her head, he gave her the 411 on the basics. "Keep the blade close to you. Both hands on the handle, point up. You need to wait until he's real close. Last resort only, you got me? This is insurance, baby. I'm not letting Cuthah get past me."

She let him adjust her fingers on the handle until he was satisfied. "You're going to stop him."

"Yeah," he said. "I will." He had to. No way he'd let her fight his battles for him. Still, he'd feel better knowing she was armed.

Holstering his weapons, he strode to the door and unlocked it. Cuthah would be gunning for him—he had no doubt of that. Plus, given Cuthah's earlier meet-and-greet in Nessa's lab, he figured the Dominion would be back real soon. So, the sooner Zer got into position and assessed the lab for a logical line of advance, the sooner he could get on with that happily-ever-after.

Sure enough, the sonic boom of Cuthah opening a portal sent shock waves rippling out before Zer even had the door fully open. "You ready?"

He felt rather than saw her nod.

"Showtime, baby." The building was shaking all around them, the power of Cuthah's arrival threatening to bring the walls down around them. Furniture crashed across the hall, the particleboard walls bowing out from the pressure.

"Be careful." Her fingers stroked a little caress down his wings. "You hear me, Zer? Watch your back out there. I want you coming back to me."

Stopping, he cupped her face with his hand, pressing a hard kiss against her mouth. "I promise you, baby. I'm coming home." Despite his promise, the anxious look on her face warned him his scientist was running the numbers in her head, and she didn't like the odds.

Well, that made two of them.

"Cuthah has to take care of business here. We can blow his cover, baby. Blow it wide open. He'll want to kill you more than ever now, because you're a soul mate."

And she knew how to find more soul mates for the Fallen. Yeah, that little secret hung in the air between them. She was a walking, talking divining rod.

For a hundred reasons, he had to stop Cuthah's violence here. The memory of Esrene's dead body taunted him, reminding him he'd failed the other female. He hadn't protected her. He should have. Worse, Cuthah had used Esrene's murder to manipulate Zer, leading to the expulsion of the Dominions.

Yeah, it was time to even the score. And all he had to do was wait. Cuthah was hell-bent on reaching him and this female.

He had to eliminate Zer once and for all, or everything he'd worked for went up in smoke.

Cuthah exploded into the far end of the narrow hallway, a freight-train roar of wings and rage. Zer tucked Nessa back into a corner. "You do what we discussed." His hand on her head pressed her beneath the desk. "You keep your head down. You don't move."

Glass blew out of the exterior windows as Cuthah strode down the hallway, unleashing a lethal storm of glittering crystals.

Inhaling sharply, she nodded and disappeared from sight.

He knew she wanted to do something, anything. Sometimes, the hardest thing to do was to stand back and let someone else fight for you.

Raising his blades, he strode to the doorway. All around him, the walls vibrated with power, and the floor rippled in long, slow waves. Like being trapped in the epicenter of an earthquake. He hoped like hell the building was less ancient than it looked. Before he could clear the door, the wall fronting the hallway exploded inward, and he lunged toward Cuthah, thrusting the blade with lethal force toward his enemy. His arms locked around Cuthah, pinning the bastard's wings shut.

Cuthah snarled, rage twisting his face. "Thought I'd flush you out here." He turned, slamming Zer into the wall.

Unfortunately, hiding beneath her desk and her newly wall-less office, Nessa had a ringside view of the violence. And there was no mistaking the cold promise of death filling Cuthah's eyes.

"Wings? Nice try," Cuthah sneered.

In a blur of speed, Zer went at Cuthah, bringing his first blade straight up and down. If Cuthah had been human, he would have been dead. Instead, he ducked, closing the space between them once again. Her breath caught, but Zer sprang away and resumed his circling. In the next moment, they were driving their blades at each other with vicious, deadly intent. Eyes locked. Arms and shoulders slamming into each other with each powerful strike. Their wings tangled, beating a harsh drumbeat accompaniment for the battle.

Zer's eyes locked on his opponent's, his face a harsh mask of determination. Driving his body into Cuthah's, he sent the other angel staggering into the far wall.

Cuthah just took the punishment, shaking off the blow and launching himself back into the fight. "That the best you can do?"

God, they were evenly matched.

Pressed up against the imitation-wood panels of her hidey-hole, she couldn't take her eyes off the fight or the deadly beauty of the two impossibly large bodies pummeling each other. Wood cracked as they crashed through a wall.

"I can do better," Zer growled harshly. Leaping at his opponent, he landed his blade, carving a deep furrow in Cuthah's forearm. Cuthah hissed and staggered, his lips tightening in a rictus of pain as he backhanded Zer with his other arm, the metal handle of his blade catching Zer on the cheekbone.

Agony blazed through their bond, leaving her shaking before Zer abruptly cut off the connection. God, she didn't know how he could stand the pain. She tried to pour love and support through the bond. She didn't know if he could feel it or not, but she needed to do something.

Zer got to his knees. That was good, right? His skin was turning purple where Cuthah had struck him.

"Ready to die?" Cuthah taunted.

Zer's second strike drew blood from Cuthah's now-useless hand. He'd cut through sinews and tendons to expose the white gleam of bone. "Not yet," he grunted.

Stepping forward, he swung the blade in an even, horizontal line. Cuthah countered as if he were hefting a baseball bat. Reversing direction, Zer cut at Cuthah's other side, scoring a long, shallow cut. Eventually, Cuthah had to feel it, but when?

Damned if she was going to sit here underneath a desk while her mate got his ass killed in front of her. Eyes narrowing, she assessed the situation. She wasn't naïve enough to think she could do anything to help with his fight against Cuthah. Not unless she had a rocket launcher tucked into her hidey-hole. Which she didn't. Oversight, there.

There was no time to formulate another plan. Cuthah vaulted into the room and over the desk, filling the space between her and the wall. Adrenaline pumped uselessly through her body, her heart making the impossible leap from her chest to her throat.

"Well, hello, darling," he purred. "I believe it's time you came out to play." Reaching under the desk, he wrapped a hand in the fabric of her blouse and dragged her up, pinning her against his body.

Cursing, she kicked desperately at his legs. There was no way she could reach the blade Zer had given her. She wanted to spit with frustration.

"No," she choked out, before his arm tightened ruthlessly around her throat. Spots of color danced in front of her eyes as the oxygen fled her lungs.

Cuthah laughed, giving her body a little shake. "Just like before, isn't it?" he taunted Zer. "Here I am. There you are. And you don't get to me unless you go through her." When he took a step backward, she went with him.

"Trust me," Zer said out loud, and she had just a moment to wonder if the message was for Cuthah—or for her.

In the next moment, Zer thrust his blade through Nessa.

CHAPTER TWENTY-TWO

Oh, God. The first two breaths were an agony, her lungs struggling to keep up the inhale-and-exhale routine even as the blade erupted through her heart and out her back, and the sight of Zer's face only made the pain worse. His eyes never met hers, never left the traitorous Dominion standing behind her, his arm locked around her neck. The sharp curse behind her was the last thing she heard before her body shut down and gave up the losing battle.

Her spirit rose up and out, clearly done with her body. She fought panic for a moment. This was going to be okay. It had to be okay. Still, she couldn't stop staring at her body. Zer's blade had pierced her heart, gone straight through her and planted the business end of all that metal deep in Cuthah's own body. She supposed that should have been satisfying, but nothing could have prepared her for the sheer horror of watching her body slide down that ruthless blade, the unmistakably bad sign of blood everywhere.

She wanted to say something, because this was the moment she was supposed to go all poetic, wasn't it? She knew instinctively that she had maybe seconds left, and somehow that time needed to count for something. But there was no way to shoehorn a lifetime of emotion—of living—into the handful of seconds she had left. Instead, all she got out was

his name—and damned if it didn't sound more like a prayer—
and then she was sucked ruthlessly away by an unseen
power. As if she'd been wrapped in warm, bright cotton
wool, she shot up and out of her body and the lab as if she'd
spent a lifetime waiting for this moment.

Oh, God. She really was dead.

Air popped around her as her feet hit ground, depositing
her somewhere unfamiliar. Instinctively, she knew she wasn't
in the world anymore. There was nothing, however, that
could have prepared her for her first sight of the Heavens, the
wide, low plain spreading away from her. By now, Zer had to
know what he'd done. He had to have seen the damage he'd
done to her. Did he care? She had to believe that he did. Tentatively, she tested their bond. The connection was stretched
thin, vibrating with tension. Like listening to a tinny, over-
seas phone call on some Third World infrastructure. *Hold
on.*

She waited, but there was no further message from the
other side. Okay. Looking cautiously around, she took in the
intense, saturated colors of the plain. The air was warm but
not too warm. On the horizon, a silver and glass city soared
up into the sky. And the sky, God, the colors of the sky made
her wish she'd been a painter and not a geneticist. Words didn't
begin to do the azure sky justice.

Mountains surrounded the plain, and it looked as if the
cosmic express she'd just taken had punched straight through
the dark rock. That ride had seemed to last forever and yet
take no time at all. Maybe that was how death worked. It
wasn't as if she'd done this before.

The sound hit her first. A pretty little melody of birds
singing. There was wind, too. Exactly like one of those relax-
ation soundtracks they sold down at the drugstore. Too perfect. Her body was all light and ghostlike. When she held her
hands up in front of her face, she could see right through
them. Definitely, not one of her better days.

She wanted to go back. She wanted Zer.

The soft beat of wings approaching convinced her now was not a good time for self-pity. She needed to pick a plan and get with it. Because, when her head came up, there was a glowing angel winging toward her. She didn't know if her day was about to get better—or worse.

God, she didn't know what to do.

She wanted to just sit down and think things through, but time was a luxury she sensed she didn't have. Zer was fighting for his life, and she couldn't bear the thought of his losing. She hadn't been able to do anything for him. She looked behind her, and it was like looking through the wrong end of a kaleidoscope, an unearthly window into the hellhole of her office.

From her office came a low, guttural sound that reminded her of a wounded animal and a keen of metal on metal like nails on a chalkboard. The sound advertised, loud and clear: death coming here. She could almost smell the thick, coppery scent of blood in the air. At least Zer finally had backup. As she stared at the unfolding picture, Vkhin and Nael joined Zer, fighting shoulder-to-shoulder with him like medieval warriors. The heavy blades flashed in their hands, the muscles bunching in their shoulders as they slowly pushed their way forward. Each brutal blow shivered the air, and there was dark purpose in their eyes. They had their fighting faces on. They were not Goblins but not quite human either. *Dominions.*

The wing beats stopped, so she whipped her head back around, praying the strange window stayed put. She couldn't bear losing that tenuous connection to Zer. The angel facing her was massively broad-shouldered, a golden-skinned threat whose dark blond hair had been cropped close to the beautiful planes of his skull in a brutal trim. His eyes were a window into hell. Dark. Fiery. Tormented. He looked over her shoulder and into her window on the familiar.

"What do you here, soul mate?"

That voice scared the piss out of her. It sounded like the end of the world. The deep basso was way beyond cold. Emotionless and ancient, that tone warned her that this new companion simply didn't give a damn about the events unfolding around her.

And she'd thought the Fallen were emotionless. This angel made them look all touchy-feely, filled with the warm fuzzies.

"Believe me," she said carefully, "I'm none too sure of that myself. One minute, I'm standing there in my office, and the next I'm being skewered like a shish kebab, and there's a hell of a pop, and here I am."

The angel seemed to look at her for the first time. His gaze traveled down over her torn blouse and skirt. Paused for a moment to take in the silvery ghost blood painting her chest. "You are a soul mate," he said again.

"News flash." She tugged at her blouse. "That doesn't seem to have mattered."

"Does your soul mate still live? With whom did you bond?" The angel stepped closer to her. Close enough for her to reach out and touch the blindingly white feathers on the massive pair of wings jutting from his back. The wings stirred, disturbing the air. Maybe, Mr. High-and-Mighty wasn't as laid-back as he appeared.

He sounded like he wanted the scoop on what was unfolding back down there in her lab.

"My soul mate is the one who ran me through. He killed me."

The angel jerked backward. "Impossible."

"Ummm. No." She indicated the blood-stained front of her blouse. "Does this look like a wound someone could survive? And now, somehow, I'm here."

"He cannot kill you because you cannot die. Not while you are bonded to him and he lives." The angel's wings beat harder.

"And you know this, how?" Because if that was all true, maybe he could send her home.

"Because"—his ancient gaze looked through her—"I am Michael."

Diplomacy could wait. "This is all your fault." She took a step forward, anger bubbling up inside her. Zer was down there, fighting for his life. And she was here. She was sick and tired of feeling helpless. "You're the one who condemned the Fallen three thousand years ago. You kicked them out of the Heavens, ripped off their wings, and exiled them. I don't give a damn what you thought they'd done—you were wrong. They didn't deserve the shit storm you handed them."

She whirled, gesturing toward the otherworldly picture window on her previous life. "Don't you dare close that. Look at what is happening, and tell me you think this is right."

Zer was fighting like a berserker now, his eyes cold and gleaming. As he whirled, he brought his blade up, and a thick crimson line blossomed on Cuthah's chest. Cuthah jerked backward, cursing, and a blade flashed in his own hand. The two edges met, and she fought not to cringe. Not to close her eyes.

The angel moved closer, frowning. "My Dominions are fighting with one of my lieutenants. What is it that you want me to do here?"

"I want you to listen to the truth!" she cried. "Whatever it is you think the Fallen did, they didn't do it. Zer told me that someone was killing off your females."

"Brutally." Michael inclined his head. "Zer is your soul mate?"

She scrubbed at the dark marks encircling her wrists. "Yes. Yes, he is."

"He was also the leader of the Dominions," the angel continued implacably. "He was responsible for all of their actions. He led them against me."

"Because he believed you were a cold-blooded killer!"

The angel shot her a hard look. "But I am. We all are. You know very little of the Dominions, human. We are bred to kill. To defend. We guard the Celestial throne. We vow to do that with our last breath, no matter what it takes."

"Well, did your no-matter-what-it-takes require innocent females to die? Because that's what Zer and the Fallen believed. They believed you were responsible for Esrene's death and the others."

Michael stared at her expressionlessly. "I did not do that."

"You said you were a killer."

He shrugged. "I spoke more generally. I did not kill Esrene or the others, but I ought to have known what was happening."

"You ought to have known that your lieutenant was a psychotic nut job. How could you let the Dominions Fall without concrete evidence?"

"There was evidence." She filed this away for future reference.

"Okay. So what about an appeal? Undoing the sentence you passed?"

"Not possible." He looked over at her. "*You* are the second chance, human. When a Fallen finds his soul mate, he is redeemed."

"Well, Houston, you have a problem." She smiled sweetly at the angel. "Because your 'lieutenant' is busy hunting down all the soul mates. Oh, and did I mention that he kills them when he finds them? Three thousand years, Michael, and there are only three soul mates found."

In another lifetime, Zer would have challenged Cuthah to a duel. There was a code. This three-on-one was not how the Dominions had lived. This was hunting. His rogue side purred with pleasure at the violence. His world narrowed to the slick slide of the blade, the familiar sensation of muscles warming up as he flowed from one familiar position to the next. He'd been born for this. Bred for this.

He couldn't look at the body of his soul mate. This was all shades of screwed up. He'd killed her, even though death wouldn't be permanent, he prayed. The mate in him demanded that he drag her body to safety. She didn't belong here. She shouldn't have seen everything he was capable of. The warrior, however, knew he'd made the smart choice, the only choice under the circumstances. She'd bought him time—and cost Cuthah his bargaining chip.

Didn't mean he had to like the truth, though, so he hit Cuthah hard, driving into the other male with a low, vicious blow. His fist punched into the other's midsection with satisfying force. Not honorable, but fuck that. He was going to finish this fight now.

Cuthah hit the wall, ribs splitting with an unmistakable crack. Inhaling painfully, he charged to his feet. And back at Zer.

Only way to kill an angel was to take off the head. Zer figured he could use Cuthah as a punching bag all he wanted, but the bastard wouldn't—couldn't—die. Stubborn as hell. Anger pounded through him.

"*You* killed Esrene." The blood running down his own face gave Cuthah's mocking smile a hellish cast. "Did you know the war her death would cause? Did you even care?

"Oh, I cared." Cuthah circled, raising his blade. "I cared very much, Zer. Her death was no accident."

Zer shifted his weight onto the balls of his feet. "So, why do it?" He wasn't going to have another chance. He needed a confession.

"I needed you Dominions discredited." Cuthah feinted, driving his blade toward Zer's ribs at the last possible second. "I needed you gone from the Heavens."

Drawing back, Zer cursed. "Why? Why go to such lengths? Why the elaborate setup?"

Cuthah surged forward. "Because you stood between me and the Celestial throne. I want it all, Zer. Control of the Dominions. Heavenly power. And I can have it. The last obstacle was you Dominions. Once Michael was convinced that you were wanton killers and corrupt"—his blade came down on Zer's—"then it was simple, Zer. Michael reacted. He exiled the lot of you, and my path was clear. I've led the remaining Dominions for the last three thousand years. And Michael feels so guilty, he's withdrawn from the front lines completely."

"Why not just kill us outright?"

Cuthah lunged forward, a wolfish smile on his face. "Because this was far more satisfying. "

"News flash." Zer met Cuthah's blade with his own. "*This* is far more satisfying." His blade cut through Cuthah's throat like the animal he was, sending the other angel's head flying.

"You hear that?" Nessa needed to hear Michael admit the truth. Admit that he'd been wrong.

"I did."

"You were wrong." She pressed the point home. "You condemned those guys. You punished them for something they didn't do. Didn't dream of doing. That's your psycho killer there."

My God. Those wings beat up and down, the sharp strokes cutting heavily through the air. She held her breath.

"Maybe," he said at last. "I know that I did not find all of the culprits. Still, your Fallen chose to fight me. They chose to ignore my authority." He shrugged slowly. "There had to be a price to pay for that rebellion."

"They rebelled because Dominion females were dying," she pressed. "They were right."

"It doesn't matter now," he said finally. "Now, it is too

late to undo what was done. They must find their soul mates, and then they can return."

"That's not fair," she protested.

Michael smiled cynically. "Life is never fair, human. Surely, you know this. This is not a matter of my not *wanting* to fix matters. This is a matter of *can't*. I can't change this. Not now. I would like to." Something dark flashed in his eyes. "Perhaps now that Cuthah has been removed from the equation, my Fallen will finally find their soul mates."

"Many of the soul mates are already dead."

"And Cuthah clearly did not work alone." He shrugged. "Life is not fair now, but there is nothing I can do to bring back the dead. I can, however, search for Cuthah's conspirators. If there are others still in the Heavens who have abetted him in his madness, I will look for them." The look on his face promised her he'd take this hunt very seriously.

But that wouldn't help the Fallen Dominions find the remaining soul mates. Which ones of Zer's brothers would go without? Could she contemplate telling Nael or Vkhin that there would be no redemption for them because of Cuthah's actions? "Send me back," she demanded.

"You want to go to him?" Those dark eyes looked at her, through her.

"Yeah," she admitted. "I love him. He's mine." She shrugged. "Somehow, we're connected."

"You're connected," he repeated. "Yes. So, you can go back. For you, it's simple now."

Frustration made her snap. He couldn't expect her to pull a *Wizard of Oz* stunt without a few directions. "Tell me how. Damn it, Michael, I don't know how the bond works. What do I do? Tap my heels three times and chant 'There's no place like home'?"

"No," he said patiently. "Hold Zer's image in your head. Feel him. Open up and follow the thread of your connection back to him."

Right. Hang a left at the corner and then take the next right. As directions went, Michael's stank. Still, he wasn't volunteering anything else, so she folded her arms over her chest and gave it a shot. Michael's dark gaze examining her didn't make it any easier, and, after a moment, she gave up.

"Try harder." Michael nodded at her. "Or stay here forever. Your choice. Close your eyes and concentrate, human."

There was motivation. Trying again, she thought of the little things that made Zer who he was. The way he prowled across a room. The half smile that teased one corner of his mouth. The thread grew, memories splicing together into a rope that took on strength and reality. When Zer's feelings flooded the growing bond, feeding it from the other end, her confidence built. Heat. Warmth. Concern. Affection. Love. *Get your ass back here, baby.* The growled command filled her mind. Her heart.

The bond tugged, pulling her back like a cosmic rubber band. Back where she wanted—had—to be. She went, and Michael's sad, knowing eyes watched her go.

CHAPTER TWENTY-THREE

Three days hadn't been enough time to work miracles in the interior-decorating department. Her lab still looked like the war zone it had been. Although the broken glass and unidentifiable bits of building had been swept up and disposed of, a blue tarp still flapped over the busted-out windows like a white flag. Given the state of grant funding these days, those windows weren't getting fixed anytime soon. Maybe she'd start a new design trend. Eco-friendly air-conditioning, right?

Boy. She was reaching.

Anything to avoid confronting the emotional elephant in the room. The threat Cuthah posed was what had brought Zer into her life. Now that Cuthah was gone, did Zer still need her?

In all the confusion of the aftermath of battle and her resurrection, she'd insisted on returning to her own office. She needed to reestablish her independence if she could. And she still wanted to destroy her research so it wouldn't fall into the wrong hands.

She jerked open a drawer particularly forcefully, cursing when a sharp metal edge made unerring contact with her shin. To her surprise, Zer hadn't objected. Maybe he was done with her. She had to face facts.

"Stupid markings," she muttered, shoving her sleeves back down over her wrists. Wouldn't you just know that she'd bond with the one Fallen who was content to let her go her own way? So much for happily-ever-after. Her calendar was free for today.

Reaching into the drawer, she grabbed a thick stack of file folders. Feeding them through the industrial-strength shredder parked on her desktop was satisfying, the metal teeth methodically chewing through the pages and pages of black-and-white data. It was surprisingly easy to erase her research. Unfortunately, it was harder to scrub Zer out of her heart.

Would he come back—would he even want to?

Thirty minutes of shredding, and her desk was as empty as her life. She double-checked the desk and shoveled the mountain of paper confetti into a trash bag. Bonfire time.

She hated the way she was hanging on to the paper, as if it was her last connection to *him*. How pathetic was that?

Except there was still that matter of her heart.

Damn.

Dropping her head onto the desk, she wondered if there was some other way to go about this. Because, honestly? She felt like she was missing half her soul, and she hated that. She wanted him, and, even though he'd sworn he was coming back, now she had to get on with the trust part of things, and, well, she'd never been good at trust. She narrowed her eyes. She was trying, damn it. Overnight improvement just wasn't possible.

It might, she figured, take a decade. Or two.

She shoved her hands through her hair, the long strands tangling around her fingers. It was damn hard to trust.

But she loved him.

That meant she had to trust him. To come back. To *love* her back.

"Good luck with that," she whispered. To her surprise, she meant it.

A noise at the window had her looking up. At Zer, stepping out of the sky through an open window.

"Dramatic entrance," she observed, her heart pounding. God. She was terrified she was going to say the wrong thing. Terrified she would scare him off. Trust, she reminded herself. She'd decided to trust him.

He shrugged, swinging his booted feet over her poor windowsill. "It worked the first time."

True. He'd broken down the lecture hall door, charged up the aisle, and saved her from a deadly predator.

"Not that you were grateful," he growled. "I distinctly recall a whole lot of protesting." He sat on the edge of her windowsill as if it was a goddamned throne. The worn leathers and black cotton T-shirt were familiar territory. She could deal with those.

But his wings. God, those wings. She wanted to tunnel her fingers through their thick, downy warmth. The unbelievable softness of the fifteen-foot span was a memory she couldn't shake. That inky blackness was as unyielding as the male himself. The Archangel had stamped him with a warning label, all right. He wasn't the Heavens' golden child. Not anymore.

"May I come in?" Was that a note of hesitation in his voice? And when had they been on an engraved-invitation basis?

Silently, she gestured toward the room.

He slid off the sill, his booted feet hitting the floor. Prowling the room, he examined the wreckage. "Bit of a mess."

That was the understatement of the year. She'd done the broom-and-dustpan bit—for three days, while she stewed over where her Fallen angel had gone.

"This is not my fault." Her eyes narrowed. "In fact, this is your fault. You're the one who decided to wage a full-on battle with Cuthah the Crazy. In. My. Laboratory."

Sure, part of her mourned the lost lab. The independence it had meant. Of course, who was she really kidding? The independence had been an illusion, her leash only as long as the dean had permitted. And answering to him had sucked bigtime.

Fuck it. She upended the plastic bag of shredded paper into the trash can and grabbed a box of matches. With a snap of her wrist, the match was in the can, merrily burning its way through three years of research. Burning her bridges. Literally.

"Fire marshal's going to be plenty pissed," he observed.

"Right," she snorted. "Least of my worries right now."

"Why?"

Shoving her hair behind her ears, she gestured toward the numerous scorch marks on the walls. The floors. Hell, there wasn't an unmarked inch left.

He tossed a cracked beaker into the trash can, "Why are you burning your papers?"

"It's up here." She tapped her forehead. "Keeping it on paper seems a little superfluous. Not to mention foolhardy" She'd seen what had happened when the rogues started keeping lists.

"So, you don't want to publish another article?"

Slowly, she shook her head. "Now's not the time, Zer. I do that, and all I've done is publish a hit list. I won't put innocent women in harm's way."

"So, you're giving it all up?" Turning away from the destruction, he started toward her, all dark intent.

"I'm not giving it all up," she pointed out. "There will be other jobs. Other chances to crack the code. Plus"—she smiled wickedly—"I believe you still owe me a favor."

She yelped and squirmed as he swept her up into his arms.

"Fly with me." His deep voice touched her to the core.

Two running steps, and he'd cleared the broken window frame, launching them out into the air.

Zer took them straight up into the night sky. What had been a pretty black carpet sprinkled with stars was now a cold, damp, *endless* tunnel of space.

"Unfair!" she yelped, embarrassed by how thin her voice sounded. The campus dropped away beneath them. How did he do this on a regular basis? She was clearly an airplane kind of a gal. Give her walls and a seat, thank you very much.

"Trust me," he growled into her ear, his arms tightening around her. "You think I'll let you fall?"

"You stabbed me. How can I trust you after that?" She'd never forget his cold, emotionless face as that blade of his cut through her. Quick and merciless. Not an ounce of hesitation in him. "You *killed* me."

His arms tightened around her. "Soul mates can't die, not while their other half lives. There was no other way to get to Cuthah." That fierce gaze watched her, waiting for her to decide where she wanted to take this. Understanding. He'd spent a lifetime fighting and hurting. He knew *precisely* how that blow had felt. "But knowing that doesn't excuse me. I hurt you, and, Christ, baby, I didn't want that. Not for you."

Those wings of his didn't hesitate, just kept beating out a steady rhythm as he took them through the night sky. One big hand dropped to her chest, tracing the spot where he'd stabbed her through the heart. She knew that if he could take away the pain and the hurt she'd suffered, he would. In a heartbeat. She'd spent hours staring at the pale white mark. The scar was fading fast. Within a month, she'd need other reminders of what had happened. Which didn't explain the sensitivity of her skin or the bright pleasure uncurling inside her chest, beneath the soft touch of his fingers.

Some things had to be said. She wouldn't lose that raw intimacy they'd found in her office. "But you did it, anyway."

His fingers paused. Rested against the hard, sharp beat of her heart. "I did what I had to do. The only way to Cuthah was through you. I'm"—he hesitated. "God, I'm sorry. It should have been a choice. Your choice."

She'd understood that on a purely intellectual level, but she'd needed the words. Words he'd given her.

"Now," he continued, "you're going to let me spend a lifetime making it up to you."

"I am?" She wasn't feeling charitable. She was feeling something else. Heated pleasure. An erotic curiosity she shouldn't admit to. "Dying, Zer? That cancels out the whole riding-to-the-rescue thing. I don't owe you. *You* owe *me*."

"Deal," he growled, lowering his head to hers for a quick, hard kiss.

A short, sharp slap of wind hit them, and Zer rode that airy wave, taking them down toward the city spread out beneath them. The steep descent sucked the breath from her lungs, left her fingers curling into his shoulders.

"Believe me," he growled into her ear, his arms tightening around her. "I'm all done Falling."

Curling up against the welcome heat of his body, she settled for listening to the smooth beat of his wings carving a path for them through all that air. He didn't look as if all this flying put him out any—or that it was an uncommon occurrence. Maybe he'd taken girlfriends flying before.

He shook his head. "You want me to drop you just to prove a point?"

Or maybe not.

"Watch the stars, baby." He twisted in midair, and they shot impossibly higher into the dark sky. Stars she hadn't seen in too long because she'd been too busy to look up. Where had he been these last three days?

"I like that skirt of yours." The sexy growl shot straight

down her spine. And lower. God, he said the most impossible things. "You know what that skirt of yours does to me, baby?"

Yeah. This close to six feet plus of Fallen, she might have more than a clue. He was thickening, lengthening, where she was pressed against him. So, maybe she'd known he'd like this particular skirt. The thick, practical wool wrapped itself around her curves, doing double duty. Warm *and* sexy.

"Are you bare underneath, baby?" His hand smoothed the material, leaving a liquid trail of fire. "You'd better hang on."

She should have been prepared for the arousal blasting through her. Zer was raw. Sensual. He'd never held back, so why would he have changed, even if he was sporting a pair of wings now? Angel or devil, she wanted him. So, she let him coax her legs around his waist, drinking in the feel of that rock-hard body moving against hers.

The movement forced the fabric of her skirt to bunch up and exposed her lace thong. Pink and pretty, she'd chosen the most minuscule scrap of silk in her arsenal. Just in case. Okay, so the thong had been a grossly impractical gesture on her part. She'd spent the day aware of every step she took, of the fabric rubbing against her sensitive skin, touching every place *he'd* touched.

"Pretty," he whispered against her ear. "So very pretty, Nessie."

One long male finger gently explored the hot valley of flesh.

"Oh, God," she moaned into his ear. "I've missed you, Zer."

"Show me." The darkly sensual command ratcheted her arousal up another, impossible notch. "Slide your panties out of the way for me."

Her flesh was liquid with wanting him, but, God, they

were who knew how many hundreds of feet in the air. Even the hard beat of those strong wings taking them away— somewhere—wasn't insurance against falling.

"Trust me," he said, and she was lost.

She badly wanted to ask if he had missed her. Instead, she slid her hand between them. Straining against the worn leather, he was thick and hard, filling her palm with delicious heat. "You missed me," she guessed, pressing against him.

His finger made another wicked exploration of her soaked panties, and she gasped. Hot and damp and needy. She was all that, waiting for him to fill her up, fill in the lonely bits.

"I'm waiting." His voice was stern and hard and dark. And a total turn-on. She loved this game they played. "Slide your panties out of the way for me, Nessie."

Trembling with need, she slid the fabric out of the way. "Good girl," he whispered, but his large body shuddered against hers. He wanted her, too. Every bit as much as she wanted him, and that made everything okay. "Now I'm going to give you what you need."

She wanted him. She wanted this, this impossible crescendo peak of pleasure as his wicked fingers parted the swollen folds of her sex and rubbed a teasing path around her clit.

"Zer," she moaned, the wind stealing his name from her.

Each strong beat of his wings drove his fingers against her throbbing clit with satisfying power. What would it feel like to have him inside her this way?

"I'm going to take you just like this, baby," he warned. "Hard and fast. Right now, where there's just you and me. You're going to have to trust me, baby." One hand threaded through her loose hair, holding her head still for his hard kiss. The other hand angled her, held her, as he slid inside her, deep and hard. With each downward thrust of his powerful wings, he hammered into her. Taking her hard and deep.

Just as he'd promised.

Her orgasm was a deep, brilliant burst of pleasure, sensation exploding behind her eyes as she held on. And he held on to her, keeping her safe as she let go and came apart in his arms.

When he gently set her feet on the ground, she wasn't sure her knees were going to hold her. His wings closed, sinking gently into the skin of his back until only an inky black outline remained.

God knew, he'd done a number—a delicious number—on her in flight.

"Where are we?" she asked, because that seemed like the safest question she could field right now. Never mind that she wanted details. Where had he been? Why had he come back? And—most important—was he sticking around, or was this a farewell fuck? Because, truthfully, she wasn't sure how she'd get on with her life without him.

He looked at her, and she didn't know how to interpret that look. Through their bond, she sensed masculine satisfaction, heat, and something else. Unfortunately, her skills as a mind reader were practically nonexistent. This was going to take practice. Centuries of practice. "We're outside of M City," he said finally. "Maybe a hundred miles or so. This place used to be a monastery." He didn't sound as if the distance bothered him any. And maybe it didn't. He had himself a pair of wings. Whereas she'd have a hell of a long walk.

"You brought me to a monastery?" Maybe he was aiming for hideous irony.

"Not just any monastery." With one arm, he swept open an ancient wooden door, the hinges protesting loudly. "Secret tsarist retreat."

Which he'd clearly co-opted for his own personal lair.

Figured.

The tumble down, butter-colored stone was silent as she

let him lead her into a half-hidden grotto and an exotic tumble of silky pillows and half-melted candles. She'd wanted romance, and he'd delivered. "It's beautiful."

"So are you." His hand on the small of her back urged her toward the bed he'd clearly made for them in the center of the grotto.

"Where were you?" She needed him to tell her. His face closed, and, for a moment, she wasn't sure if he would. If they were going to have any sort of a future, however, he had to let her in. This couldn't be a one-way street. They were both bound to this relationship. Weren't they?

"I have responsibilities," he said finally.

"Armies to lead," she said lightly, but she knew it was no joke. Zer was a warrior—he always would be.

"Yes." His eyes examined her face. "That's part of the deal. I fight."

"Right." She got that. And, she realized, she could even accept that. The hard part was figuring out what her role in his world could be. She had to do something, because she couldn't imagine being the little woman at home. If what he wanted was to stick her away on a shelf somewhere until he needed some companionship, that wasn't the life she'd imagined for herself. But that was the point of talking. Get it all out there, in the open. Still, she wondered if she'd be able to keep the bitterness out of her voice. "And I find soul mates for you."

He gently settled her on the nest of pillows, and the look of hesitant tenderness on his face was killing her. Maybe there was a place for her here, after all. She turned her cheek into his palm and waited.

"The soul mates are important." Understatement. "But," he said hoarsely, "if you don't want to find them for us, that's okay." His dark eyes never left hers. "That's your choice. You make it."

"You'd trust me with that?"

He raised her hands and pressed a kiss against her knuckles. "That's your right. I need you to keep them safe, though. You know who they are, so if you choose not to tell us, you make certain they're safe."

"So, what else do you want from me?"

"Love me." His voice was all rough command, a liquid reminder of the lazy sensuality of their bond. His fingers traced the marks that curled around her forearms. "I need you to love me." The vulnerability in his voice made her own heart ache.

She wrapped her hands around his arms, sliding them over the hot skin.

"That's all?" Damn. That hadn't come out right. "I mean, if we're soul mates, isn't there something else?"

"You mean, like a special ritual?" The look of masculine satisfaction flashing across his face warned her. That hesitation was all gone now. "We already did that part." He threaded his hands through her hair, tugging her closer. Delicious heat and the scent of him sent the words tumbling right out of her head. God, he was dangerous. "And you already got your favor, baby. All of me."

"Forever."

"Forever, baby. All yours. You going to return that favor?"

That note of vulnerability was back in his voice now. He wasn't sure what she wanted, and that raw emotion was doing something to her.

"I want all of you," he said, and that hoarse note was back in his voice, squeezing her heart and turning her insides molten.

She pulled his dark head down to hers, closing her eyes because all this was almost—but not quite—too much. She hadn't been asking for love, but that was what she'd found when she'd found Zer.

"You got it. You've got me. I love you," she whispered, sensing rather than seeing his slow smile as the wicked shadows wrapped around them and he filled her world.

He leaned into her. "Falling or flying," he promised, taking her mouth—and her heart—in a hard, hot kiss. "We do it together."

Try these other great titles available from Brava!

Sweet Stuff by Donna Kauffman

*Double Fudge . . . Toasted Coconut . . . Key Lime . . .
Strawberry Cream . . .
Every bite is a mouthful of heaven.
And the women of the Cupcake Club are bringing
their appetite . . .*

Riley Brown never imagined she would find her bliss on Georgia's quiet Sugarberry Island after years of Chicago's city life. With a new career and fantastic new friends, she's got it all—except for eligible men. But a gig staged at a renovated beach house delivers a delicious treat—six feet of blue-eyed, gorgeous writer as delectable and Southern as pecan pie. Quinn Brannigan has come to Sugarberry to finish his latest novel in peace, and suddenly Riley has a taste for the bad boy author that no amount of mocha latte, buttercream, or lemon mousse will satisfy . . .

Riley's friends are rooting for her to give in to her cravings and spice up her life, but it's Quinn who needs to learn that life's menu just might include love, in all its decadent, irresistible flavors . . .

Matthew by Emma Lang

It is a vast spread in the eastern wilds of the newly independent Republic of Texas, the ranch their parents fought for . . . and died for. To the eight Graham siblings, no matter how much hard work or hard love it takes, life is unthinkable without . . .

In the wake of his parents' murder, Matthew Graham must take the reins at the Circle Eight. He also needs to find a wife in just thirty days, or risk losing it all. Plain but practical, Hannah Foley seems the perfect bride for him . . . until after the wedding night. Their marriage may make all the sense in the world, but neither one anticipates the jealousies that will result, the treacherous danger they're walking into, or the wildfire of attraction that will sweep over them, changing their lives forever . . .

And check out *Touch of a Rogue* by Mia Marlowe, coming next month!

He can keep her safe . . . or be her very ruin . . .

Jacob Preston has three requirements for a woman desiring access to his bed: She must be enthusiastic in affairs of passion, jaded in matters of the heart, and—to ensure the first two qualifications—she *must* be married.

Lady Julianne Cambourne has all the makings of a passionate lover, and she certainly shows no signs of sentimentality . . . but her unmarried status should render her firmly off limits to Jacob.

Instead, it proves only a temptation. One that grows stronger when she comes to him in desperation, looking for the kind of answers only he can give. For beyond his rakish reputation, Jacob is known for the mysterious—even other-worldly—power of detection he commands through his sense of touch. And Julianne, surrounded by long-hidden secrets that threaten to ensnare her in a deadly trap, will do whatever it takes to recruit his skills . . . using every form of persuasion at her disposal . . .

GREAT BOOKS,
GREAT SAVINGS!

When You Visit Our Website:
www.kensingtonbooks.com

You Can Save Money Off The Retail Price
Of Any Book You Purchase!